Regan Black, a *USA TODAY* bestselling author, writes award winning, action-packed novels featuring kick-butt heroines and the sexy heroes who fall in love with them. Raised in the Midwest and California, she and her family, along with their adopted greyhound, two arrogant cats and a quirky finch, reside in the South Carolina Lowcountry, where the rich blend of legend, romance and history fuels her imagination.

COLTON P.I. PROTECTOR

REGAN BLACK

MILLS & BOON

First Published in Great Britain 2018
by Mills & Boon, an imprint of HarperCollins*Publishers*
1 London Bridge Street, London, SE1 9GF

Colton P.I. Protector © 2018 Harlequin Books S.A.

Special thanks and acknowledgement are given to Regan Black for her contribution to *The Coltons of Red Ridge* series.

ISBN: 978-0-263-26574-3

39-0518

MIX
Paper from
responsible sources
FSC™ C007454

This book is produced from independently certified FSC™ paper to ensure responsible forest management.

For more information visit: www.harpercollins.co.uk/green

Printed and bound in Spain
by CPI, Barcelona

For Alexis, dog lover extraordinaire and daughter of my heart, with a big thank-you for your service with the police department.

Chapter 1

In her office at the Red Ridge K9 Training Center, Danica Gage finished the reports for the day and shut down her computer. From the kennels, she heard the faint whining of the newest arrivals, two Belgian Malinois puppies. At three months old, they were beginning their journey to become working dogs. Danica loved this first stage when the goal was to teach a dog basic obedience and uncover the inherent strengths.

Whenever new dogs arrived, they were often lonely from leaving their mother and littermates, and uncertain about the new surroundings. This pair was no exception. The staff always scheduled an overnight trainer to supervise and ease the transition. Working these shifts, just her and the dogs and the expansive quiet of the South Dakota nights, gave Danica a deep sense of peace and purpose.

The puppies had been snuggled together when she'd been in the kennels half an hour ago to give a fully trained protection dog named Nico one last walk for the night. Also a Malinois, he was solid black and all the more intimidating for it. At this stage of his precise training, he was allowed only limited contact with a few members of the staff while he waited for the assignment of a permanent handler. Danica hoped it didn't take long. Nico was one of the smartest dogs she'd had the privilege to support and he needed to get to work. With his inherent pride and defensive drive, the dog would be an asset to any handler or security team.

She opened the door between the offices and the kennels and the whining turned to a keening plea. She smiled as the puppies scrambled to the front gate. Other dogs nearby woke to the noise, but only one or two gave any verbal reaction when they saw Danica. The puppies, however, were wide awake and ready to go. Typical of their breed, this pair was bright and eager, their intelligent eyes gleaming from dark-masked faces. The tan fur still had plenty of puppy-fluff in it and on the rare occasions when they were still, she indulged in petting the soft coats.

She gave the command to sit, something dogs were expected to do whenever a trainer came to their kennel. Both puppies hesitated, but were too excited to completely comply. At this point, seeing them hesitate at the command was a sign of progress. They wriggled through the first available space as the gate opened and she let them rush out at her. After slipping a lead over each fuzzy head, she ushered them past the row of other dogs in various states of curiosity and out into the backyard.

Outside, she let the puppies off their leads and gave the command to relieve themselves. Not a difficult command for them to obey and she praised them repeatedly. The positive reinforcement paved the way for successful training. She let them romp and wrestle, burning off a little energy so they'd sleep well until morning. Once the puppies were tucked in after this outing, Danica had a mystery novel waiting for her in the office that she was eager to dive into.

The night was clear and cool, and stars dotted the midnight-velvet sky above the dense trees that backed the training center. Born and raised in Red Ridge, she never tired of the quiet, removed atmosphere. The modest city had every convenience and Danica felt safe here, and apart from the troubles of more populated areas.

More than a few of her friends had raced out of Red Ridge almost as soon as high school graduation was over. She didn't understand it. Danica's roots were inexorably tied to this northwestern corner of the state. She'd known at an early age that her affection for and loyalty to the area would weather any storm, be it a flood of the typical minutiae of life in a small city, a winter blizzard or the current drama of a murder spree that had started with her brother.

Grief wasn't anything new to Danica or her family. As Grandpa Gage often said, the key to living was being courageous enough to find and pursue the joyful moments. In the case of losing her brother, she found joy in the memories and by moving forward in the K9 work they both enjoyed. Finding her life's work right

here at the training center, a source of city pride, had
given her a new dream when her first goal to join the
police force had been crushed. As a Gage working on
the periphery of law enforcement, she had more freedom and less of an uphill battle against the lingering
skeletons rattling around in her family's closet.

She softly called the puppies back to her. For the
next year, she would train these two on the basic tasks
every dog should know and all working dogs were required to master. Additional training would follow,
according to the type of service or task the dog would
provide. Danica knew many of the Malinois wound up
as security and protection dogs like Nico, capitalizing
on their natural strengths and instincts.

Despite the late hour, the puppies were making
the most of the outing. At this age, they could be indulged a bit. She had to smother her laughter at their
antics. After slipping the leads back on them, she urged
them toward the kennel door and heard the snap of
a twig somewhere close. Turning toward the woods
that backed up to the training center, she called out.
"Hello?"

A heavy silence from the deep shadows answered
her, interrupted by a sudden flurry of barking from the
puppies. They tugged at the ends of the leads, trying
to get to the fence. Someone was out there, though it
wasn't the right time of day or the right season for a
hunter. *Probably kids on a dare*, she thought, willing
herself to remain calm. "Who's there?"

She was safe in the yard, behind the five-foot privacy fence and the locked gate. Trying to get the puppies to the kennels became more of a challenge as they
were convinced there was something to see. Her nerves

getting the better of her, Danica reined in the puppies and hurried toward the open door of the kennel.

She'd taken only a step or two when someone grabbed her from behind. One heavy hand clamped over her mouth. She struggled, pushing and pulling up on the forearm, ducking her chin so she could shout for help or even bite. It was no use. A moment later, she felt a sting at her neck and her legs went limp immediately. She fell to the ground in a boneless puddle and watched the stars overhead wink out as blackness swamped her vision. She heard the whimper of the puppies, felt them head-butting her arms, but she couldn't move.

Shane Colton and his K9 partner Stumps, a talented Pembroke Welsh corgi, were taking a long late-night walk. Shane needed the clear night air to think, and walking worked out the kinks after the long drive. They'd just returned to Red Ridge after spending several days on the road, running down a potential lead in an ongoing illegal firearms case for his cousin Finn Colton, chief of the Red Ridge Police Department K9 Unit.

Shane wished he could say the trip had been productive. On the department payroll as a private investigator/informant rather than a police officer, he had a little more leeway with how he collected information for a case. Everyone in local law enforcement had noticed an increase in criminal activity and nearly everyone suspected two brothers, lifelong residents of Red Ridge, were at the heart of the trouble.

Noel and Evan Larson, identical twins, had been a year ahead of him in school and had been raised by their grandmother, Mae Rose, after their parents were tragically killed in a car accident. No matter what the RRPD did, they couldn't connect the recent criminal activity with the Larson twins. Despite suspicions, no one they'd arrested so far would name the twins and no one in law enforcement dared to embarrass Mae Rose. The softhearted and generous widow was a beloved and respected fixture in town.

Despite their best effort, neither he nor Stumps had found any indication that the Larson brothers had been present at the site where the guns had been delivered. Though Shane had never cared much for the twins, he refused to express a public opinion on a case based on suspicion alone. There was either solid evidence to bring in a suspect or there was more work to do. That black-and-white philosophy had served him well since day one of his career as an investigator.

Shane handled his own investigations in addition to working cases for the RRPD that could take them anywhere in the region if he and Stumps were called to search or support. When he was on a police assignment, he considered it a top priority to make sure evidence was gathered properly and no corners were cut in the quest to close cases.

Off duty now, Stumps led the way at the end of his lead, his white backside waving like a flag as he trotted along, taking in every scent. When he was working, the short and stocky red-and-white corgi was a genius at pinpointing evidence. The finds he and his dog made frequently helped identify the right culprit in their various cases.

From the rear pocket of his jeans, Shane's cell phone chimed and vibrated with an incoming text message.

The display showed the number as unknown, but it was the text message itself that froze Shane in his tracks.

I'm innocent. D

At the other end of the lead, Stumps glanced back, his ears cocked as he waited for a signal from Shane. Shane was floored. The message had to be from his half sister, Demi. It was the first he'd heard of her making contact with anyone since she'd disappeared under the shadow of a murder charge earlier in the year.

He quickly sent a text message back. I know. You okay?

No reply. He waited, willing her to answer. As nothing came through, he sent another text, hoping to prod her into a response. The baby okay?

Still nothing. What was he supposed to do now? More than likely, Demi was texting from a burner phone that couldn't even be traced. She was tough and capable and if anyone could survive her current ordeal as a pregnant murder suspect on the run, she could. Still, he worried.

Growing up, Shane hadn't been particularly close to Demi or his other half siblings. Rusty Colton wasn't an exemplary father, and his four children had four different mothers who didn't always get along. Lately, though, it seemed as if the four of them were looking to redefine family ties. Shane hadn't quite decided how he felt about that yet.

So, in the good news category, Demi was well enough to text, but the bad news was that the Groom Killer case was spiraling out of control. To date, four would-be grooms had been shot through the heart right

before saying their vows. Demi was the prime suspect after being dumped by the first victim, Bo Gage,
who'd been killed in the parking lot of the bar where
his bachelor party was about to take place. He was
set to be married to Hayley Patton, his new fiancée,
when it happened. Based on the scene, it appeared he
had died in the act of spelling out her name with his
blood. A piece of her jewelry had been found near the
crime scene. A witness claimed to see her running in
the shadows of the parking lot soon after the murder.
Worse—another witness claimed to see her shoot another Groom Killer victim, same MO: groom-to-be,
shot in the chest, black cummerbund stuffed in his
mouth. The FBI had sightings of Demi far away from
Red Ridge at the time of the last murder. But no one
knew what to think.

It didn't help to have the media hyping up every
assault and accidental gun discharge as a potentially
linked crime. Media aside, public opinion remained
divided between Demi as the prime suspect and someone successfully framing her. Shane couldn't help clear
her name if she wouldn't communicate.

He glanced at his patiently waiting dog and sighed
as he pocketed his phone. "Let's go." Clearly delighted,
Stumps trotted forward once more.

Shane's thoughts moved away from the gun deal
case to Demi's situation. He supposed the best first
step would be sharing this text with his half brother
Brayden. Like Shane, he would be relieved to have
some news from her. Brayden was also a K9 officer in
the RRPD unit and more importantly, he'd never had
a moment's doubt about Demi's innocence.

They were on one of Stumps's favorite routes this

evening, following a walking path that wound away from the street and circled the K9 training center, where he'd met and trained with the dog to become an evidence team.

Smart as a whip on the job, Stumps knew how to have fun when he and Shane weren't working. They were strolling along, Stumps sniffing out every detail of what he'd missed in recent days, while Shane continued to ponder the Groom Killer case. Suddenly, Stumps halted, ears perked. He sat down, his nose pointed at the training center fence.

"I know," Shane said absently. "We have more classes next month." He spent working time with Stumps every day, regardless of their caseload. A few times a year, they returned to the training center for various classes to keep them both sharp on the job and current with techniques.

Distracted with two cases playing bumper cars in his head, Shane took another step or two before he realized that Stumps was at alert. Giving the area his full attention, he paused and listened, hearing the unmistakable whine of young puppies on the other side of the fence. Underneath the whimpers, he heard an occasional spate of barking from the kennels. That didn't make any sense. He shouldn't be able to hear those sounds so clearly unless a door was open. Something had the dogs riled up. How had puppies wound up in this part of the yard alone?

The training center staff didn't make mistakes like this with their dogs. Concerned, Shane put a hand on his gun and signaled Stumps to lead the way. Casual walk or not, with a killer roaming around Red Ridge, he didn't go out unarmed anymore.

Silently, they approached the fence, the sounds of the distressed puppies growing louder. Stumps abruptly sat again, back straight, and nose aimed at the gate as if he could see right through it. Something out of place had grabbed his attention again. Shane peered over the fence and swore.

Sprawled on the ground, her head lolled to one side and one leg bent awkwardly beneath her, was Danica Gage. Two fuzzy puppies, obviously training center newbies, were doing their best to rouse her. The shadows of the woods behind him swallowed the light, and the glow of the security light over the open back door wasn't enough for him to tell if she was alive or dead.

"Danica?" he called in a hoarse whisper.

Why did it have to be *her*? Since his return to Red Ridge nearly ten years ago, he did his best to avoid anyone named Gage. Not an easy task in a town originally founded by the Colton and Gage families. Although the dark bitterness lurking inside him urged him to believe the worst of her, that she'd landed in that pose due to her own errors, he knew better.

Danica was a top-notch professional. She'd been their lead trainer when he and Stumps first began working together three years ago. With enough fiery energy packed into her petite body to power the sun, she was dedicated to her career and the dogs entrusted to her. And though he hated to dwell on it, by pairing him with Stumps she'd breathed new hope into his life when he'd been on the verge of giving up.

He glanced at Stumps. "Good boy." Gage or not, they couldn't just call this in and walk away. In a perfect world, he'd give his dog a treat and let the police take over. This scene had too many unknowns to wait.

"Danica?" he tried again. The lack of any sounds other than the dogs made him nervous. If her attacker was still lurking around he—or she—was being damn quiet about it.

He thought she was breathing, but it was hard to tell in the lousy light, with the puppies crying and climbing all over her, leads trailing in their wake. They were stepping on her hair and hands, tripping over her legs, and she gave no visible reaction. "Please don't be dead," he muttered as he pulled out his phone and dialed the police station for backup.

With the promise of assistance on the way, Shane pocketed his phone again and let Stumps know they were back in working mode as they moved toward the back gate. He was pleased the gate was closed, but it was unlocked. Shane had spent enough time at the training center to know the policy was to keep the gate locked for the protection of the dogs, the staff and the community.

Drawing his gun, he flicked off the safety and let Stumps take the lead as they walked into the yard. One of the hinges squeaked as he closed the gate behind them for the safety of the puppies that were loose. He knew he was potentially contaminating the scene, but he wasn't about to leave her there until it could be cleared.

Stumps didn't alert Shane to any further trouble as they crossed the yard and approached Danica's unmoving form. The worried puppies cranked it up another octave, bracing at the sight of Stumps, while staying close to her.

Shane hoped their behavior meant she was alive, but he didn't lower his guard. "Stay," he said to Stumps, before he released the lead. His dog sat, ears perked, eyes on Shane.

Curious, the puppies lurched forward and then tumbled back to Danica, over and over. "Easy now," Shane crooned to the puppies as he knelt down. Malinois, he saw now, recognizing the distinct black faces, fawn coats, huge ears and long tails. "Have you been keeping an eye on her?" They were so obviously untrained that he didn't think the puppies posed any threat, but he wasn't in the mood to wrestle or deal with needle-sharp puppy teeth.

"All right, you two. Move over and let me have a look." Shane pressed his fingers to the pale skin of her throat, relieved to find a pulse. Slow and steady, it seemed much stronger than her shallow breathing. Fortunately, an ambulance would be here soon. "Danica?" He smoothed her red-gold hair back from her face, trying to ignore the silky texture against his fingertips. "Can you hear me?"

One of the puppies whined, his tail sweeping across Danica's face as he strived for Shane's attention, and the other shoved his head under Shane's elbow, seeking comfort. "She'll be fine." He wasn't sure if he was trying to convince the puppies or himself.

Glancing back, he saw Stumps watching as if such raucous displays were beneath him. When his corgi was working, that was true enough, yet Shane made sure he got plenty of time each day just to be a dog and give his innate silliness an outlet.

Drawing the puppies aside, he continued to look Danica over. She was slightly built, but her confidence in the training classes gave her such a big presence he always forgot that she was short. Lying at such an awkward angle, her hair tangled, she looked almost breakable. His temper flared at the idea of anyone assaulting her.

There was no sign of blood and he struggled against the urge to straighten out that bent leg. He wouldn't risk moving her, in case there were injuries from the fall that he couldn't see. Nearby, a siren wailed and flashing lights darted into the night sky. The police department was nearby but an ambulance dispatched from the hospital on the other side of town might take a bit longer.

"She'll be fine," he said again, gathering the leads on the puppies. He should take them back into a kennel, yet he didn't want to leave her out here alone.

Needing a distraction, Shane picked up the puppies. "Stumps, come." The corgi hustled into action, stopping at Shane's foot. "Seek."

He didn't have any better direction to give the dog. If there was something that didn't belong in the area, Stumps would find it. The stocky legs carried him all around Danica, and he snuffled where the puppies had rubbed against Shane's running shoes and jeans.

As he systematically explored the rest of the yard, Shane soothed the puppies and tried to sort out what had happened that Danica landed just like this.

She moaned, her limbs shifting slowly as if she was moving through thick sand. The puppies squirmed in his arms, eager to reach her. Shane was surprised how much he shared the sentiment. He kept a firm hold on the puppies as her eyelids fluttered open. Eyes he knew to be the pale green of springtime stared up at the sky before darting about, finally landing on him.

"Relax, Danica," he said. "You're safe now."

Chapter 2

Danica knew that voice. *Shane.* Through the fog in her mind, she wondered why she wouldn't be safe. This was Red Ridge. She'd always been safe here. She blinked, or tried to. Her eyelids were so heavy they just wanted to stay closed. Maybe she should give in. Sleep sounded like a good plan. Her arms and legs felt as if they were weighted or buried. As she rolled her head from side to side, her neck ached and the scent of grass tickled her nose. How had she wound up out here on the ground?

"What happened?" The words were hard to get past her parched lips. And why was *he* here?

"Stay still," that deep voice rumbled, dark as the night sky overhead. "Help is almost here."

"Help?" It didn't sound like the worst idea to wait, but her pride was taking a beating as she lay here while he stood over her. She heard the yip of puppies and recalled the new Malinois. "Are you holding the new puppies?"

She would like a better look at the tough, inscrutable Shane holding a couple of energetic three-month-olds. Ignoring her aching muscles, she tried to make out his expression through the weak light and her blurry vision. She knew he lived nearby, but she was a Gage. It seemed more likely Shane would be here to gloat over a Gage in trouble than help her out of any crisis.

He didn't like her or anyone in her family—with good reason.

Her gaze moved to the wriggling Malinois pups, one cradled on each of his forearms, his large hands supporting their chests. "Where is Stumps?" She tried to take a deep breath and sit up. Her body fought her on both actions.

"Stay put," Shane said. "Stumps is working."

This time when she looked up, she could see the hard line of his square jaw and the grim set of his lips. His blue eyes would be stern and cold. It was the expression she privately referred to as *judge and jury*. Since his return to Red Ridge several years ago, he seemed to look at the world through that singular mien. "Why are you here?" she asked. Of everyone in the RRPD, why did Shane have to be the first at her side? And who had called him in?

"I guess I'm that kind of lucky," he replied.

Her thoughts were too muddled to make sense of any of this. Ignoring his suggestion to stay put, she sat up. "How did the puppies get out?"

"I assume you brought them out," Shane replied, lowering himself to a knee as puppy feet pawed at air, scrambling to get close to her. "Do you remember anything?"

She took one puppy into her arms, soothing herself as much as the dog as she tried to think. "Not really." Her eyesight cleared much faster than her mind. Logic said she was on the overnight shift for the new arrivals, but her memory was a blur. "Who called the RRPD?"

"I did." His sandy eyebrows drew together. "Stumps and I were on a walk and he sensed something wrong here in the yard. RRPD and an ambulance should be here any minute."

She glanced around for Stumps and found him sitting in an alert position, his gaze trained on the door to the kennels. "I'll thank him later." She tipped her head toward the building. "Looks like he's still on the job."

Shane's expression tightened even more. "Is there another way inside?" he asked, his voice low at her ear.

"Only the front and back doors you know about."

"Where is the ambulance?" he wondered aloud.

"You need to investigate," she said.

"I don't want to leave you out here alone." He scowled. "Do you think you can stand?"

At her nod, he helped her to her feet, both of them dodging the antics of the excitable puppies. When she had the leads in hand and the puppies under control, they walked to the door where Stumps waited.

"Hang on." He drew his gun. He and the dog went through the door first. He moved into the shadows, peering down each row. "Hit the lights," he called.

She did. Several of the younger dogs were restless, whining, barking or up and pacing in their crates. The fully trained dogs sat quietly, or were stretched out, curious but patient. Somewhere out of sight, a beagle bayed pitifully. Danica recognized the voice of Stella, a sweet-natured two-year-old being trained for a tracking career.

Shane walked back into view, squinting against the bright glare of the fluorescent lights with Stumps trotting at his heel. "Best way to your office?"

She was a little surprised he didn't know. "Straight ahead, through the door, second door on the right. Shouldn't we kennel the puppies?"

"Not yet," he replied, his voice flat. "Stay close." His gun raised against any threat, he cleared the hallway and her office. Lowering his weapon, he held the door for her. "Lock yourself in and wait for backup," he ordered. "I'm going to see what Stumps can find."

She tried to protest but he pinned her with that unrelenting, chilly blue gaze. It wasn't a look any argument would overcome. She sat down at her desk and soothed the puppies with soft words and warm caresses. She wanted to be out in the kennels, sorting out the situation. Helping. The dogs needed a familiar face and the quickest possible return to their routine. At this rate, tomorrow's training plans would fall on deaf dog ears after the disruptions tonight.

Despite the sirens they'd heard outside, it seemed to be taking forever for anyone to actually arrive. She wondered what he'd told them when he made the call after Stumps had found her. What had they been doing walking out this way? She supposed it could have been a case. Knowing he worked private cases as well as assignments for the RRPD, that thought didn't give her much comfort.

When Shane had been training to partner with Stumps, she'd tried time and again to reach out and bridge the abyss of resentment between him and the Gage family. Shane hadn't been the least bit interested in her efforts. Stumps she remembered fondly from those days and enjoyed whenever he returned for a refresher.

His partner, Shane, not so much. Tall and ripped, with sandy blond hair and hard eyes, he'd given her shivers—not all of them good. He was wonderful to look at, but he carried a chip on his shoulder the size of the nearby mountains, though she could hardly blame him.

As she pulled a bag of dog treats from her lower desk drawer, she trembled at the memory of asking Shane about his choice to become a private investigator rather than going through the academy to become a police officer.

"Someone should keep cops honest," he'd replied in that flat tone that unnerved her. "I nominated myself."

The Colton and Gage families had been feuding since the first days of Red Ridge. But Shane harbored more resentment than all the generations before him. His words, dripping with well-aged hatred, were a clear warning to mind her own business. Danica considered herself a quick study and she'd lost her courage to share how his predicament had affected her own career choices.

"His predicament," she muttered to the puppies. What a pathetic understatement for wrongful imprisonment. Weary and inexplicably sad, she managed to get the puppies to sit and rewarded them accordingly as she tried to purge the past she couldn't change from her mind.

That exchange years ago had convinced her Shane

would never find a way to forgive her grandfather for the dreadful mistakes that had cost Shane his freedom and so much more. She understood why he hated them all collectively, but she'd never quite been able to stop wishing she could fix it. She studied the bright eyes in the two attentive faces watching her. "Why can I remember the past just fine and have no idea what happened to us tonight?"

With Danica as safe as possible, Shane backtracked with Stumps. He heard vehicles out front and the flashing lights were bouncing off the side of the brick building, spilling into the yard. At the door between the yard and the kennel, he drew his gun once more and set Stumps to searching again. Stumps moved with purpose, Shane's encouragement following him, as he confidently trotted into the kennel and searched the rows.

Shane noted the various dog breeds along the route. Had this been a visit for a refresher course, he would have appreciated the soft-eyed basset hound or given reassurances to the enormous Newfoundland who watched Stumps work with obvious concern. It was easy to judge the progress of each dog's training by how they reacted to the disruption. The fully trained dogs were quietly observant. The dogs still in progress whined or barked as Stumps and Shane passed.

Stumps abruptly turned down an aisle that seemed deserted. He'd clearly caught the scent of something that didn't belong. Stumps walked a bit further and then dropped into a perfect alert pose in front of an open kennel. Shane read the tag on the door and swore.

Nico. Belgian Malinois. Protection.

"Great." If this dog had been released without authorization, the training center had a brand-new crisis on their hands. Shane took a picture of the tag with his phone and another picture of Stumps at alert. Then he released his dog and gave him a reward.

"Shane? It's Carson. You in here? Where's Danica?"

At the sound of Carson Gage's voice, Shane called out, "I'm in the last row. Danica should be locked safely in her office." He should have known the dispatcher would notify Danica's oldest brother, a detective with the RRPD. Though Shane avoided the Gage family whenever possible, Carson was notoriously thorough on his cases and had earned Shane's grudging respect through the years.

"Is she hurt?" Carson asked as he hurried forward through the rows of dogs.

Shane hesitated. He wasn't a paramedic and yet he didn't want to worry the other man. "She made it to her office under her own steam. I found her in the yard with two new puppies. I assume by the way she came around that she'd been drugged."

"Found her?" Carson echoed with a scowl.

"Stumps sensed a problem during our walk. I looked over the fence and found her out cold on the ground."

Carson put his hands on his hips, looking up and down the empty row. "Someone took her down to get in here?"

"That's my guess." Shane pointed to the sign on the empty kennel door.

Carson gave a low whistle. "That's a problem."

Both men knew a missing or stolen dog trained in protection could pose numerous threats to the thief as well as the community. The odds of this ending well for the dog or the people who'd taken him were slim.

"Maybe the tag is leftover and Nico was relocated earlier," Carson said.

Shane shook his head. "Stumps would disagree."

"I figured." He glanced at Shane. "Can I tell him he did a good job?"

"Sure." Shane knew that Stumps considered Carson an extension of his pack after they had collaborated with the detective and Justice, his K9 partner, on a few cases.

Carson dropped to a knee and rubbed Stumps between the ears, praising him lavishly. Shane nearly laughed. If Stumps had been a cat, he might have purred. He was definitely preening.

Standing again, Carson said, "Let's go see if Danica can shed any light on this."

Shane knew what Carson hoped to hear, but his money was on Stumps's assessment of the situation. Leaving a tag on a kennel and the door open was sloppy work and no one at this facility would make that kind of error. There was too much time and money invested in each of the dogs trained here to let that casual approach stand. Especially not in the case of a protection dog.

As they all headed toward the offices, Shane had no doubt Danica had been attacked for the sole purpose of stealing the dog. Now his questions revolved around who would want to steal a dog with lethal potential, who knew such a dog was here, and how they'd known to strike tonight.

Danica barely managed to escape the care of two dedicated paramedics. Her office was too small for a medical team, their gear, the puppies and the thoughts racing through her mind. She knew the paramedics meant well. They might even be right about her needing a full exam, since no one had any idea what drug the attacker had used to incapacitate her. She promised to see her doctor tomorrow and sent them along.

She pulled the band from her hair and scrubbed at her scalp, combing her hands through her hair before pulling it into a ponytail again. Dragging the back of her hand across her mouth, she tried to erase the memory of that heavy palm smothering her mouth, strong fingertips pinching her jaw. A tremor slipped down her spine as she glanced out her office window to the darkened training yard. No one was out there—she knew that. No one was watching her talk to a couple of puppies. Still, she walked over and lowered the blinds, twisting the handle to block the view.

Right now, she had a job to do. It was past time to restore calm to the dogs in the kennels. After that, she could focus on restoring herself. Expediting the process, she scooped up the puppies to carry them back to their kennel for what remained of the night.

In the hallway she paused, listening and looking around for Shane and Stumps, relieved they didn't seem to be in the building. Whenever she bumped into Shane, here or in town, she felt an awkward and uncomfortable secondhand guilt. Until tonight, she'd always managed to maintain her professional footing when he was nearby.

Her arms full of the puppies, and her head a bit woozy, she pushed through the door to the kennels backward. Turning, she found herself face-to-face with Shane—or rather her face to his chest. Did everyone have to be taller than her? When she glanced up, she caught a wisp of concern in his gaze before his eyes iced over with the familiar reserve and disdain.

"What are you doing?" he demanded.

"My job," she replied calmly, in deference to the puppies and fussing dogs nearby.

"*How* are you doing?" Carson asked.

She hid her jolt of surprise behind the wriggling puppies. How had she overlooked her brother standing right behind Shane? She knew they occasionally teamed up for cases, but seeing them together was unexpected. Giving Carson a smile, she walked down the row and settled the puppies into their kennel. She closed the latch and made a note of the time on the clipboard attached to the door.

The instant she finished, Carson pulled her into a big, lingering hug. She eased out of the embrace to get a deep breath and to make sure she wasn't caught wallowing in front of Shane. "I suppose when they got the call about trouble here, they dragged you out of bed, too?"

"You're my little sister. I'm allowed to worry." He looked her up and down, his gaze stopping at her neck. "That looks like a needle mark."

She nodded, brushing at the sore spot with her fingertips and pulling her ponytail around to hide it.

"Why didn't the paramedics transport you?" Carson demanded.

"Because I'm fine," she said. Did they have to do this in front of Shane, of all people? If Carson kept up the big brother routine, she was likely to lose Stumps's respect, as well. "And I'm an adult," she reminded him.

"I'd feel better if—"

She held up her hand and cut him off. "Can we take

this somewhere else? The dogs really need to get back to normal."

"Not quite yet," Carson said, clearly unhappy with the answer. He waved her over as he moved down toward another aisle of kennels.

Her stomach knotted as he tipped his head to the side and pointed. "What can you tell me about this dog, Nico?"

Danica rushed forward, her shoulder bumping Shane in the process. She ignored the sensation, consumed by more bad news tonight. Whatever she'd expected to find, it wasn't the door to Nico's kennel hanging open, the kennel empty. "You found it this way? He isn't anywhere inside?"

"Stumps found the kennel," Shane replied. He held out his phone to her. "The dog isn't here."

She glanced down at the picture of the corgi, frozen in the quiet alert stance in front of Nico's kennel. "Oh, no." She pressed her fingers to her lips. "This can't be happening."

"Talk to me, Danica," Carson prompted, pulling out a notebook. "Has this dog been stolen?"

She nodded. "Must have been," she said. Worry and misery swamped her in waves as she reached for the clipboard log they kept on Nico. "According to this, I took him out to the yard one last time before ten. That was a little earlier than usual because of the puppies."

"You don't remember taking him out?" Carson asked.

She closed her eyes tight, searching for the memory. "I remember opening the gate and clipping the lead to his collar." That had to be today, she thought. She'd had the last two nights off. "I don't really remember being outside with him." Yet she must have done it or she wouldn't have written it on the chart.

It occurred to her that if someone had attacked her to get to Nico, they could have stolen the dog more easily while she was in the yard with him. She mentioned it, but neither Carson nor Shane seemed as convinced.

"What's his status?" Shane asked.

"Nico is fully trained attack/protection, but not yet assigned to a handler." She turned to her brother. "Dogs with Nico's training are kept separate and we limit their interactions. Other than his trainer, only the vet and I have had any contact with him."

"So he bonds best with the handler," Carson said.

"Right." She wrapped her arms around her middle, willing away the tremors. This was a disaster.

As both Shane and Carson took notes, Danica watched Stumps. The adorable corgi was Shane's partner and companion, but she had worked with him through his initial obedience training and she had written the recommendation for him to become an evidence dog. "You've had a long day," she said to him in the same tone she'd use with her human colleagues. "Can we *please* take this elsewhere?" she asked again.

She rubbed her hands up and down her chilled arms. Her knees were like jelly and her mind kept fogging over. The whining from nearby dogs normally didn't bother her but right now it was giving her a pounding headache and she wanted to shield her eyes from the lights overhead.

Carson nodded. "A crime scene unit will be here shortly, but you don't have to guide them through."

Great. More disruption for the dogs tonight. She couldn't argue. Nico needed to be found and recovered immediately, and gathering evidence was the first step. Hopefully the RRPD would put a tracking team on the case.

The three of them, along with Stumps, returned to her office, and she was thankful for the quiet after the noisy kennel. Carson walked in and sat down in a guest chair while Shane leaned against the doorjamb, Stumps at his feet. On weak knees, she sank into the second guest chair rather than circling around to sit behind her desk. Shane's tall, muscular form blocked the only way out. Inexplicably irritated, she bit back a request to have him move. She'd never been claustrophobic before, but tonight everything was different and it bothered her to think she couldn't get up and walk out whenever she chose.

"What can you tell us about the attack?"

She hesitated, thinking her brother's question should have ended with *dog.* "Oh. You mean what happened to me?"

He nodded, pointing over his shoulder to Shane. "They found you unconscious in the yard with the puppies. Do you remember anything about your attacker?"

"No. Not really." She closed her eyes again. "I heard a noise. The gate maybe?" She scrubbed at her face. "No. A twig snapped near the gate—that was it." She was sure that had been while the puppies were out.

"You need a hospital," Shane stated.

He was studying her so intently, she pressed her hands between her knees to warm them up.

"When did you find her?" Carson twisted around to face Shane.

"About ten forty-five." He consulted his phone again. "Log says I called dispatch at ten forty-seven."

"Based on the log on Nico's cage, she could have been out for up to an hour."

"Hospital," Shane murmured.

Restless, she pulled the tie from her hair once more and left it loose. "I just need to get home and sleep it off."

Carson started to answer and stopped, interrupted by his cell phone. He checked the display and then looked from Danica to Shane and back again. "I need to meet with the crime scene unit. Shane will drive you to the hospital."

Turning to go, he paused at the doorway, waiting for Shane to move. At first she thought Shane held his ground, simply being a jerk because Carson was a Gage. Then she realized they were talking. About her, she assumed, since Shane's cool gaze rested on her and they kept their voices to a murmur. Too bad Stumps couldn't share the details with her.

When Carson was gone, Shane's judge and jury expression landed on her. "Let's go."

"I can't leave," she protested. "It's my overnight." She could handle it now that she didn't have to go out in the yard again.

"Hayley is already here to fill in for you."

Danica rolled her eyes. "That's silly. I'll be fine."

"She's here," he repeated. "You need a hospital. Come on."

When had her adult status been revoked? She didn't want to owe Hayley Patton any favors. The woman was a great dog trainer and a nice person underneath her passion for gossip and her tendency toward the self-absorbed end of the scale.

Danica scolded herself for being petty. Hayley

would be her sister-in-law by now if someone hadn't murdered Danica's brother Bo on the night before their wedding. She'd never quite understood what Bo had found so irresistible about Hayley, though they shared a love of animals, working dogs in particular. Maybe they really had fallen in love over the common ground of Bo's German shepherd breeding business.

From her chair, she matched Shane's cool gaze. After all, *his* half sister Demi Colton was the prime suspect in her brother's murder. The situation was just one more point of strife in the latest generation of the Colton-Gage feud. The Gages were perpetually certain the Coltons put family ties above the law and yet the Gages had made plenty of mistakes through the years. Shane might be the most glaring of those mistakes.

Though she personally refused to put too much stock in the circumstantial evidence found to date, the facts weren't lining up in Demi's favor. It was a balancing act for Danica, caught between grieving and knowing the investigation needed time to run its course so the right person ended up in jail.

"Come on," Shane said.

She didn't like the way he watched her as she pushed out of the chair. "I'd rather go home. I've already told the paramedics I'm fine."

"Great." Shane extended a hand, urging her forward. "You can tell the doctors, too."

She started to shake her head and thought better of it.

On a grumble, Shane closed the distance and seized her elbow. His grip was firm and gentle and sent a burst of tiny sparks up and down her arm. "Do you know what they injected me with?" she asked.

"No," he said. "Stumps didn't find anything in the yard, so the attacker must have kept the syringe he used."

On the way out of the training center, they passed Hayley sitting at the front desk, looking as polished and composed as ever. Even when she dissolved into tears over Bo, Hayley always seemed to be the epitome of beauty and polished grace.

Though they were both twenty-five, Danica always felt like the awkward younger tomboy around Hayley. It never surprised her that Hayley's long blond hair, blue eyes, sweet smile and generous curves drew so many admiring glances. Beside her, Danica's figure would best be described as streamlined and easily overlooked. It didn't bother her. Much.

Even now, she caught Shane's appraisal of Hayley as they walked out. She couldn't care, having no claim on where his eyes or interest wandered. The cool fresh air and velvet darkness of the South Dakota night refreshed her immensely.

"Where's your car?"

"I walked to work today."

"Can you walk down to the police station?" Shane asked. "If not, it looks like the ambulance is still here."

A trick question, she decided, following his gaze. The paramedics were leaning against the rig, chatting with another RRPD officer who had responded to Shane's call. One of them waved to Shane. "If I walk it, will you drive me home rather than take me to the hospital?"

"No," he replied.

She'd rather not continue the conversation, and being outside was helping. For a time there was only the muted sound of the corgi's toenails on the sidewalk as he trotted beside Shane. Neither her shoes nor his made any noise.

"You were drugged," Shane pointed out. "We shouldn't take any chances."

His insistence on helping confused her. "Why do you even care?" She was a Gage. He was a Colton. On top of that, her grandfather, a decorated officer in the RRPD, had railroaded an investigation and sent Shane to prison for a crime he didn't commit.

His hand tensed on her arm. "I don't know," he admitted. "When I looked over that fence and saw you, I wanted to keep right on going."

She appreciated the honesty, though it was hardly comforting. In Red Ridge, Shane was as well-known for his stark candor as he was for surviving the wrongful conviction and carving out a new career with his spunky K9 partner.

At last they reached his dove-gray SUV parked at the curb in front of the police station. The parking lights flashed as he pressed a button on the key fob and opened the passenger door for her.

"What were you doing out here anyway?" she asked when he had Stumps settled in the back seat.

"We were walking off a long drive from the other side of the county," he said. He took advantage of the complete lack of traffic and pulled a U-turn to go to the hospital. "Stumps likes to walk out this way every chance he gets."

"He probably still thinks of the training center as his territory," she said, thinking out loud. "He wouldn't be the first." She couldn't help wondering about Nico.

How had a stranger gotten him out of the training center without incident?

"Could be," Shane allowed.

The street seemed to do a slow spin around her head. She used the headrest as an anchor, distantly thinking a medical evaluation might not be a bad idea. "Whoever took Nico drugged him, too," she said under her breath, her eyelids growing heavy. "No way he'd let a stranger lead him away."

She was thinking about what that might mean for recovering him swiftly as a blanket of blissful black enveloped her once more.

Chapter 3

Her voice was so faint Shane leaned as far across the center console as he dared to hear her, hoping Danica was recalling something helpful. "What would they use to drug him?"

When she didn't reply, he took his eyes off the road and discovered she was unconscious again. He reached over and gave her shoulder a shake. All that did was cause her head to loll forward, that heavy curtain of red-gold silk falling over her face.

He swore and, thankful for the complete lack of traffic at this hour, stomped on the gas pedal. Better a speeding ticket than another Gage falling into trouble at the hands of a Colton.

He didn't for a moment believe Demi killed Bo, but the Red Ridge rumor mill loved to toss gasoline on the fire of the Colton-Gage feud. As if they couldn't manage the mutual hatred without outside interference. Until the RRPD identified a better suspect, the going theory of the Groom Killer case was the only theory.

For the first time in his career, he understood the sense of pervasive helplessness that came with an inability to bring justice to a victim. It wasn't a comfortable sensation and he refused to dwell on anything that gave him common ground with the decorated Sergeant Gage, the officer who'd inexplicably framed him.

He pulled up at the emergency room entrance and told Stumps to stay while he went around and lifted Danica from the passenger seat. He carried her inside and gave her name to the nurse at the information desk.

The nurse's eyes went wide as she recognized Danica's name and his face. Shane nearly snapped that he was the rescuer, not the perp. Similar claims had never helped him before so he didn't bother now. He could feel the speculation from people in the waiting area close enough to overhear them, but he resisted the urge to glare at them.

"What happened?" the nurse asked, escorting him through the doors to an available treatment bay, and he situated Danica on the bed. A male nurse hurried in, asking for information.

"She was drugged earlier and found unconscious." He pushed a hand through his short hair as he explained what he knew. "She came around on her own just before 11:00 p.m. and was doing fine. She refused to let the paramedics transport her. On the way over, we were talking and then she just blacked out."

"All right. We'll take it from here," the nurse said, nudging him clear so he could do a blood draw.

"I'll notify her brother that she's here," Shane said as he ducked out.

He'd done his part getting her here and he could leave with a clear conscience. So he had no logical explanation for why he parked the car and walked back into the hospital with Stumps at his side. In the waiting room, he sent Carson a text message that Danica was being evaluated.

Telling himself it was a simple courtesy and he'd leave as soon as someone from her family arrived, he found an out-of-the-way corner to wait. Stumps stretched out at his feet, resting his chin on his paws. Soon soft snores were coming from the tired corgi. Shane thought he had the right idea. He leaned back against the wall and tried to rest his eyes.

Instead, his mind tortured him with the images of Danica sprawled awkwardly on the grass and her disorientation when she'd come to. Contrary to public opinion, he didn't actively wish her or any of her siblings harm. He was thankful the attacker had used a drug to clear a path to steal the prized Malinois rather than overpower her with brute force that might have been deadly. For all her skill as an expert dog trainer, she couldn't change the fact that she was petite.

He sat forward and scrubbed at the stubble on his jaw. It was impossible to shut down his investigator's mind-set. The attacker's decision not to simply kill her had Shane thinking maybe the thief knew her. Probably even liked her. How did that shift the suspect pool? Although he avoided the Gages on principle whenever possible, he was in the minority. Danica had plenty of friends as well as plenty of sympathy for her recent loss.

Unlike him,

His connections were irrelevant. He didn't want friends or sympathy anyway. Being selective about whom he spent time with was a survival tactic. When he'd been young and stupid, his casual acquaintances had landed him in a world of trouble. In prison, it had taken him less than a week to learn having the wrong friends was worse than having no friends.

He couldn't stop the errant thought that even at eighteen his explanation of his presence a few blocks from a crime scene should have been enough to keep him out of jail. Unfortunately, Sergeant Gage decided otherwise and railroaded Shane for murder because of his last name and lousy-neighborhood address.

Growing up in the rougher neighborhoods in Red Ridge would have been challenge enough to outgrow and overcome. Being one of Rusty Colton's kids made his childhood exponentially worse. The familiar frustration with all the things he couldn't change gripped his shoulders and coursed down to his hands. Deliberately, he relaxed his clenched fists and smoothed his open palms over his knees. The past was gone. He was here because he'd rebuilt his life. He had a better address and a lucrative career with an excellent partner.

Right now, his intuition said this was definitely a case about a dog, but how the thief had chosen to take that dog made him curious. Had someone's fondness and respect for Danica changed what should have been a more aggressive approach?

He rested his elbows on his knees and let his hands fall between them. Familiar with the gesture, Stumps took advantage, sitting up so Shane could pet his ears while he gave the situation more thought.

Why did he care? He'd stumbled onto a crime scene—that was all. "Come on," he said to the dog. "The Gages can take care of their own." He stood up, waiting for Stumps to stretch and yawn. They had other cases and a hefty to-do list waiting at home. Writing up the report from their week of tracking down the site of the gun deal topped the list. He'd be far more effective after a few hours of sleep. And he definitely wanted to go into the station fresh tomorrow when he had to share the text message from Demi. He kept hoping that the next time he checked his phone there would be another text from her. So far, only more silence. He was nearly out the door when a nurse called his name from the reception desk.

He turned. "Yes?"

"Follow me." Her gaze dropped to the dog, her lips pursed in disapproval.

Shane lifted the hem of his shirt to show her the K9 badge clipped to his belt. "He won't be any trouble."

With a dubious sniff, the nurse led him back to the treatment area. "The patient has been asking for you," she said over her shoulder as they neared the curtained bay where he'd handed Danica over to the medical staff.

Disbelief rendered him speechless. No matter that he'd been out of prison for nearly a decade—the hard lessons died harder. Shane knew it was always better to wait and see about a situation rather than start asking questions too soon. The person who spoke first lost the advantage.

As the nurse swept aside the curtain, he saw Danica sitting up a little. "Thank goodness. I knew you'd stay." She looked to the doctor. "I signed the paper. You can inform him about anything." Her eyes snapped back to him. "Tell them you'll take me home."

Before Shane could sort out how to respond, a doctor in blue scrubs stepped forward. "We'd like to keep her for observation overnight. I don't have the blood work back to know what she was dosed with. Based on your statement, I'd rather she wasn't alone."

"Then she'll stay overnight," Shane stated.

"Don't side with them," Danica protested. "I need to get out there. You need to get out there and track down Nico."

She was more agitated now than when she'd woken in the training center yard. What was going on? "I'm sure your brother is organizing those details."

"Stumps already knows what to look for," she insisted. "There's no time to lose." Her green eyes were wide and a little dazed in a face that was far too pale. The freckles dusting the bridge of her nose stood out more than ever.

She knew Stumps wasn't a tracking dog. "She wasn't like this earlier." Shane glared at the doctor. "What did you give her?"

"Nothing that should cause an adverse reaction." The doctor shook his head. "Whatever is in her system is presenting almost like a rebound effect."

Shane wasn't particularly familiar with the term, but he assumed the drugs used on Danica were messing with her system. Danica started to swing her legs over the side of the bed. "Wait a minute," he said, stepping forward to stop her. "Stay put," he said.

"Nico could be anywhere," she wailed.

"Is Nico her child?" the doctor asked quietly.

Good grief. The doc had to be from out of town if he

didn't know Danica. "No, he's a working dog," Shane explained, using as few details as possible. "We believe whoever drugged her stole the dog from the K9 training center this evening."

The doctor arched his eyebrows. "I see."

Danica was crying, her green eyes swimming with tears, her hands clutching the sheets. Shane moved closer to the bed and put Stumps in her lap, hoping the dog could calm her. The medical staff clearly wasn't having any luck. Though Stumps was his dog, the corgi knew and trusted Danica. Stumps wedged his nose under her hand until she was stroking his head and ears. Within a minute, the crying slowed and the tension in her face evaporated.

"Thanks," one of the nurses murmured as she passed behind him.

Someone brought him a chair. Resigned, he sat down. He wasn't leaving without his dog which meant he wasn't going home anytime soon. He watched the clock over Danica's bed as she dozed restlessly. Another hour passed with no sign of her family.

Eventually, the doctor returned and a nurse added something to Danica's IV bag, though they didn't tell him what it was. It was nearly 2:00 a.m. when they moved her to a room and he and Stumps followed. He wanted to go home and yet he didn't feel right leaving her here alone. When she finally came out from under the drugs, she'd have questions. Shane wondered what was keeping her family. With Stumps snuggled beside her, Danica fell asleep again and Shane tried to do the same.

It didn't come easy. Hospitals and prisons had that same institutional atmosphere, every surface designed to withstand bleach cleaning with a pressure washer. The background noises were different and yet too similar. Shane could hear the faint undercurrent of machinery peppered with conversations and the occasional moan of pain or weeping. At least the hospital antiseptic smell was an improvement over the general stench of men oozing hate, fear and resignation with every breath and bead of sweat.

Shane jerked upright at the squeak of a shoe on the linoleum. Instantly awake and braced to defend himself, he glared at the shadow coming through the door.

"Easy," Carson said, walking over to the other side of Danica's bed. "I didn't expect her to have to stay." He scratched Stumps behind the ear. "I thought she was okay when you left."

"She was." Shane pushed at his hair and reached for a bottle of water the nurse had left for him. "She had some weird delayed reaction to the drug. She passed out in my car on the way here. Didn't you get my text?"

"Had my hands full," Carson replied.

Right. Carson had been working the crime scene where his sister had been attacked. "Well, when she woke up in the ER, she was in a frenzy to find Nico. They came and got me by default." It was becoming a pattern in his life, getting stuck in situations with members of the Gage family by default.

"Weird." Carson's eyebrows furrowed. "And you stayed with her."

Didn't seem like he had much choice at the time. Shane shrugged. "Stumps gave her some peace."

At the sound of his name, the dog snuggled closer to Danica and rested his chin on his paws. Shane knew that look. The dog wasn't in any rush to leave his comfy spot.

"This is above and beyond for you, Colton," Carson said. "Thanks. I guess it's a good thing they kept her overnight."

"Guess so." Shane's mind kept cycling through recent events. "Did you find anything promising in or around the kennel?"

"Nothing conveniently obvious. The crime scene unit did their thing and will report back. You know how it is. Everything is calm over there now." He looked to his sister. "Here, too. You should go on home."

Shane agreed. He was so tired he was tempted to mention the text message from Demi, just to get an opinion. As much as he respected Carson, Shane knew it was better to discuss that with his half brother, Brayden, before he mentioned it to anyone else, including their cousin, the chief. "You'll be at the station in the morning?" He checked his watch. "Well, later this morning?"

At least Carson could see for himself that his sister would be okay. Not knowing what was really happening with Demi and her pregnancy was like a rain cloud following Shane, threatening to drench him at any moment.

He stood up and approached the bed. Her color was better and her breathing had evened out. The freckles on her nose were nearly invisible again. He'd always thought she was cute—from a distance. Up close, she always treated him with that guarded professionalism that set his teeth on edge. At least this encounter was over and he wouldn't have to see her again until his next recertification with Stumps.

Careful not to wake her, he eased his dog away from Danica's side. She curled into the space as if hugging the warmth left behind, and tucked her hand under her chin. In that pose, she appeared far younger and more innocent than any Gage could possibly be.

Clinging to his familiar and reliable ire, he walked out of the hospital with Stumps. His gut knotted with the misplaced attraction he had often experienced around Danica and the more appropriate suspicion of the methods of the dog thief.

When at last he was home, he let Stumps out into the backyard. While he waited, he sent a text message to Brayden that he needed to talk first thing in the morning. Then he and Stumps retreated to the bedroom for a few invaluable hours of uninterrupted sleep.

Danica woke, momentarily disoriented by her surroundings, jerking away from the woman holding her wrist.

"Good morning. I'm your nurse, Anna." The woman said. "You've spent the night in the hospital."

"Why?"

Anna only smiled. "How are you feeling?"

"Better. I think." Pieces were coming back to her. What should have been a peaceful night had turned chaotic. She remembered walking to Shane's car, being dreadfully upset and snuggling with Stumps. It didn't make much sense but, curling her fingers into the blanket, she smiled at the red and white dog hairs scattered there.

"Any headache?"

Danica thought about it. "No." She purposely looked toward the brighter light spilling through the door and didn't feel the need to cringe or hide. "Definitely an improvement."

"Wonderful news."

"What time is it?" Danica asked.

"Nearly 7:00 a.m. The man who stayed overnight with you just went in to take a shower."

Did the nurse mean Shane? Had he stayed all night? Feeling better didn't mean she felt ready to deal with Shane. As she heard the water running in the bathroom, her imagination offered up a picture of Shane on the other side of that door and she felt her cheeks heat. Embarrassment flooded through her as details of last night flitted through her mind. Trying to regain her composure, she looked around the room for Stumps. "Where is the dog?"

Anna grinned. "He left before I got here. I heard he was a big help when you were upset."

So that wasn't Shane in the bathroom. The two were inseparable, as it should be with a K9 team. She tried to tell herself it was relief rather than disappointment trickling through her system.

"When can I go home?"

"The doctor will be around in another hour or so to explain everything."

The nurse sailed out of the room, leaving Danica bristling over the vague reply. She felt fine—her thoughts were clear at last. The water in the bathroom stopped and a few minutes later an electric razor buzzed. When her brother Carson emerged wearing dark slacks and a crisp white button-down, he looked fresh and ready for another day.

"You're awake." He crossed over in a hurry, a big, warm smile on his face.

"And feeling normal," she said, her mind drifting back to last night. "Finally."

He studied her closely. "You've said that before."

"I have?" She chewed on her thumbnail. "Did you bring Justice?" She hoped asking about his K9 partner would divert the conversation.

Carson didn't take the bait. "Shane said something happened when he brought you into the hospital." His brow furrowed. "And something worse in the ER."

She was tempted to smother herself with a pillow as another wave of embarrassment crashed over her. "You remember how normal meds do the unexpected in my system."

"Yeah." He chucked her under the chin. "You're too small for your own good."

"Ha. Not funny." Her small stature had always been a point of contention. It wasn't her fault the tall genes in the family skipped her. Desperate to hold her own, she'd studied martial arts for several years and proved she was perfectly capable of taking care of herself. As long as that fight was fair and came with a referee, apparently. It would take years to live down this attack. "Did you call Dad?"

"Only to let him know you're all right," Carson replied with a knowing wink.

The lack of her father stalking around the bed demanding the best treatment was proof Carson had sufficiently downplayed the whole incident. She owed him one. "Do they know what I was drugged with?"

He shrugged. "Something I can't pronounce. It was a hefty dose, way too much for your system, obviously."

"Obviously." She swallowed. "Was the thief trying to kill me?"

"Doubtful. It wasn't that type of drug. I know you've only been awake a few minutes, but anything could help. Do you remember new details?"

"Not really." She tried to think. "He came up behind me. I heard that twig. And then he was there, his hand over my mouth." She used her hand to demonstrate. "A pinch." She tapped her neck. "Then I couldn't move." Her palms started to sweat at the memory.

"Take it easy," Carson soothed. "You're safe and we'll make sure it stays that way."

How? "Have they started searching for Nico?"

"Yes. Based on where Shane found you, the attacker must have come through the back gate. Don't you keep that locked?"

"Yes." She heard the quiver in her voice and hated it. Bad stuff happened to good people all the time. She hadn't even been hurt. Not really.

She would *not* cry, not with Carson watching and worrying. He'd lump her into the Victim column and coddle her. She couldn't be sidelined during the search for Nico. He'd been taken on her watch. What she wouldn't give for a long, hard run to purge all these feelings. It would have to wait. "Is there coffee or something?"

He arched one eyebrow, but he left the room to track down coffee for her. She took advantage of the moment and managed to get into the bathroom with her IV pole. When she finished, she splashed water on her face and tried to comb her hair into some semblance of order. She was back in the bed when Carson returned with two tall cups of coffee. "Enjoy." He set one in front of her, "Sugar and cream already added."

"Thank you."

Carson got right back to his interview. "Shane said the gate was unlocked when he came through to help you. That it squeaked."

"The hinges need oiling," Danica said. "I don't recall hearing the squeak." Did that mean the attacker was hidden *inside* the yard when she walked out with the puppies? Goose bumps chased over her skin.

"We'll sort it out. Forensics is on it," Carson assured her gently.

She set the coffee cup aside when her hand trembled. "Are you sticking around until they spring me? I'll need a ride home."

"Yes. I had Vincent bring over clean clothes for you. And he said he'll feed your cat this morning."

"Thanks." Her cat, Oscar, wouldn't be much happier with the change in routine than her little brother, but she would make it up to her cat after work tonight. Everyone should have a big brother like Carson in a crisis. He understood she would want to get straight back to work.

Suddenly, her stomach rumbled loud enough to make Carson chuckle. "Sounds like what would help most is breakfast."

"That's a good sign." Carson grinned. "I'm on it."

Alone again, she fended off the persistent vulnerability lurking at the edge of her mind by focusing on the details of the theft that didn't fit together. Who had left the gate unlocked? What had the thief used to take Nico without a fight?

Nico wasn't the type of dog just anyone could manage. She said a quick prayer that they wouldn't find him after he'd caused someone serious harm. Restless, she checked the clock, willing the doctor to come by and release her.

The thief might have a few hours' head start, but RRPD had the best K9 unit in the region and the resources to track down a valuable animal like Nico and the person dumb enough to steal him.

Chapter 4

Shane and Stumps entered the police station and walked straight back to his half brother's desk. Echo, a yellow Lab that worked as Brayden's search and rescue partner, was stretched out on the cool floor. Shane placed one of the two coffees he carried in front of Brayden.

Brayden's dark eyebrows arched. "What's the occasion?"

Other than sharing a last name, they were polar opposites. Brayden's coloring was dark and Shane's fair. Both men bore a strong resemblance to their respective mothers. Aside from their height and build, very little of their father showed in either man. Neither of them would ever complain about that happy genetic coincidence.

"I have a problem," Shane said.

"No, you don't" Brayden removed the lid from the coffee and let the aroma waft up, inhaling deeply. "Detective Gage called in and said his sister is awake and feeling better."

Shane buried the surge of relief and pressed on. "Not his sister." He leaned closer and lowered his voice. "Ours." He pulled up the text message and handed over the cell phone.

Brayden paused in the act of sipping his coffee and carefully returned the to-go cup to the desktop. He stared at the phone display for far longer than required to read the brief message and swiped the screen to read the replies Shane had sent back.

"Still no word," Shane pointed out unnecessarily. "What do you think?"

"We have to tell the chief."

Shane pocketed the phone. "I figured you'd say that."

Brayden took a big gulp of the coffee. "This isn't a secret you can keep, Shane."

"I know, I know."

"You were hoping she'd give you a clue to follow so you can find her."

"We're all hoping that," Shane replied, irritated at Brayden's ability to see right through him. He might prefer the old distance after all.

"For different reasons," Brayden added, glancing around the station.

The brothers drank coffee in silence, their K9 partners keeping an eye on the activity swirling around them. Putting the mounting questions and worry into words wouldn't help Demi.

"She didn't kill Bo or anyone else," Shane muttered.

Brayden shot Shane a warning glance. "And yet we have to work the case. Anything else leaves us open to—"

Shane cut him off with a hard look. "I'm the last person here who needs that lecture."

Brayden snorted. "I'm just saying even you could benefit from an open mind once in a while."

"If your mind is too open your brains fall out." Shane winked. "Might be the only useful bit of wisdom our father passed along."

Rusty Colton's reputation was less than stellar in the Red Ridge community. The people who patronized the Pour House, his bar anchoring the rough side of town, wanted stiff drinks to dull the pain life frequently dished out. No one looking for sound advice on anything asked Rusty for more than beer or whiskey.

The slacker, no-good reputation had posed several hurdles for Rusty's offspring when they tried to improve themselves. Shane caught the gazes darting his way from various points around the bull pen and realized not all of those hurdles were out of the way, even after all this time. Though he sat here with Stumps in an official capacity on the right side of the law, he still didn't fit in. He really should be used to it by now.

"Come on." Brayden smacked Shane's shoulder. "You shouldn't put this off any longer." Together with their K9 partners, they went over to the chief's office.

Finn Colton, the chief of the K9 unit, listened intently to Shane's explanation of the text message and the subsequent delay in reporting it. He wasn't any more encouraged about a successful trace on the source than Shane. "She used a burner phone," Finn said flatly. "Assuming that's her and not someone messing with you."

Shane bit back the insistence that it was his sister on the other end of those two words.

"If you get another text, report it immediately."

"Of course," Shane promised, tension thrumming in the obedient reply.

"I'll just get back to my desk," Brayden said, making a swift exit with Echo.

"Do you have anything else for me?" Finn said, stopping Shane's attempt to follow.

"I was about to write it up." At Finn's obvious frustration, Shane relented. "We didn't find anything at the site of the exchange to connect the gun deal to the Larson brothers."

Finn swore. "I'm not surprised." His gaze shifted to the window and the view of the street outside. "Thanks for trying."

"Um, sure." The gratitude was unexpected considering he'd basically failed, and Shane tried to leave again.

"Can you take on one more investigation?" Finn asked as Shane reached for the door.

He paused, unwilling to volunteer for what he feared was coming next.

"Everyone is working overtime on the Groom Killer," Finn said. "I really need you and Stumps to take point on the missing Malinois."

Shane smothered a groan and barely resisted rolling his eyes. "How is Danica this morning?" The question was out before he could stop it.

"Carson said she was good as new when he called in earlier." Finn raised his chin toward the bull pen. "Looks like you can ask her yourself."

Shane turned to see the redhead in question walking in with her brother and his K9 partner, Justice. She was dressed for work. Why wasn't she *at* work?

"I know with your history this is the last case you want. I sympathize."

Sympathy never fixed anything, Shane thought. Working the missing Malinois case inevitably meant more time with Danica, prime witness. "There has to be something else, another investigation we can help with." Shane dropped to one knee and gave Stumps some affection, soothing both of them. He didn't consider it hiding.

"You can't hold her grandfather's mistakes against her," Finn said. "She had nothing to do with your incarceration."

"I know." She'd been a kid, fifteen or sixteen, maybe. At barely eighteen, he'd only been an adult in his mirror and in the eyes of the law. Still, the resentment was easier than forgiveness for so many reasons.

"Under normal circumstances I wouldn't push it," Finn was saying.

Shane stood up, folding his arms over his chest. "But?"

"Damn it, don't make me beg." He came around the desk and went toe-to-toe with Shane. "You know as well as I do we can't have a trained protection dog out there." His face clouded, the dark blond eyebrows casting deep shadows over his blue eyes. "Take Danica and start with the Larson twins." It was clearly an order. "They were mad as hell when Darby wouldn't sell them any puppies. They were specifically looking for protection dogs at the time."

"Not good," Shane muttered. Darby, Bo Gage's ex-wife, had recently taken over the German shepherd breeding business.

"Not at all," Finn agreed. He opened the office door and called Danica over to join them. After a brief exchange and assurance that she was well, Finn explained that Shane had been assigned to her case and they would be working together.

Though Danica's lips lifted into a polite smile, Shane noticed the strain of the news in her eyes. Well, at least they found common ground with their mutual distaste for Finn's orders. Maybe working closely with her—away from the training center—would help him purge the last of his lingering attraction to the one woman in town who would never want anything to do with him. The one woman in town he shouldn't want at all. As she crouched to chat with Stumps, he supposed the dog gave them two common points to work from.

She looked up, her green gaze misty and warmer than usual. "Thank you," she said.

He would have been less surprised if she'd punched him.

"Thank you, too," she repeated to Stumps.

"What?" Behind him, Finn mumbled something that might have been advice, but Shane's attention was locked on Danica as she stood up.

"For everything last night," she said. "You let Stumps stay with me. I heard that you, um, stayed, too." Her lips twisted to the side. "I appreciate it."

"Okay." The sincere gratitude threw him off. Struggling with it, he shoved the conversation back onto the proper track. "We'll start with the Larsons," Shane began, ignoring more muttering from Finn. "As long as we also pursue the theory that the attacker knew Danica personally."

"Pardon me?"

There—the familiar wariness was back in her eyes and the world settled under his feet once more. "You could easily have been severely injured," he explained. "The attacker drugged you when he might as easily have bashed you over the head or just killed you."

Her green eyes went wide and her face paled. Those freckles reappeared. A heartbeat later her eyes sparked and her cheeks flamed with temper. Good recovery. He pressed his point. "For that matter, why didn't he kill you once you were down? It would have been a smarter move. No way to be sure what you might remember. A stranger probably wouldn't care whether you lived or died, but someone who knows you might."

"Might?" Her auburn brows challenged his choice of words and she folded her arms over her chest. "I only know of one person in town who'd like to bash me or mine over the head." She gave him a pointed look, clearly accusing him of being that person.

She wasn't exactly wrong, though he kept his Gage-bashing urges under wraps by simply avoiding them as much as possible.

"Moreover, anyone who knows *me* probably knows better than to steal a trained attack dog. Without a handler, Nico might as well be a loose cannon—"

"Enough," Finn interjected. "Figure out a way to work this case together," he ordered. "Shane is in charge," he said to Danica. "And keep me in the loop on your progress."

"Yes, sir," Shane said.

Danica echoed him and when he opened the door,

she passed him with her pert nose high in the air. Just like a Gage to be certain they knew everything about everyone before all the facts were in.

Danica fumed in silence over the shift in her circumstances. The only silver lining she could see was that proximity to Shane kept her mind well away from the bone-deep sense of violation haunting her. She'd argued that driving from the police station to the training center was a waste, but Shane had pointed out that every minute of walking was a minute they weren't looking for Nico.

"Do you really think the Larson twins would stoop to this?" she asked as he parked the car.

"At the moment, I think they're capable of most anything."

They'd come over so Danica could pick up a microchip scanner before they questioned the Larsons. If the twins did have Nico, she wanted to be able to scan his chip and prove the dog belonged to the K9 training center. The sooner they got him back on his schedule, the safer everyone would be.

She felt a tremor in the air as she walked inside. Glancing at Shane and Stumps, she saw they didn't seem to indicate anything was amiss. Maybe the tremor was inside her or apparent only to those who worked here every day. She knew this building as well as she knew her condo and until last night, she'd felt equally safe here and at home. Today the energy was off, as if no one wanted to speak too loudly and bring on more trouble.

A form of grief, she supposed, after the violence of last night. Though she'd been the only human victim, everyone here would be upset by the invasion and theft. And everyone here, understanding the great risk of having Nico out there without a certified handler, would be on edge, hoping for the best and braced for the worst.

As efficiently and graciously as possible, she accepted the concern from her colleagues. Although she was impatient to get out there with Shane, she was glad to hear the dogs were only slightly off today and new security guards had been hired to prevent another mishap.

Mishap. As if a missing attack dog was on the same level as a puppy's bladder giving way indoors.

With the microchip scanner in hand, she was nearly out the door when she noticed Tyler Miller hanging back as if he didn't want to intrude. A little shy, he was a smart kid willing to do any task and was good with the dogs. In her eyes, he was as valuable to the program as any of the trainers. Smiling, she walked over to speak with him. At fourteen, he was already taller than her. They'd met at the community youth center. It had taken a few months, but she'd finally convinced him to visit the training center. Now he spent every available hour here. Through the course of working with him, she knew he didn't have a great home life and his experiences at school, the youth center and the training center might be the only good examples he had.

"How are the puppies doing today, Tyler?"

He shrugged a bony shoulder, his long, dark hair falling over his brown eyes. He gave up studying his shoes to meet her gaze. "They seem a little bummed. What about you?"

"I'm just fine now." If she said it enough it might feel true. Physically, it was true. She thought he could use a hug, but she kept her arms to herself. Tyler had told her early on he didn't do hugs.

He shuffled his feet. "They said you were in the hospital." His gaze slid away, then back, hot with temper. "Were you hurt bad?"

"No," she replied. He seemed so angry on her behalf she tried to downplay it even more. "The overnight observation was only a precaution. I promise you, I'm fine. I had a weird reaction to whatever drug was used on me."

"As long as you're okay. I was worried when I heard about it." His eyes drifted over her shoulder and he took a quick step backward. "I'll get back to work. Take care." He gave her a half smile as he turned and disappeared down the hallway to the kennels.

She only noticed Shane and Stumps had come up behind her once Tyler was gone. Knowing what she did of Shane's background, she'd wanted to introduce them.

"You seem a little rattled," Shane said as she walked out with him and Stumps.

"I'm fine." In a perfect world, she would have broken into a run. She fought the urge to look back over her shoulder. Doing so would only reveal too much to an investigator as observant as Shane. "More security is a good first step," she said, hoping to shift his attention to a safer topic.

"You're pale again."

Clearly, that tactic failed. "I'm fine," she repeated.

"What happened last night—"

She cut him off with a look as he opened the passenger door for her.

"All I'm saying is that no one would blame you if you took the day off."

"We need to find the dog." Her eyes didn't hurt anymore, but she donned her sunglasses anyway and closed the door herself. Staying home wouldn't help Nico. Right now, she wasn't even sure she could stay home alone and stay sane.

"Let me do the talking when we question the Larsons," he said, pulling away from the curb.

It was a reasonable request. He was trained in investigation. She was trained in dogs. "As long as you let me give the commands if Nico is there."

"Deal."

That might be the first agreement between a Gage and a Colton in a long while. Well, if she didn't count her little brother Vincent's lovesick vow to marry Shane's cousin Valeria Colton. At nineteen, they just couldn't seem to accept they were too young for that kind of pledge. "What do the Coltons think of Valeria and Vincent?"

"How should I know?" Shane muttered. "We're not a hive mind."

Did the man have to be so aggravating? "What do *you* think of their relationship?"

"I think nineteen is too young to make any lifelong commitment," he replied. "And despite their claims to the contrary, I'm sure they're still dating."

She shouldn't have been surprised they agreed on that point, too. It was common sense. Both families had voiced worry for Vincent's safety, with the Groom Killer on the loose.

"He's your brother," Shane said. "Can't you reason with him?"

"He's nineteen," she laughed. "No one can tell him anything he doesn't already know. We've all tried."

She remembered the challenges of being a teenager, when every choice felt like it carried life-and-death consequences, and her childhood had been nearly perfect. Just one reason she invested her time at the youth center, mentoring teens like Tyler. "Do you ever volunteer at the youth center?" she asked.

Shane snorted. "I'm hardly role model material."

"I disagree," she blurted without thinking.

He parked the car on the street, across from the Larson offices. "Care to elaborate?"

"Not really." Why couldn't she keep her mouth shut? She looked over at the modern-style glass building. It wasn't exactly out of place, yet something about it felt too shiny to be real.

"Nice building," she murmured, refusing to turn and risk meeting Shane's hard blue gaze. The sign stated the Larson brothers owned a real estate company. If that was true, they'd made some smart or lucky deals to come into their fortune so suddenly.

"Ready?" She reached for the door handle.

"Tell me why you think I could be a role model," Shane demanded.

"That can wait."

"Call me an in-the-moment kind of guy." The words were full of a bitterness that made her feel terrible.

She was sure that was exactly what he wanted by the not-so-subtle reference to his eighteen months in prison. A year and a half stolen from Shane when her grandfather manipulated the case to pin a murder on him.

"You haven't let circumstances define you." She hoped that would be enough. They had a dog to find. His choked laughter told her otherwise. Pushing her sunglasses up to the top of her head, she faced him at last. "People admire you for what you've accomplished."

"People?" His eyebrows lifted. "Evidence and confessions aside, people have been waiting nearly a decade for me to do something that proves I should be locked up."

"That isn't true."

"Isn't it?" He barreled on. "We both know my sister is the prime suspect in your brother's murder because our father is Rusty Colton and we were raised on the rough side of town. Blood tells."

"When the victim spells out her name with his own blood it sure does." She regretted the words immediately. She held up her hands in surrender. "I'm sorry. That wasn't fair. I don't really believe Demi killed Bo." She was surprised she didn't get frostbite from his brittle, cold glare. "I do believe you could be a benefit to those kids."

He leaned across the console. "Being exonerated by a good DNA test and a witness who found God doesn't make me role model material."

"No, it doesn't," she agreed, refusing to let him intimidate her further. "What you've done since as a business owner and a K9 officer *does*. Your perseverance and determination to build a life and reputation against steep odds would be a big inspiration to kids struggling to find a way out of their own challenging situations."

He eased back in his seat, studying her with that hard blue gaze.

"Have I grown a second head?" she asked.

"No."

"Then let's go get Nico." She reached for the door handle again.

He hit the power lock button. "Hang on. What hardships make you qualified to mentor at the youth center?" he demanded.

"Oh, no hardships at all." She sweetened the words with a sugary smile. "My life's been utterly perfect." She dropped her sunglasses back into place. "I volunteer out of the goodness of my heart, wearing rose-colored glasses on my quest to change the world."

She flipped the lock button manually and exited the car. Clinging to the last of her dignity and composure, she managed not to slam the door. Whatever had possessed her to speak to him that way, she wasn't going to apologize. Someone should have knocked that chip off his shoulder years ago. He had no right to assume he *knew* anything about her.

Of course, prison must have been dreadful, but life didn't hand out free passes to anyone. Frustrated with herself as much as with him, she stalked across the street and waited in front of the building.

Gripping the microchip scanner, she reminded herself Nico was the top priority. Going in riled up and anxious would only put them all at risk, especially if Nico was inside. She took deep, slow breaths and pulled herself together for the task ahead.

Chapter 5

Shane didn't appreciate her gratitude or this nonsense that he could be any sort of mentor or asset to a teenager. Those were absurd concepts. He'd take her temper and disdain over her kindness. He didn't have enough practice dealing with the softer side of life.

Still, that didn't give him the right to trump her hard knocks with the prison card. She was keeping it together after being attacked. He commended her for convincing everyone but him she was over it already. He recognized the deep shock lurking in her gaze and the fearful expectation that another attack was imminent, having seen it often enough in his mirror.

And why did her sarcastic claim of a perfect life rouse his anger toward an unseen, unnamed foe? Other than last night's attacker, who had hurt her? His distraction gave her a head start across the street as he helped Stumps out of the car. For a split second, he worried that she'd storm into the Larson offices in a petite imitation of Wonder Woman, but she waited for them to join her. One positive didn't erase a host of negatives, but he supposed it was a start.

He refused to take all the blame for the bickering. Danica wasn't the professional, cheerful dog trainer she seemed, or at least she wasn't *only* that. It made him curious about the other layers under that sweet packaging, which irritated him on general principle. They were working a case, not building a relationship.

No matter that she was beautiful and clever with a smile that could go from innocent to wicked in a blink—he had no right to be curious about Danica Gage. *Who had hurt her?* he wondered again as he and Stumps joined her on the sidewalk. Good grief, what was wrong with him? Her past wasn't the issue. He had to derail that pointless train of thought and focus on the missing dog investigation.

"You ready to do this?" he asked.

She nodded. "If they have Nico, I'll recognize him," she said.

"And the scanner will confirm it," he agreed. "If he's here, we'll have Nico back where he belongs soon." He wanted to bang his head against the nearest brick wall. Was this his first day on the job? An investigator never made promises he couldn't keep. The woman tangled him up. He pulled his thoughts together and opened the door for her to walk inside first.

His first impression on this side of all the gleaming glass was simply *high-end*. From the marble floors to the sleek information desk, everything in this lobby screamed new money. Shane walked over, easy smile in place, and asked to speak with the Larson brothers. After a short wait, he and Stumps and Danica were shown into the office.

Stumps's ears immediately perked up as they walked in. Shane knew he and his partner were cataloging all of the details simultaneously.

At one side of the room, two sleek German shepherds in their prime lounged on thick, luxurious dog beds in the wash of sunlight from the windows. Curious, but at ease, Shane had no doubt either of those two dogs would have happily clamped jaws over his neck if either Larson gave the command.

"Hello, Evan," Shane addressed the man at the closer desk. "Noel." He gave a nod to the man behind the desk situated further back. "Did we catch you at a bad time?"

"Not at all," Evan replied. "Just taking a break for lunch."

The identical twins were difficult to tell apart. Both men had gray-blue eyes, were clean-shaven and wore their blond hair trimmed in a similar tousled fashion. They kept mansions next door to each other on Bay Boulevard, the best street in the most coveted neighborhood in Red Ridge, where new money liked to plant large houses.

Shane believed the twins thrived on creating doubt and uncertainty about which of them was which. He'd always differentiated them by Evan's tendency to talk first and think later and the subtle ways he typically deferred to Noel. Telling them apart had been easier for Shane since he'd partnered with Stumps because he cued into the signs that Evan didn't care for dogs as much as his twin did. He wondered if that's why

Evan's desk was as far from the German shepherds as possible.

The calculating gazes of the twins studied their visitors, giving Shane the eerie sense that they were being viewed as potential prey by a couple of hungry wolves. Wolves with trained protection dogs in the pack. He glanced again at the German shepherds, named Hans and Fisher. The twins claimed the dogs were merely devoted companions, and served as an intimidation factor when they were showing rural properties in the area, but everyone in town gave the twins and their dogs a wide berth.

Beside him, Danica tensed when her eyes lit on the third dog in the room. Seated near Noel's desk, the dog fixed a dark gaze on the three of them while he panted lightly. The dog was definitely a Malinois, a little smaller but no less deadly than the bigger German shepherds at the window. Judging by Danica's bristling reaction, she believed this was Nico.

He trusted her assessment, on the canine at least.

"What brings you two by?" Evan said, coming around his desk to greet them with a handshake. "Looking to put your house on the market and upgrade to something better, Colton?"

"I'm content where I am." He'd moved when he'd launched his business, investing in a better area of Red Ridge that was closer to the police station. The location made it easier to fulfill his role as part of a K9 evidence team.

Evan's leering gaze raked over Danica with enough interest that Shane nearly stepped in front of her. "So you must be in the market for something new," Evan said.

"Danica, are you here about real estate?" Shane asked.

"Love my condo, thanks," she replied, her gaze locked on the Malinois.

"There's a new development planned—"

Danica cut off Evan's pitch. "Give it a rest. You know we're here for Nico," she stated.

Shane caught the slight shift as Nico's eyes latched onto Danica. It was the dog's only movement. With the twins suspected of so much illegal activity from the gun deal to laundering money, Shane had no doubt there was something incriminating in this office beyond the stolen Malinois. It was tempting to give Stumps a seek command. Only the awareness that doing so would likely get his corgi attacked kept Shane in check.

"Nico? Who's Nico?" Evan asked, eyes wide with feigned innocence. The dog continued to watch Danica. "You know anyone by that name, Noel?"

Shane took a half step forward before Danica said something else. They couldn't afford to blow this rare opportunity by getting thrown out too soon. "Nico was the name of a dog stolen from the K9 training center last night," Shane explained. "Naturally, Danica and everyone at the training center are upset by the loss."

"Naturally." Evan's sympathy was far less convincing as he leered at Danica again.

Shane shifted closer to her. "We're simply checking in with dog owners in the area, asking them to keep an eye out."

"What kind of dog did you lose?" Noel asked.

"Belgian Malinois. Stolen," Danica corrected him.

"That's a shame," Noel said. "Well-trained dogs are invaluable."

"Yes, they are," she agreed.

Shane was amazed she could speak at all through her clenched teeth.

"You should get better security out there," Evan observed. "Y'know, if you want to protect the dogs and the investment." He returned to his chair and propped his feet on the corner of the desk, stacking his ankles. "The dogs you train are worth a fortune."

"I'm aware," Danica replied.

Again, Shane noted the uncanny resemblance of the twins to the dogs under the window. Casually alert to any action and willing to dispense with trouble should it arise. With opposable thumbs, the twins were more lethal than the dogs, but it was a close race.

"When did you get that shepherd?" Shane asked, deliberately getting the breed wrong. "He's a beauty even if he's on the small side."

"Last night," Danica murmured under her breath.

He threw her a quelling look that bounced right off her impervious stubborn hide.

"He's a Malinois," Evan said proudly. "We bought him as a pup some time ago."

Shane caught the displeasure Noel aimed at his brother. God bless Evan's inability to keep his mouth shut.

"He just finished his training so we took delivery," Noel added.

"You're becoming quite a collector," Shane said. "Or did something happen that you're expanding the pack?"

"Real estate has risks," Noel said. "Hans and Fisher are good, but this guy will be better."

"When was that delivery?" Shane asked, pulling out his investigator's notebook. "Because he's the same breed as the stolen dog. It would be great if you could show me a receipt. Just to clear up any confusion."

"I don't have the receipt here," Noel said before Evan could reply.

"How convenient," Danica said. The snarl on her lips belied her neutral tone. "I know *where* you took delivery," she said.

Noel arched one golden eyebrow, then turned his head to the dog. "Come."

To Shane's astonishment, the dog padded over to Noel.

"Good dog." Noel rewarded the dog with a bite of steak from his sandwich. He stared down Danica. "I know it's hard to admit a mistake, but clearly you can see this isn't the dog you think it is."

She tapped the microchip scanner against her palm. "If I'm mistaken, you won't mind if I scan his microchip."

"Be my guest," Noel said.

His utter confidence planted a seed of doubt in Shane's mind. Yes, Danica knew her dogs, but she was recovering from being drugged and attacked. Although he agreed with the general consensus that the Larson twins weren't operating aboveboard, Shane wasn't willing to make them the scapegoats for every recent crime in Red Ridge.

Shane kept an eye on Evan, hoping for some sort of tell as Danica walked toward the dog. Unfortunately, Evan didn't flinch.

From the sunny spots, the German shepherds tracked her progress, and beside him, Stumps almost came out of his seated position. It was a rare situation that unsettled his corgi.

While Evan and Noel and the dogs watched her with equally assessing and predatory gazes, Danica scanned Nico's shoulder where the training center would have implanted his identifying microchip. Shane didn't hear a signal.

"Anything?" he asked her.

She shook her head, her golden-red ponytail rippling down her back. "Give me a second. You know they can move."

"By all means, be sure," Noel said in a tone that made Shane's teeth ache.

She tried, moving the scanner back and forth between the dog's shoulder blades until at last the device made a noise. Danica's triumphant smile evaporated in an instant as she read the information on the scanner's display. "This can't be right," she said. She whirled on Noel. "What did you do?" she asked, pulling out her cell phone.

"I had my dog chipped," Noel replied. "Like any responsible dog owner." He fed the Malinois another bite of steak and watched Danica with an amused gaze.

Shane realized she must be calling the microchip registry for confirmation. When he saw her brace for battle, he knew she was searching for any target after last night. Noel wasn't a fight she could win. Not today. "Let me see," he said, beckoning Danica back to his side. He didn't want her within grabbing distance of either the twins or the dogs any longer than necessary.

She marched back to him, her temper nearly overriding her self-control. "Look." She shoved the scanner at him. "It's Nico, but the chip isn't our frequency. The registry says this dog belongs to Noel and Evan Larson."

"All right," Shane said. Questions chased one after another through his mind, but with this result, they couldn't argue about the ownership of the Malinois further right now.

"Shane." She turned her back on the twins. "It's him," she whispered, staring up at him, her eyes pleading for him to do something. Stumps was gazing at him with a similar intense expectancy.

He believed her. Danica knew her dogs, especially those she'd trained. They would have to find a different way to prove it. He didn't have a viable option as an investigator, not to mention the threat from the men and their dogs if he tried to take Nico back by force. If he stepped over the line here, the chief would have his hide for giving the Larsons a legal loophole to slip through. Stealing Nico was only the latest crime they suspected involved the twins.

"Clearly, we're mistaken and I appreciate your patience." He hated the betrayal that twisted Danica's features. "If you'd just answer a few questions about your whereabouts last night, we can button this up for the chief."

"Our whereabouts?" Evan's feet hit the floor with a thud. Hans, Fisher and the Malinois previously known as Nico locked onto him. "We just proved the dog is ours. You've got no right asking—"

"Forgive my brother," Noel said, rising calmly. "He's overtired. We had a rough night last night."

Danica folded her arms over her chest. "Yeah, I hear stealing dogs can wear a person out."

Shane shot her a sidelong glance. "You'd rather wait in the car?" She stood her ground, her lips pressed together. "What happened last night, Noel?" Shane asked.

"We were at the hospital until sometime after two this morning," Noel said. "Our grandmother called you around eight, right?" he glanced at Evan.

"Eight thirty-two," Evan replied, holding up his cell phone. "Said she was having chest pains." He swallowed. "She'd called an ambulance and wanted us to meet her at the hospital."

Noel offered his phone as well, the screen displaying his call history. "Evan called me and we went over to the ER to wait it out."

Airtight, Shane thought. It was a wonder he hadn't bumped into the twins while he'd been there with Danica. All of this would be easy enough to confirm with the ambulance logs and ER intake records.

"Took them forever," Evan groused. "They moved her all over with various tests."

"Is she still in the hospital?" Danica asked with sincere concern.

Shane understood her reaction. Although no one trusted her grandsons, everyone thought of Mae as an extra grandmother.

"No," Evan said. "She's home resting."

"According to the tests," Noel added, "her heart is fine. She'll follow up with her doctor later this week."

"That's great news," Shane said. "We appreciate your time."

Noel's gaze slid over Danica. "Our pleasure."

"When you get time, send a copy of that receipt for the dog over to the police station," Shane said. "Just crossing the t's and dotting the i's."

"I'll take care of it," Noel agreed.

"Thanks." Shane opened the door, keeping himself between Danica and the dogs and twins. "I'll tell the chief to look for it."

Neither Shane nor Danica spoke until they were in his car driving away from the Larsons' fancy office.

"You're angry," Danica said. "With me or them?"

He couldn't deny it. "Not entirely with you," he hedged. "You told me you'd let me do the talking."

"I tried," she said. "When I saw Nico, I knew him. He knew me, too," she insisted. "They can't be allowed to keep him. He wasn't even on a lead."

"I noticed."

"How are we going to get him back?"

"Forget it." He couldn't let her entertain ideas of rescuing a dog. "That dog is officially registered to Noel and Evan. If he disappears, the Larsons will name you as the prime suspect." He checked her expression to see if the jab landed, but she was staring out the window. "Where would you stash the dog if you did manage to steal him back?"

"'That dog' was Nico," Danica said.

He noticed she didn't answer him. "I believe you." He flexed his hands on the steering wheel.

"You do?" She twisted in the seat to stare at him.

He kept his eyes on the road. "Of course. You know your dogs."

"Then why—"

"If there had been a way to take Nico with us without you, me or Stumps becoming Hans and Fisher food, he'd be with us right now."

She sank a little deeper into the seat. "Where are we going?" she asked after a few minutes.

It had been just enough time for his mind to get back on the case. "Nowhere, really." Sometimes a meandering drive helped him think. At the moment, they were headed west, toward the mountains in the near distance. The sun was high and the views expansive.

"In the office, I was sure you believed them."

"Noel's initial confidence planted a seed of doubt in my mind," Shane admitted. "But it withered and died under the airtight alibi." Had they sent in the thief when they heard Mae Rose was ill, or had they decided to move last night and gotten lucky that their grandmother's crisis gave them a more legitimate alibi?

Sensing the scowl, he glanced over and confirmed her auburn eyebrows were drawn tightly together over her pert nose. "That makes no sense."

He didn't expect it to make sense to her. She'd never been framed for a crime she didn't commit. Since he'd been cleared and released, he'd been labeled a cynic and much worse. Contrary to popular belief, he didn't have it out for the cops. He was just a realist about human nature. People did dumb stuff and they did mean stuff and they did truly inexplicable stuff when they were backed into a corner.

"I'm sure Mae Rose had a health scare, but it felt too rehearsed when they told us about it," he said. "Once the chief has this information, he can get the ER visit and ambulance ride verified. I'm sure it will check out."

"Me, too." She twisted her hands in her lap.

He struggled against an annoying, persistent urge to soothe her. "The only way for the Larson brothers to have Nico today is for someone to have stolen him for them last night."

"How do we prove that when the microchip says he's their dog?" she asked.

No idea. The town faded in his rearview mirror as the mountains grew from the horizon ahead. The bright spring sky above was an endless blue curve. Nothing relaxed him or reassured him more than the freedom to roam wherever he pleased across the wide-open countryside. He passed the junction with the state road that he'd traveled home on last night, wishing he and Stumps had found something at the site of the gun deal.

"We'll focus on finding who attacked you," he replied. He had some concerns and a brewing theory about where and why she'd been drugged last night. So far, no one working for Noel and Evan had flipped on the brothers. Finding the weak link was the crux of this type of investigation. Eventually, someone would crack. Someone had to.

"But they couldn't have known Mae Rose would go to the ER last night," she said, echoing his thoughts.

"I'm sure they had another alibi lined up, ready to go."

"You're right." She drummed her fingers on her knee. "They must have a veterinarian lined up and ready to go at a moment's notice, too," she muttered.

"What do you mean?"

She stopped fidgeting. "That was Nico, but he wasn't acting like himself."

"How so?" Shane recalled how he'd come to attention when Evan got upset. "He looked pretty alert to me."

"You noticed the panting, right?"

"Yes." And now that she mentioned it, he recalled that was typical behavior postanesthesia or when medication was involved.

"He's a trained attack dog, Shane. The thief must have drugged him to get him out of the kennel without losing a limb."

He was warming to her veterinarian theory. "Sedatives can be acquired any number of illegal ways," he pointed out.

"Sure, but you can't learn veterinarian surgical skills on YouTube. I looked him over. There wasn't an obvious incision so it was someone with skill. Nico's original microchip was registered to the training center. This wasn't a case of tampering with a computer record. They removed our chip and inserted their own. Only a vet could do that."

"The dog had to be sedated?"

"It would be pretty cruel to remove a microchip without some form of pain relief. And Nico wasn't showing any signs of discomfort or aggression when I was using the scanner."

Huh. A new direction was better than another roadblock. Feeling better about the update he could give Finn, Shane turned back toward town. "That's great information. I'll see where it leads. Where can I drop you?"

"We're supposed to work this case together," she said, her hands twisting in and around themselves again.

He managed to keep the exasperated sigh to himself. Not wanting to be alone was a classic postassault reaction. The only togetherness Shane was interested in was his work with Stumps. His K9 partner was reliable. People let him down way too often. But the idea of making her fend for herself pricked his conscience.

"To the police station, then," he said. "You can sweet talk your brother into getting the confirmation out of the hospital while I report to Finn." Maybe Carson would see through her bravado and take care of her.

She agreed with that plan, which eased his mind more than it should have. After the report was turned in, Shane intended to take Stumps on an evidence-hunting walk behind the training center yard and he wouldn't let any inquisitive, tempting dog trainers tag along.

There was no reason for her welfare to be his concern, yet he kept wanting to leap between her and the rest of the world.

Weird. Doubly so, considering who she was. The protective urge was probably just fallout from the interview with the Larson twins. The way they'd looked at her, as if she'd make a tasty snack, would stick with him for some time.

Danica struggled not to fill the silence with nonsense as Shane drove back to town. The shock and fear and denial of being overpowered kept sneaking into her mind. She couldn't quite accept the way her arms and legs had simply failed and the stars were swallowed by the drug's effects. Logically, she knew it was over, yet deep in her heart she kept trying to go back and do something different.

Shane might not be mad at her, but she wasn't very happy with herself. She didn't fight hard enough last night and she'd given up too easily today. She should have grabbed Nico's collar and dared Noel to do something. And if she had, all three of them would probably be dealing with serious injuries right now. Hans and Fisher were big, strong dogs and having seen them around town with the twins, she recognized they'd been trained well beyond basic obedience. However they appeared, lounging in the sunshine, she had no doubt they would follow whatever command Noel or Evan gave, including an attack or protect order.

Although she'd initially wanted to criticize Shane for not taking decisive action, she knew he had to work within the law. As a private investigator, he had more leeway, even on a RRPD case, but he could lose his career and his K9 partner if he did something rash. She didn't want to be responsible for more loss in his life.

She twisted around to check on Stumps in the back seat. The adorable corgi shared an unbreakable bond with Shane, and she'd heard the bits and pieces about the cases they'd solved for the RRPD as well as his personal clients. Usually, it gave her a sense of pride and partnership when the K9 officers succeeded.

With Shane and Stumps, she did her best not to feel anything. Not pride in training done well, not remorse for the eighteen months Shane spent in the state penitentiary, and certainly not regret that she'd never know why her grandfather had railroaded Shane.

"I should have told Noel that was a ticking time bomb eating his steak, not a new dog." She couldn't quite figure out how the twins had managed to gain Nico's loyalty so fast, drugs or not. Fully aware of how the young Malinois had been trained, Danica knew that didn't bode well for anyone who opposed them.

"What do you mean?" Shane asked.

"About what?" Had she said something else without realizing it? Maybe she would be better taking the rest of the day off. She rubbed at the goose bumps on her arms, chilled by the idea of only her cat and her thoughts for company in her condo. Tonight would be bad enough. She wouldn't lump in what was left of a workday, too.

"You said Nico was a ticking time bomb."

Thank goodness she hadn't said something more personal. "He is. You know protection dogs have a unique training protocol because of what is expected of them. The Larsons stole him at the perfect time. They wouldn't really be safe with him if he was already bonded with a handler. To have him up there without a lead around other dogs is begging for trouble. He's out of his element. Any sign of aggression from the dogs or people could set him off. He's been trained to bite first and bark later. Noel seems determined to become his handler, but bonding with a dog like Nico requires expertise, discipline and consistency."

"It'd be something if Nico took down the Larsons on his own," Shane muttered.

Understanding the sentiment, she wanted to laugh, but if Nico attacked his registered owners, he'd be put down immediately and that would be tragic. "Without the original chip, we'll never prove Nico was stolen," she grumbled. "They'll get away with it."

"We'll find a way to link them to the theft," he said. "Stumps put us on the right track last night and we'll keep following those clues."

"What clues?" she asked. Either he wasn't sharing everything or she was too unfocused by the situation. Discouraged and frustrated, she glared at the police station as it came into view.

Shane shot her a look. "We're on this case together," he said. "We'll stop at the station first and talk to Finn. Then we can walk over to your office, review what we know and make a plan."

She took a measured breath to stifle her immediate resistance to going back to the training center. She'd done it once. She could do it again. "I've told you everything I remember about last night."

"Think of Stumps as the brains of this partnership," he suggested with a ghost of a smile. "Hearing it again may spark more questions. Unless you need to rest."

The little dig, intentional or not, irked her. She had the pride and stamina to keep up with him. "I'm rested enough."

"Great," he said. He parked the car and opened the back door for Stumps.

In the station, they learned the chief had time so they didn't part ways. She gave her brother a small wave as the three of them walked into the office. Danica listened with half an ear as Shane relayed the results of their interview and the surprising change in the microchip registration. Finn asked questions of both of them and encouraged Shane's plan to find her attacker.

She understood the nature of police work thanks to the officers and detectives who peppered her family tree all the way back to the original founders of Red Ridge. The tools were better now and the laws more comprehensive, but the inherent desire for justice seemed to be imbedded in the Gage DNA.

She didn't share Shane's outward confidence that there would be a happy ending for Nico. While the chief and Shane tossed around additional ways to connect the thief to the twins, her inability to truly help became more and more evident.

The short walk to the training center wasn't enough time to clear her head, and fifteen minutes later, the sense of futility pressed in on her from all sides as they reviewed everything about the attack and the theft behind her closed office door.

Shane had folded his tall form into one of her chairs, an ankle propped on one knee and Stumps relaxed at his feet. Sitting behind her desk, she felt the room shrinking with every question she couldn't answer definitively. Someone had opened the blinds, and the sunny view through the window mocked her with its illusion of safety and security.

"How often do you train protection dogs?" Shane asked.

"Everyone works on basic obedience with all types of working dogs." She could see her answer didn't please him. "I've never been part of the bite work, only the basic care and evaluations of prey drive."

"Have you ever wanted to train one of the attack dogs?"

Where is he going with this? "It isn't my first choice, no."

"Why not?"

"The training relationship is different. At some point, a trainer must be the bad guy to get the dog to shift from avoidance to controlled aggression. It's rewarding for the trainers who do it well." She pointed at Stumps, flopped on his side on the cool tile floor by

Shane's foot. Even half-asleep, he looked like he was smiling. "I'm more comfortable with working dogs like Stumps who enjoy a personal bond and real downtime in the course of their careers."

Shane glanced down, his lips twitched at one side of his mouth and then a true smile bloomed, full of affection for the corgi. Danica's breath backed up in her lungs. The man was sexy enough when he was serious, but that devoted smile made her knees weak and sent her pulse skipping.

For years, she'd blamed her interest in his welfare on his rocky history with her grandfather, but her underlying fascination with him went back before those dreadful days. In high school, he'd walked that fine line between good guy and bad boy, and it had always been the wide smile loaded with charm that drew her in. The smile had become a rare occurrence, too often eclipsed by the judge and jury expression.

"Do you know who was supposed to take Nico as a partner?" he asked.

"That's above my pay grade," she joked. Surely someone else from the training center had covered this stuff last night or earlier this morning.

"I'll ask around." He stood up, his gaze holding hers. "Would you be more comfortable walking with me through the yard and the woods or would you rather stay here?"

Another question she couldn't easily answer. Staying here gave her a break from him but left her alone. Going outside with him meant revisiting the scene of her failure. Too bad she couldn't come up with a third option.

Outside in the yard, she wanted to ask if the crime

scene unit had found anything conclusive, but she was afraid Finn had given that update while she'd been zoning out. No sense in offering him more proof that she was useless as an investigative partner.

Despite the warm afternoon sun pouring over the yard, she fought chills. She zipped her windbreaker, shoved her hands into her pockets and kept her gaze away from the gate while she tried to come up with a valid reason to go back inside.

Shane looked around but didn't give Stumps any kind of command yet. Relaxed, the stocky corgi snuffled each blade of grass. He perked up his ears when the kennel door opened and the Malinois puppies tumbled into view, trying to drag Tyler.

For a split second, the teenager looked more like himself until he spotted Danica and Shane and his expression turned sullen.

"Give me a second," Danica said to Shane. If something serious was going on with Tyler at home, she wanted him to be able to speak with her privately.

The puppies raced up to her and she jutted her knee out to discourage them from jumping. When they mostly succeeded in controlling themselves, she lavished them with praise.

"Did you find Nico?" Tyler asked.

She probably shouldn't tell him, yet she thought he could use a little good news. "Not officially. I believe the dog we found today is Nico, but his microchip is registered to a new owner."

"Wow. I guess the dogs can look alike." Tyler shuffled his feet, mindful of the puppy playing with his shoelace. "Will you be at game night tonight?" he asked.

On Thursday nights, the youth center sponsored a game night to help kids connect and find positive distractions. Cards, board games and some video games were always available, along with plenty of pizza, cookies and soft drinks.

"Wouldn't miss it," she said. Hours surrounded by people having fun would be divine.

"You don't have to be here?" he asked, perking up a little.

"No. Everyone wants me to take it easy, even though I feel fine."

"That's good." Tyler wouldn't quite look at her. "I'll be there, too."

She jumped on the opening. "Will you tell me what's going on with you?"

He wrinkled his nose and shrugged, his gaze on the puppies rolling around on the grass. "Nothing," he said. "I'm good." He jerked his chin toward something behind her. "Is he a bodyguard, too?"

"What?" She glanced back to see Shane stalking over. "Oh. Not at all. I should go. I promised to help him and Stumps look for anything that might lead to the thief." She moved back to intercept Shane. "We'll talk tonight."

"All right," Tyler said. "Be careful." He easily corralled the puppies so they wouldn't follow her as she walked away.

"He really has a gift for this work," she said to Shane.

Shane scowled at him. "How can you tell? He's just a kid."

"A kid motivated to improve his life, with the common sense and grit to do it."

"And your impeccable guidance," Shane added, his voice sour.

Why did he have to make her sound like one more challenge in Tyler's life? Not all Gages were out to ruin the lives of young men, although she understood why Shane would be wary.

That was one of her flaws, understanding an opposing viewpoint. Her teachers and bosses often praised that characteristic, but Danica didn't think it was really a positive trait. Seeing someone else's side of the equation left her open to ridicule from family who expected automatic loyalty and made it challenging to take a hard line with people who deserved it. She'd learned to hide her frequent internal conflicts, but that only left her feeling alone even when she was surrounded.

She wondered what Shane would say if she blurted out all her thoughts about his past and admitted her long-standing infatuation with him. She nearly laughed at the idea of how quickly his expression would shift from judge and jury to abject horror.

"Why do you get on with Carson so well?"

Shane stopped and stared at her. "How is that relevant to anything?"

"He seems like the only Gage you trust. If we're working together—"

"I don't trust him. I respect him," Shane interrupted. "There's a difference."

Difference, yes, but she thought trust and respect went hand in hand. You couldn't have one without the other. "You respect him because?"

"He works his cases objectively." Shane halted, his hand poised on the gate latch, the line of his square jaw tight. "For the record, I respect your work, as well."

The admission startled her, but before she could ask a follow-up question, he opened the gate. The hinge squeaked and she shivered like the last leaf of autumn. She had *not* heard that sound before the thief grabbed her.

Shane gave Stumps the command to search and she watched the dog eagerly go to work. Seeing him in action made her feel marginally better. If there was any sign of the thief out here in the woods, Stumps would find it. Her forced proximity to the human half of the team might be uncomfortable, but she knew the corgi's skills.

Chapter 6

Shane could practically hear Danica thinking. He just couldn't quite pin down any of her conclusions. Much like the Larson brothers and this stolen dog case. It should have been simple and might have been if the chief had left her out of it. She was a witness, not an investigator. The proof of that was all over her automatic protection and defense of that kid, Tyler.

Something was up with him and Shane intended to find out what. It meant waiting until Danica wasn't around, which could get tricky. Why had he invited her on this search? Oh yeah, because she'd looked so miserable in her office trying to ignore the window at her back.

He really should give her brother a heads-up that she wasn't nearly as okay as she let on. *Mind on the case, Colton*, he chided himself. His partner was excellent at picking up details that didn't belong in a certain area, but a search required Shane's full attention, as well.

"How many cases do you work in a year for the police department?" she asked.

He paused, enduring a long-suffering look from Stumps, unwilling to risk missing a clue because she sidetracked him. "About half my caseload each year involves official police cases here and around the county. Why?"

"Curiosity," she answered with a shrug.

Of course. It seemed he would forever be the curiosity of Red Ridge. Shane returned to the task at hand, hopeful Danica wouldn't interrupt again.

"Why didn't my attacker strike earlier in the evening when I had Nico in the yard?"

So much for hope. He figured she didn't remember asking this same question last night since she'd passed out in his car not long after. "Must have seemed too risky," he replied, "even if he had a drugged treat for the dog."

He wished she'd let him concentrate, yet he could hardly admit to her that she distracted him. It was more than the conversation—it was just her. That whisper of warm scent in her hair, the graceful way her compact body moved, and the barely-there version of her typically bright smile she reserved just for him.

How ridiculous to be flattered that she had a smile she used only on him, especially when it was a less-than-happy smile.

There was something in her gaze, too. Something indecipherable in those green depths when she looked at him that made him twitchy. He was used to people who had known him since he was a kid watching him with a measure of suspicion or pity. Suspicion he could handle, though it fueled his perpetual anger toward Sergeant Gage, Danica's dead grandfather. The pity was much worse, as if no one believed he could ever come all the way back to a normal life after eighteen months in the state pen.

It had been here, or rather in the training center classroom, when she'd first aimed that inscrutable look at him. He dragged his mind back to the task at hand, only to have her wrecking his concentration again.

"I suppose you're right," she said. "If Nico sensed aggression he could easily have attacked the thief when the man came after me."

"Better to drug one victim at a time," Shane agreed. He paused as Stumps continued searching. "What do you think the Larsons are using to mute his aggression now?"

"If the vet cooperating with them has any sense, it will be something as mild as Benadryl."

"Great, they can pick that up anywhere," Shane muttered. No chance of connecting them that way. He looked back toward the gate. They'd come at least a hundred yards and Stumps hadn't found anything. He knelt down, gave the dog praise and then turned the search in a different direction.

"You were hoping to possibly track veterinarian drug records?" she asked as they reset.

"It crossed my mind," he admitted. "I wouldn't expect the Larson twins to be that sloppy, but luck breaks cases open more often than not."

"And sooner rather than later, I hope," she said. "For Nico's sake."

As they passed the gate, Shane took a hard look at

the signs left from the crime scene evidence collectors. Stumps was a master at the search game, but he wasn't coming up with anything today.

"He had a long night last night," Danica said, as if she'd read his mind.

Shane wanted to sigh, but he was careful not to telegraph any of his own emotions while Stumps was working. "I don't think fatigue is the problem." Shane kept his tone upbeat. "I'm not seeing anything out of the ordinary back here either. We might be working on the false assumption that this is how the thief got in."

She frowned, her auburn eyebrows knitting over her pert nose. "You're back on the theory that someone I know is involved."

Shane kept his gaze on his dog, watching for the slightest signal that Stumps was onto a clue for the case. "The chief dumped this case in my lap."

"Our laps," she said.

He ignored that. "Knowing where Nico is *should* make it easier to connect how he got there." At least he hoped having a location would be more helpful in this instance than it had been in the case of the gun deal. "But how did they find out about Nico in the first place?"

Danica seemed to fold in on herself, trudging along in Stumps's wake. She'd resisted the known-assailant theory in Finn's office, though she agreed that identifying the thief was the best way to connect the theft to the Larsons. "Questioning the staff is obviously my next step," he said with far more patience than he would typically use. "Any idea who I should start with?"

"No one I work with would do this," she said, her voice tight.

Stumps turned back, his head tilted and ears perked up.

Shane glared at her.

She pointed at the fake smile she'd pasted on her face. "It's all good," she said in the neutral tone she used for training.

Not all good. That smile was a little scary. He encouraged Stumps to keep searching while he did the same thing. Resigned at the lack of progress, he gave up. "You should find something else to do while I handle the interviews," he said.

She rolled her eyes. "If that's how you want to waste your time."

"A thorough investigation is *never* a waste of time." Anger rushed over him like heat lightning on a summer night. "Stumps, come." He bent down and gave the dog high praise, telling him this exercise was over.

"I didn't mean—"

"Didn't you?" He had no use for her excuses. "Is it in the blood? This assumption that what *you* know is the truth and damn any facts to the contrary." He heard himself overreacting, saw her go pale and still he couldn't rein it in. "A good investigator learns as much from the dead ends as he does from the solid leads."

"My grandfather was a good cop," she murmured.

Another time or topic and he might admire her tenacity. "Your grandfather came after me with a single-minded purpose and a leaky theory."

"After…after that happened with you, all of his cases were reviewed," she said. "None of his other convictions were overturned." She folded her arms over her chest, her chin high, utterly defiant.

He wanted to shake the smug expression off her

face. Did she expect *him* to apologize for being in the wrong place at the wrong time? "Well, bully for the honorable Gage name. That makes *me* feel so much better about being locked up for eighteen godforsaken months. I suppose I shouldn't be upset at all."

Her bravado evaporated instantly. "Of course you should be upset." Her hands fell loosely to her sides. "Of course you should hate all of us. Forever."

Were those tears glistening in her eyes? He couldn't allow himself to care. He shoved aside yet another impulse to soothe her. She didn't deserve any kindness from him. He suddenly wished he'd never looked over that fence last night.

"Nothing I can say or do will replace that year and a half for you. There's no way for me to restore what you lost or make a dead man pay for his sins. I was only trying to be clear that the training center staff is like family."

As if that made it any better from his perspective. "Family isn't all unity and bliss."

She winced. "I know that, too. Everyone in that building cares about what we do and they know Nico's theft is a danger to the community as well as our reputation. I was only trying to point out that no one has a motive to steal Nico for the Larson brothers."

He stared at her a long moment, then looked down to his partner. Off duty, Stumps had moved between them, as if he could somehow defuse the fight that had exploded as abruptly as a land mine. Taking a deep breath, Shane attempted to make his point without shouting again or losing his temper. "Did you ever learn why your grandfather framed me?"

She jerked back as if he'd slapped her, her eyes wide. "No," she admitted with a tiny shake of her head.

"Is that enough proof that you might not know or comprehend what motivates everyone around you?"

She caught her lower lip between her teeth, her eyes on the trees behind him. "I understand what you're saying." She stood a little straighter and at last she met his gaze. "It's hard for me to accept, that's all. Make sure you apply the same objectivity to your interviews as my grandfather should have used with you. Please."

That left him reeling. "That's low." He wondered when such a fine-boned and petite woman learned to wield that intensity like a weapon. Looking at her now, he marveled that her attacker had prevailed.

She shrugged a shoulder and then turned on her heel and marched off. Rather than go through the training center gate, she walked the reverse of the path he'd taken last night, skirting the fence.

"Where are you going?" he called after her.

She didn't reply, though he knew she'd heard him. He started after her and stopped short. Danica wasn't his priority. As a witness, she'd given him all she had. It was broad daylight and people were out and about. She was safe. Besides, the case was about the stolen dog. Danica had merely been collateral damage in the theft.

So why did it make him uneasy to let her go off alone?

He leaned back against the fence until his heart rate slowed and his mind was clear. Conducting interviews would be useless otherwise. He was about to head inside when he noticed the pale yellow-green of young box elder leaves flipped upside down. Common enough when leaves were tossed by wind or rain, but the day was clear and calm. He moved closer, noticing the sapling had been crushed a bit, leaning away from the surrounding underbrush in the trees butting up to the training center.

"Back on the clock, bud," he said to Stumps. "Let's see what we see."

Shane had to bend at the waist to duck into the break someone had made. The air was markedly cooler on his face and arms under the cover of the trees. A few paces up the hill, the ground cover had been flattened as if someone had stretched out for a nap. Shane crouched low, confirming his intuition. Someone had watched and waited right here, enjoying a perfect view over the privacy fence surrounding the training center yard.

Questions nagged at Shane as Stumps nosed around, sorting out what belonged here and what was different. With Hans and Fisher, why did the Larson twins feel the need for another attack and protection dog? Were they expecting Nico to protect the stash that the police were sure existed and could not pinpoint?

He'd basically accused Danica of being too trusting and assuming the best of the people around her. This find gave him cause to take a hard look at everyone who knew about Nico, but until he came up with a motive for better direction, the investigation was doomed to stall out.

Stumps sat down suddenly, his gaze locked on a small pile of debris at the base of a tree just to the left of the window in the shrubs.

"Good boy," Shane said. He took a picture of the alert. His habit wasn't exactly standard practice for all K9 teams, but it helped him with his logs when he was working a case. Carefully, he nudged aside the top layer of debris to find a red temporary badge with the K9 training center logo stamped on the front. Only two ways to get one of these: take a class or volunteer.

So much for Danica's naive belief that no one at the training center would ever be involved in the theft. He called the police station and requested a crime scene unit while he debated his next steps.

Danica stalked around the outside of the training center and forced herself to turn for the front door. She wanted to go back to the Larson offices, though it was a ridiculously stupid idea. She could just imagine the lectures from everyone if she wandered off in search of trouble.

If only she didn't feel like such deadweight on this case.

Shane was the investigator and he was probably used to dealing with grumpy witnesses or reluctant informants, yet she couldn't sit around and do nothing while the twins ruined a good dog.

She gave half-hearted greetings and assurances to her coworkers that Shane was on the Nico case as she arrowed toward her office. Having been ambushed, they had no real lead on her attacker. She remembered only the feel of a hairy forearm and a body much bigger than hers. That hardly whittled it down. Most everyone in town was taller than her. If she couldn't identify the attacker, they couldn't make the subsequent links to Nico's theft and then to the Larsons having the dog.

While Shane grilled the training center staff, Danica would find a way to contribute to the case. The Larson twins had a vet working with them. There was no other explanation for only one microchip in Nico. At least researching vets gave her something to do.

She pulled up a directory of veterinarians in the county and grumbled at the idea of any of them working with the Larsons.

"Problem?" Hayley asked, rapping on Danica's open door.

"Too many to list," Danica admitted. She clicked over to her screen saver to hide her search and groaned when a snapshot of Nico was the first in the rotation.

"Are you feeling all right?"

"Yes." She pushed her hands into her hair and rested her elbows on the desk. "I want Nico back."

"We all do." Hayley walked in and sat down. "No one blames you, sweetie."

The pat reassurance made Danica want to laugh. Bitterly. Hayley wasn't being snide or even passive-aggressive, but the words added to Danica's guilt. "I blame me."

"You're sure it was Nico at the Larson office?"

"Absolutely." Giving up, she folded her arms and rested her forehead on them. Was there any legal way to dig through a vet's client records? Who could she ask? Although vet records weren't protected like personal health records, it seemed like the wrong thing to do without permission.

"I'm sure Shane will find a way to get Nico back," Hayley stated confidently. "Do you think he's seeing anyone?"

The non sequitur had Danica sitting up. "Shane?" The woman had nearly been her sister-in-law. She couldn't be interested in *Shane*. Men flocked to Hayley every day of the week, all day long. It was part of life in Red Ridge. "I really don't know," she managed to reply.

And why was she getting so riled about it? She and Shane weren't anything to each other but wary acquaintances, if not outright enemies. She was merely a useless witness on one of his cases. Cocking her head, she tried to picture them together. They'd be gorgeous. She could see them lighting up Red Ridge like some celebrity couple, all that blond hair and big smiles, both fit and tall.

She wasn't up for this conversation. Covering her face with her hands, she worked to smother the imminent threat of both tears and growling curses. Maybe she should go home.

"Oh."

Danica dropped her hands. "Oh?" she echoed. "What does that mean?"

Hayley flicked away the question with a long-fingered, manicured hand. Danica always wondered how she managed to maintain such lovely nails in their profession. It was another mystery of Hayley's unfailing perfection.

"You should never play poker, Dani." Hayley smiled indulgently, as if she was so much older and wiser. They were the *same age*. "It's obvious you have feelings for him. That's great news. You haven't gone out with anyone in a long time."

Great news? Danica's cheeks flamed with embarrassment. There were times she hated being a redhead. "Feelings?" Her voice cracked and she plucked a pencil from her desk, twirling it in her fingers. "Well, sure. I'm grateful he found me when he did. That's all."

"Mmm-hmm."

"Please stop," Danica said. "Every girl in Red Ridge has crushed on Shane Colton at some point."

Hayley's lips curled with fond memories. "It was that smile and singular focus. He was such a charmer back in high school. Do you remember?"

Danica remembered all that charm fading out of him through the course of a murder investigation and trial that ended with a life sentence. Since his return to Red Ridge, exonerated and a free man, he had a hard edge in both his smile and his eyes that kept people at arm's length.

"Add in the bad-boy factor," Hayley continued, "and it's no wonder you're crushing on him again."

"Not me." Infatuation sparked by associative guilt did not a crush make. It was a recipe for disaster in a relationship.

Hayley's lovely eyes filled with tears, yet miraculously none spilled over her lashes to mar her makeup. "Take it from me, Dani, don't wait on love."

Love? That escalated quickly. "You're reading too much into it," she said. Shane was the last man on the planet she could or should love.

Hayley stood, a fragile smile wobbling on her glossy lips. "I mean it." She sniffled delicately. "None of us know how long we have. I loved your brother and as much as I miss Bo—" she laid a hand over her heart "—as hard as each day is without him, I don't regret a moment. If you care for Shane at all, don't waste a minute. Love is a gift, Danica. Make time to find out if it's mutual."

Before she could ask for advice on how best to do that, Hayley walked out.

Danica appreciated the sentimental speech, but there

were bigger obstacles between her and Shane than how best to express any feelings. There were things she'd wanted to say to him from the moment he'd returned to Red Ridge. Things she kept locked deep inside because she was a Gage and he was a Colton. She'd let prime opportunities slide when he was initially training with Stumps. And there had been more casual moments since. She chickened out every time.

Contrary to Hayley's theory, she didn't want to tell him she had a crush or wanted to go out. She wanted to tell him how the worst time in his life had irrevocably changed her, too.

More frustrated than ever, Danica pushed all of her cluttered thoughts about the past out of her mind and resumed her computer search for the vet who had changed that microchip for the Larson brothers.

After an hour or so, she had a short list of the nearest vets in the county and a raging headache. She printed out her findings for Shane to investigate further and planned to grab a bottle of water from the break room before paying a visit to the puppies.

She stepped out of her office and nearly ran headlong into Shane and Hayley, blond heads close, voices friendly as they chatted about something. Shane scowled at her and Stumps wagged his whole body happily. The corgi was definitely her favorite half of this particular K9 team.

With a smile for the corgi, Danica handed the printout to Shane.

Changing her mind about staying, she decided what she needed more than another conversation disguised as an argument or unwelcome advice was a nap, even if that meant going home alone. Let him do his interviews. It was the only way to prove she was right about the training center staff.

Shane extracted himself from Hayley and caught up with Danica in three quick strides. "What am I supposed to do with this?" He skimmed the list of names, phone numbers and addresses. Veterinarians, he noticed, every last one of them.

"Hopefully you'll find a real lead," she said. "Enjoy your interviews."

"You can't leave," he said as she walked through the front door. He and Stumps hurried after her. She wasn't going to talk to these vets, was she?

She glanced back and cocked an auburn eyebrow. "I am leaving. If you need me, I'll be at home."

The glint in her eyes dared him to follow, to stop her. He wouldn't. Recognizing her bravado was a thin, brittle shell, he let her walk away. He'd been there, unsure if he could recover from a harsh surprise attack in a place he'd always considered safe. No one could make this easier for her.

Shedding the shock and betrayal were only the beginning. He'd rebuilt his life after prison with little outside help. Stubbornness and perseverance were the cornerstones of his reputation as a private investigator. Through it all, the bigger challenge had been rebuilding his self-confidence and those shattered pieces of his soul he kept hidden from the world.

Chapter 7

Danica gripped her keys in trembling hands. No one was behind her. No one had been hiding in the back of her car or in the elevator or lurking to jump her at her front door. Despite the voice in her head screaming to the contrary, she was not in danger here.

She shoved the key in the lock and got herself inside. Leaning back against the door, she heard a deep, heartwarming rumble. Her cat, Oscar, a Maine coon shelter rescue, peered down at her from his favorite perch on top of the kitchen cabinets. Grumpy with almost everyone else, he doted on Danica. It was mutual.

She needed the unconditional acceptance right now. He came down to the counter and she scooped him into her arms, rubbing at his ear while his purr got louder and louder. She gave him the quick version of events since she'd left for work last night, apologizing for not being home overnight. He butted his head against her jaw and she set him down. At the pantry, she unlocked the treat jar, rewarding his patience.

Appeased, he padded out toward the main room. Danica turned off her phone and set the kitchen timer for half an hour. Everything would look better after a power nap. She flopped onto the couch and Oscar joined her, stalking over her legs and nuzzling her hands. When he settled, rumbling contentedly on her chest, she finally dozed off.

She dreamed of a man with clear blue eyes so cold she got a chill when he glanced her way. *Shane.* Her dream propelled her into his strong arms and she watched that chilly gaze heat when she dared to kiss him. It was a perfect dream-kiss on a perfect dream-day as they walked happily hand in hand along the trails outside town.

The view changed, a summer storm rolled down from the mountain and crashed over them. He shoved her away and she stood apart, drenched by the cold rain, pinned by that colder gaze.

An alarm clanged, breaking through the dream turned nightmare. She sat up suddenly and Oscar complained as he leaped to the floor. She felt as if gravity had magnified exponentially in thirty minutes. Scrubbing at her face, she considered resetting the timer for another half hour.

No, naps like that were worse than no sleep at all. Dream-kisses aside, spending time with Shane was clearly dredging up a past she wanted to leave buried. She got up and walked to the kitchen for a glass of water. At least her headache had dulled to a nearly imperceptible throb at her temples. That would make the inevitable volume of game night easier to bear.

She fixed a peanut butter sandwich and took it out onto her small balcony overlooking the western horizon to think. Or not think. She couldn't make up her mind which might be better. Her thoughts tossed and turned with ideas to rescue Nico and various impossible scenarios in which Shane didn't look at her with disdain because of her last name.

Shane had better reasons than the bad blood of the original Red Ridge founders to hate the Gage family, but for some reason she'd never quite lost hope that he would eventually forgive her grandfather. It was an outrageous premise. In Shane's shoes, she wouldn't be able to let it go, either.

So much had been stolen from him and yet she'd give anything to ease that hard, suspicious glint in his eyes. It wasn't like her to fixate on things that could never happen. Things like kissing Shane Colton or even just making him smile. Hayley had been right about his charismatic smile, the one that drew people in and made them feel special. The smile he'd been so generous with before his life had been torn apart.

At fourteen and fifteen, she'd been too young to be noticed by Shane. She wouldn't have known how to react if he *had* noticed her. Still, like most of her friends, she enjoyed casting him as the ideal dream date in her imagination.

When he'd been charged with a local girl's murder, she hadn't wanted to believe it. The rumors and conjecture and community judgment against him had been terrible. She'd struggled to reconcile how a guy who'd seemed so nice and fun could kill someone.

It had been little more than a year later when a witness who had testified against Shane recanted. The new information had blown the case open and Danica's worldview shattered when it came out that her grandfather had *deliberately* ignored standard investigation protocol and framed an innocent young man to swiftly close the case.

Community conjecture and judgment had landed squarely on Sergeant Gage and the RRPD. The old feud between the Gage and Colton families roared back to life. All eyes in Red Ridge were on her Grandpa Gage, waiting for him to do the right thing, though several people disagreed about exactly what the right thing was. When he died suddenly, her friends and neighbors whispered that he'd gotten off easy.

To this day, she marveled that any of her siblings had gone into local law enforcement. Though she'd been on that track herself, she couldn't bring herself to follow through. In the days after Shane's conviction was overturned, she'd hated her grandfather with an anger that blazed like a forest fire out of control. In the grip of that dreadful anger she'd made an irreparable mistake, discovering firsthand that no one was perfectly righteous.

Shane had returned to Red Ridge and made the most of his second chance, distancing himself from his crotchety, negligent father and starting fresh in a new direction. He'd done a tremendous job as both a K9 handler and a private investigator. She couldn't help comparing Shane then to Tyler now. The fourteen-year-old needed healthy, strong examples to overcome the hindrances of parents who were, at best, disinterested in his future.

Danica closed her eyes tight against the sting of tears. Crying didn't change anything. She would never have an opportunity to correct the biggest mistake of her life. Being young and idealistic would haunt her the rest of her days. The terrible accusations she'd shouted at her grandfather would always be the last words between them. Not words of love or joy. None of the corny jokes they'd shared all her life.

She'd verbally assaulted him, demanding an explanation for his appalling mishandling of the murder case. He'd cried. The only other time she'd seen him cry was when her grandmother had died. He'd promised to beg Shane's forgiveness. Riding that fury, she hadn't been moved, claiming she'd never forgive him. Hours later, her father had found Grandpa Gage dead in his bedroom, a victim of a massive heart attack. Days, months and years passed, but Danica had accepted that the guilt never went away.

On that point, Hayley was right. Love was too important to ignore and far too valuable to throw away as she'd done nearly a decade ago. Everyone had looked at Shane suspiciously when he'd returned, wondering if he was a killer despite the new evidence, and she was the one who'd managed to kill a man, however indirectly.

She swiped away the tear rolling down her cheek. She didn't want to work with Shane any more than he wanted to work with her. For her it was the burden of the old guilt. He would never have the closure he deserved from her grandfather because of her. For him, she figured it was akin to getting in bed with the enemy.

She had no illusions that working with Shane

would ease the strain of the age-old distrust between the Gages and Coltons. Building a bridge between the feuding families was better left to her little brother and his devotion to Valeria Colton. They were young, yes, but who was she to judge whether or not he'd met his soul mate? Better to be young, idealistic and in love instead of young, idealistic and full of hate and anger as she'd been. As long their relationship didn't make Vincent a victim of the Groom Killer.

Her thoughts quashed her appetite. After taking the remains of her sandwich back inside, she tossed it in the trash and went to get ready for the evening ahead at the youth center. She couldn't let any of this old stuff cloud her focus while she was there to help the kids.

She showered, washing her hair and scrubbing all the places she knew the attacker had touched her. With deliberation and care, she dried her hair and left it down. Dressed in a casual lavender tunic over black cropped leggings, she felt feminine and strong. Hopefully the feeling would last. She fed Oscar and promised him she wouldn't be out all night and then left her apartment with her head held high.

It took more effort than she'd ever admit to keep her head high as she stopped to fill up the car with gas. Sweat popped on her palms and she caught herself looking over her shoulder too often. Sheer determination had her driving to the grocery store for supplies to make treat bags for the kids on her way to the youth center.

The only way she knew to get over this irrational fear dogging her heels was to simply keep moving forward. This was her home. *Her* home. She wasn't going to let a lousy thief dictate her feelings and reactions.

Even with the stop at the store, she walked into the youth center quite early. It gave her some time to put the treat bags together without jumping at every noise and shadow. She didn't bring treats every week, but whenever she did, the kids got a kick out of it.

No, a small treat wouldn't suddenly improve tough circumstances, but it usually brought out a smile. Setting an example of small, kind gestures also went a long way, in Danica's opinion. The kids who frequented the youth center were often generally ignored—or worse—in their homes, the one place every child deserved to feel safe.

Grandpa Gage had often said stability and a sturdy roof could change everything for a kid. Shane's mom had been his stabilizing force. She'd been the one who kept a sturdy roof over Shane's head. She'd died unexpectedly during Shane's incarceration, believing her son was a killer. Though Danica tried repeatedly, she couldn't reconcile her grandfather's wisdom with the way he'd railroaded Shane. What had he been thinking to knowingly send an innocent kid to prison?

Some questions weren't meant to be answered.

As preteens and teenagers trickled in, she greeted most of them by name. Soon volunteers arrived with coolers of drinks and stacks of hot pizzas. After helping set up the serving table, she sat in on a couple of card games and laughed as she watched a spirited board game involving plenty of bargaining. She conceded to a video dance game when she was breathless and clearly outclassed by the younger players. While it all helped her feel more normal, none of it was enough to distract her from Tyler's absence.

He'd made such a point of asking if she'd be here;

it seemed strange that he wasn't. In these moments, she often wished she could drop in and check on Tyler, or any of the other kids in similar situations, but that crossed a fine line. No one wanted a parent to feel judged and pull a kid who was getting something from the program.

She was paring down leftover pizza slices, combining them into whole pies for kids to take home, when Tyler finally showed up. He was wearing a T-shirt advertising a classic video game and his dark hair fell across his forehead, hiding one eye almost completely.

"Hi," he said with a half-hearted wave.

"Hi." She put two slices of pepperoni on a plate for him, and he grabbed a can of grape soda from the ice chest at the end of the serving table. Inwardly, she winced. Pizza, soda and candy didn't make for the healthiest of meals, but when they served salad and veggies, they typically wound up with more wasted food.

"How are things going?" she asked.

"Okay." He wouldn't quite look at her.

She followed him to a table and sat down in the chair next to his. Had Shane's interviews made Tyler feel uncomfortable? If so, she'd put a stop to his witch hunt. No one at the training center would have helped the thief. She wanted to pepper him with questions, but experience had proven that would only put him on the defensive. Instead, she chattered about the action on various games until he almost smiled.

Acting this sullen was unusual for Tyler when his parents weren't around. On his own, here and at the training center, he was much more animated and lively.

"I wish you'd tell me what's bothering you," she said quietly. "You know you can trust me."

"Uh-huh." He folded a piece of pizza in half and took a big bite. "It's no big deal," he said after he'd chewed and swallowed. He tipped his head back for a long drink of soda and his hair fell away from his eye.

Danica didn't stifle the gasp in time. His hair had been hiding an eye nearly swollen shut, already turning violent colors.

Tyler scowled and let his hair flop down again.

"Who did that?" she demanded.

He shook his head.

"This is no time to be stubborn. Tell me what happened right now." If she had to call protective services and pull him out of his house, she'd do it. Tyler was one of the good kids. He had a future if they could only get him through high school without a serious misstep.

"I walked into a door." The innocent tone lost its effectiveness when he sneered.

"Was that door at home?"

He shook his head quickly, his mouth set in a grim line.

"Tyler." He'd been fine this afternoon. School had ended last week, so when could this have happened?

"Forget it." He crumpled his paper napkin and added it to the two skeletal pizza crusts on the paper plate. "I got clocked by a bully, that's all. Nothing to do about it but let it heal."

She sensed that piece was true. Pockets of his neighborhood could be brutal. He was growing up only a few blocks from where Shane had lived…before he'd been sent to prison. Maybe Shane could get him to talk about whatever trouble he was trying to handle on his own.

"You have friends," she said at last. "And friends listen. They help each other." At his grimace, she gripped her hands in her lap to keep from shaking some sense into him. It wasn't that easy to get through to teenagers. "Remember that." She patted his shoulder. "And go have some fun tonight."

She slid out of the folding chair and walked away. If he wouldn't open up, she couldn't do anything. No, Tyler didn't have much reason to trust adults. Still it stung that he refused to open up. Yet, she reminded herself, in the past he often sorted out issues in his head first before sharing his process and conclusions with her. It was a trait she admired most of the time.

She kept an eye on Tyler, pleased that he stayed through the rest of game night, playing card games with a few friends. Hearing him laugh with his peers went a long way toward reassuring her. When game night ended, he rode home with a few other kids in the youth center van. His parents were either working late or not in the mood to come out and pick him up. Danica's family was far from perfect, but she'd never doubted how much she was loved.

She helped the other volunteers with the cleanup, needing the distraction and the companionship to re-inforce her courage before she headed home. Finally, she couldn't stall any longer, and she walked out to her car. If she checked the back seat before she got into the car and overused her rearview mirror on the drive home, she was the only one who knew about it.

Unfortunately, she had to quickly put her brave face back on when she reached her condo. Shane was looming in the lobby, his arms folded over his chest and a glacial chill in his eyes. "Where have you been?" he demanded as she walked in.

"That's none of your business." The clock on the wall showed it was just past eleven. Surely any interrogation could wait until morning. She tried to pass him and he blocked her. When she glanced up, he was studying her too closely. "What are you doing here?" The question did nothing to back him off.

His gaze raked her from head to toe. "What are you wearing?"

"Clothing." This wasn't the first time he'd seen her in something other than training center gear. "Excuse me." She moved toward the elevator.

"You didn't pick up my calls," he said. "Were you on a date?"

He'd called her? She'd silenced her phone to give the kids her full attention. "That also falls into the 'none of your business' category. Why are you here?"

"We need to have a conversation."

"So talk," she prompted when he didn't continue.

"Privately," he said through gritted teeth.

It finally dawned on her that Stumps wasn't with him though his K9 badge was clipped to his belt. It was the closest he ever came to a uniform. "Where is Stumps?"

"Off duty at home," he replied.

For some reason she would feel better if the little corgi were here too. She waved an arm toward the empty lobby. "Seems we're alone enough."

"Danica."

The way he growled her name sent a delicious shiver down her spine and put visions in her head of far more intimate situations. Damn that dream-kiss. She was never going to take a nap again. A different explanation for his calls and presence occurred to her. "Have you figured out how to recover Nico?"

"No." He scrubbed a hand over his face. "Can we please go up to your place to have this conversation?"

"No." She had enough trouble with her imagination and Shane as it was. Having him in her house? Not a smart play.

Clearly frustrated, Shane crowded closer and bent his head to her ear. "There was another theft at the training center tonight."

"No." Her heart tripped and stuttered. "That's impossible."

"They took one of the Malinois puppies," he said, his jaw hard as granite.

She clapped a hand over his forearm and jerked it back as if she'd been burned.

"I need to know where you've been," he said.

Sure, he was investigating a case, but she was offended anyway. "I was not stealing a puppy," she said when she could get the words through her clenched teeth. With her contacts, she could have a dog through legitimate means anytime she wished. "Am I a suspect?"

His stare felt as tangible as a caress. "No." He shook his head. "The guard was bludgeoned and you don't have the leverage."

She pressed her fingers to her lips and stifled the groan building in her throat. She'd forgotten all about the new guard. "Was he killed?" she asked from behind her hand.

"No. But not for lack of someone trying."

She turned on her heel, pacing the length of the lobby along the floor-to-ceiling windows that fronted the modern building. First Nico, fully trained and about to be assigned a partner, and now a raw puppy who could be turned to any purpose. The odds of two different dog thieves targeting the training center at the same time were laughable. "You *know* the Larson twins are behind this."

He tipped his head. "I strongly *suspect*, since they have Nico, but I need proof. And motive for this second theft." He folded his arms over his chest again. The pose did fabulous things for his biceps. "Right now I'm focused on finding the dog thief," he continued. "It's our best bet. If we do that the police can make him give up his buyer or whoever hired him."

Of course, that made sense. "Where is the guard now?" She hadn't even met the man and she felt terrible for him.

"Hospital," Shane replied.

"Can we go see him?"

Shane's muscular shoulders rippled under his T-shirt. "I doubt he's up to talking. If the blow had gone an inch one way or another, he'd already be dead."

"Who found him?" she asked.

"He called it in himself when he came to. RRPD responded and phoned to let me know."

How was it that two violent attacks in two nights ended with successful thefts on both occasions? Her temper started burning through the shock, temporarily muting her dismay for the fate of the dogs.

"I'd really prefer to discuss the rest upstairs."

There's more?

"Or at the station, if you're worried I'll stain the carpets. This can't wait until morning."

"What?" It took her a second to register what he meant. "Oh for—" She marched over to the elevator and punched the button. When they were inside and the doors closed again, she whirled around and drilled a finger into his chest. His tough, unyielding chest, she noticed. "Stain the carpets? That's beneath you, Shane."

His eyes widened under arched eyebrows.

"Drop the self-pity," she said. "I'm sure prison sucked."

That blue gaze iced over. "You have no idea."

"But you were exonerated," she continued as if he hadn't spoken. "You've recovered and rebuilt—"

"Have I?"

"—your life into something remarkable. Your past isn't why I didn't invite you up." The elevator doors parted at her floor and she stepped out, marching down the hallway. At her condo, she shoved the key into the lock and pushed her door open.

"Go on in," she ordered. He did, eyeing her warily. She followed and slammed the door behind her. "Only one of us is a killer and we both know it isn't you."

Chapter 8

Shane couldn't have heard her correctly. "What did you say?" And why would she say it? He'd been accused of murder and had met hardened killers. Danica was *not* in that league. Hell, she had perpetual innocence stamped all over her, despite the fighting-mad sparks in her eyes. With her hair down around her shoulders, and that soft fabric skimming her body, he wanted to gather her close and learn the textures of her hair, her skin. He shook it off.

"Let's focus on one crime at a time, Colton." She dropped her purse on the kitchen counter and leaned back.

He liked it better when she called him Shane. It was as if she couldn't make up her mind how to address him. Maybe, like him, she needed the reminder that he was a family enemy.

He corralled his errant thoughts, wishing he hadn't left Stumps, his best friend and partner, at home.

"Fine," he said, not at all convinced she'd ever committed a crime of any nature. "I need to speak with Tyler."

She frowned. "You didn't interview him this afternoon?"

"Not officially. He's a minor."

Although she didn't reply, she rubbed her upper arm, her teeth nipping her lower lip. He recognized the evasive body language from his P.I. training and prison before that. Danica was hiding something. Interesting. What didn't she want him to find out? Maybe she wasn't as sure about the kid as she let on.

"He had nothing to do with these thefts."

"I'd like him to convince me." Before she could toss him out, he stepped deeper into her space and checked to see her reaction.

She rolled her eyes and then gestured for him to continue. "Take the grand tour," she said. "That was the kitchen. This is the great room." She gestured to the wide sliders. "Mountain view is that way."

He moved toward the sliders. Overall, the place was neatly kept and still felt homey. She hadn't decorated with an overtly feminine style. That wouldn't have fit her anyway, though he couldn't pinpoint why he held that opinion.

Her midnight-blue couch was flanked by two comfortable-looking chairs. The seating area was anchored by a coffee table made from an artistic slice of a tree that would have been at home in an art gallery. The television was a respectable size and the dining table had room for six. He supposed that fit, considering her family.

He assumed the hallway she did not label led to the bedroom. "No dog?" Hearing a hiss he thought came from Danica, he spun around.

"Hush." She wasn't even looking at Shane. "Be polite, Oscar."

He realized she was speaking to an enormous creature padding into the room from the darkened hallway. "What is that?" Based on the sounds, it was feline, but it outsized a normal house cat. It was big enough to pass for a bobcat or lynx that should be roaming that mountain view.

"Be polite." Danica said to him this time. "This is my cat, Oscar."

"You're a dog trainer," Shane said as she bent to let Oscar head-butt her hand. "Shouldn't you have a dog?"

"I have plenty of dogs at work." She rubbed the cat's ear. "A good cat doesn't mind the hours I put in at the training center. He's a Maine coon and completely tame."

"If you say so." He wasn't sure what to do with himself or how to get the conversation back on point. She hadn't exactly invited him in for a drink. Had she been on a date? "You weren't stealing puppies and you weren't trying to rescue Nico dressed like that." He ignored the challenging eyebrow she aimed at him. "Would you please tell me where you've been?"

"Game night at the youth center," she replied. "Tyler was there, too."

"The entire time?"

She bit her lip again. "He was late," she admitted.

"That's what you wear to game night?" he asked before he could stop himself.

Her gaze sharpened and her lips pursed. "You are not criticizing my wardrobe."

He shook his head, trying not to laugh over inadvertently offending her. "More likely you ignited a few crushes among the teen set."

"Quit teasing me," she snapped. "Tyler couldn't have been involved."

"You said he was late," Shane said. "Did he tell you why?"

"Would you like something to drink?" She started back toward the kitchen. "Tyler isn't the thief," she added as she walked away.

The flowing tunic and snug leggings drew his gaze, showing him a different, stylish side of Danica. He liked the view more than he should have. "You keep saying that without giving me any reason to believe it." He leaned against the wide pass-through between the kitchen and dining area.

"My word should be enough for you," she said. "Beer or water? I'm having wine."

"Water, please." He accepted the bottle of water she handed him. "I didn't say he did it," Shane pointed out. "I just said I wanted to talk with him. Although he might have been able to drug you, he's too scrawny to have successfully taken out the guard tonight."

"Then why drag him into the investigation at all?" She poured a glass of red wine, came back around into the main room with him and curled into a corner of the couch.

"He knows the training center," Shane said, barely keeping a leash on his exasperation with her. "*Some-*

one left the gate unlocked last night. Tonight too, most likely. Stumps and I found a temporary training center ID where we think the thief watched and waited for his moment to attack you."

Her eyes rounded. "When were you going to tell me?"

"You went home early." He purposely evaded the precise time of the discovery. "And then you didn't answer your phone." He'd been far too concerned with her safety, but he kept that to himself, as well.

"Tyler loves his work," she insisted. "He wouldn't do anything to put the team or the dogs in jeopardy."

"Is he acting normal?" Shane demanded.

"Not exactly," she replied. "That doesn't mean he's acting criminal, either. Who knows what's going on at home?"

"You clearly have a soft spot for the kid." He decided to test her a little. "And if I take your word on Tyler, I should take your word on that comment about you being a killer too, right?"

She blanched, but rallied quickly. "Yeah, actually."

He rolled his eyes and strolled over to the sliding door, though all he could see was the reflection of her. "Tyler is hip-deep in this mess, whatever you want to believe," he said, turning to face her.

She shook her head stubbornly.

Shane tried to appeal to her protective and compassionate nature. The same facets of her character that would never allow her to kill anyone. "The sooner I have the information, the sooner I can protect him. If it is Tyler, he's vulnerable to the thief and whoever hired him to take those dogs."

"You've got it wrong." She didn't sound so sure this

time. "There has to be another explanation. Tunnel vision is bad for investigative work."

Why was she baiting him? "Don't you dare accuse *me* of tunnel vision. If there are alternative reasons for Tyler to be upset, all he has to do is give me one." It would put him back at square one, but that was how things went sometimes. "Dropping a suspect too soon is also lousy investigative work."

She set the wine aside and hugged her knees to her chest, looking as fragile as he'd ever seen her. It put an uncomfortable itch between his shoulder blades.

"You know the thief might have killed you." Though she trembled, he plowed on. He had to find a motivator that would get her to cooperate with him. "If the dose had been a little stronger, if Stumps hadn't alerted me when he did."

"Stop it." She shoved to her feet. "I survived last night. I am *fine*. No part of Tyler's life intersects with the twins or their business. Can we please focus on a way to get Nico away from the Larsons?"

Shane groped for the patience that had served him well behind bars. "People can surprise us." She sure as hell was surprising him regularly in just the past twenty-four hours.

"What if we work backward?" She tucked her hair behind her ears. "If the Larsons were at the hospital with Mae Rose, how and where did they take delivery from the vet who removed Nico's microchip?"

It wasn't a bad idea. He'd explore it tomorrow. There was no way the thief was successful without some inside help at the training center, and her insights could help. "Are you worried I'm right about Tyler?"

Her eyes blazed to life. "I'm worried you questioning him officially will make his home life worse."

She was fighting him harder than ever. "You said he was basically in a neglectful situation."

"So I thought," she muttered.

"What happened?"

She raised her gaze to the ceiling and blinked away tears. "He was late to the youth center as I said." She sucked in a deep breath. "And he had a black eye."

Shane's intuition kicked up a notch. "Did he have an explanation?"

Her watery laughter held more bitterness than humor. "First he said he walked into a door."

"You didn't let him get away with that answer."

"Of course not." She retrieved her wineglass, looking miserable as she drained it. "My interrogation skills aren't up to your standards. I couldn't grill him over a couple of slices of pizza."

He stared at her. "You thought about it."

"Of course I did, though he typically clams up when he's pressed that way." She put the empty wineglass on the counter and pushed at her hair again. "He told me it was a bully, but that's all he'd give me."

"Will he be at the training center tomorrow?"

"Shane, you can't go after him," she protested. "He'll never trust me again."

He wondered if Tyler had any idea how lucky he was to have an ally like Danica. Many nights before and after he wound up behind bars, Shane had wished for just *one* person willing to take his claim of innocence at face value. Instead, they all believed the illustrious Sergeant Gage's version of the crime.

"You should trust me." He crowded her between his

body and the counter. "You act like I want to haul the kid to jail and throw away the key."

She shoved at his chest, clearly annoyed that she couldn't budge him. He should back up, would have, but the feel of her hands scorched the last of his common sense. He trapped her hands against his chest with one hand and caressed the nape of her neck with the other. Before he could change his mind, he bent his head and kissed her.

That first, sweet contact gave him a jolt. He explored her lips with his until she softened. When she kissed him back, she surprised him by reflecting the same intense need pounding through him.

Her hands relaxed, drifting across his chest, then fluttering higher, twining around his neck. He wanted to feel those hands everywhere. Her sigh sifted through him and he changed the angle of the kiss, sinking deeper. She tasted of wine, and the silk of her hair cascaded through his fingers, over his arm.

Her slender body was supple against his and he wanted to drag her close, closer, lending her his strength while taking in her soft tenderness. His hands smoothed down her back, over the slight curve of her hips down to the hem of her tunic. He gathered it up, tormenting himself with feel of her toned thighs, every hint of the heat of her body waiting for his touch under her clothing.

Everything about her was a blow to his senses. Her head fell back and he indulged the unspoken request, trailing kisses up and down the column of her throat, along her jaw. Her green gaze shuttered by long auburn lashes, she lifted her lips to his for another long, luscious kiss.

What was he doing? He released her, reluctantly, making sure she was steady on her feet, though his knees felt weak as his pulse slammed through his veins. Her cheeks were rosy, her eyes wide and unfocused.

"I—" Words failed him.

"Yeah." She pressed her fingertips to her mouth as her lips curved up in a shy smile. "That was, um…" She'd apparently run out of words, as well.

He barely kept himself from laying claim to that amazing mouth all over again.

Though the kiss rattled him, he savored the lingering taste of her. He struggled to regain his balance now that his world had been tipped sideways. "So you must have a soft spot for hard-luck kids." The joke missed the mark.

Her gaze dropped to the floor. "You should leave," she whispered.

"I only meant—"

"I get it." She started to reach out for him and jerked her hands back. "Please go."

Smart. If she touched him again, there was no doubt in his mind where they would end up.

"Okay." He'd leave, but this wasn't over. It was marginally easier to go when it was obvious she was as breathless and unsettled as him. "I'll meet you at the training center in the morning."

Out in his car, he had to wait for his hands to stop shaking before he could drive away. Now that he'd had one taste of her he wanted more. He'd lost his mind, kissing Danica Gage. And she'd kissed him back.

At least he wasn't alone in the insanity.

* * *

Friday morning arrived too quickly, leaving Danica wondering how long a person could safely go without sleep. She'd tossed and turned all night. When she wasn't wrestling the irrational fear of being alone and defenseless, she was reliving that kiss…imagining what could have followed. When she had slept, Shane's sexy face and body had invaded her dreams.

Not that any of those dreamy moments would come to pass. She was still a Gage and he was still the man with a rightful grudge.

A little voice in the back of her head chimed in with the reminder that he'd kissed *her*. What did that mean? If she hadn't asked Shane to leave, both of her problems would be solved. She wouldn't be alone, jumping at every shadow, and she'd *know*.

Despite the early hour, she tossed back the covers and went about her morning routine. Going in early was probably smart after leaving early yesterday. Being at work, with plenty of people and responsibilities, would also give her a buffer from Shane.

She had no idea how she was going to look him in the eye or work the case with him after last night. Not only the knee-melting kiss but also her idiotic claim that she'd killed someone were hanging out there between them now.

She would find a way, she thought as she fed Oscar breakfast. Because barring the Larson brothers' willing return of Nico and the puppy, assuming Shane found him there as well, they had a job to do. She wasn't sure either one of them was thinking clearly or what that meant for their chances of rescuing the dogs.

At the training center, she wasn't the only one in

early. Everyone on staff was equally unsettled, sad and somber after the thefts. Danica bypassed her office and went straight back to check on the dogs. The awkward vibe of loss and uncertainty clouded the air in the kennels, as well. The Malinois puppy that had lost his littermate was nervous and lonely.

To combat her anger over the circumstances she couldn't control, she took the puppy out into the yard, doing her best to lead by example for the little guy. If she could be brave out here, it would convey a sense of stability and reassurance to him. That was the core of her job, after all, to give the dogs confidence in themselves and their human partners.

At the morning staff meeting, the training schedule was modified and still more security precautions were introduced. They were given an update on the investigation that amounted to little more than a plea for patience, and told the guard was improving. She wondered if that update had come directly from Shane.

Belatedly, Danica felt the gazes around the room shift to her. "I'm feeling much better," she assured everyone with a smile. "I was thinking it would be good to get the new puppy on the agility course today," she added as notes and plans were solidified. "Just to give him something fun to focus on."

Being out in the yard would be good for her, too. Working the puppy on fun and challenging skills would require her full attention. Any success would be another step in restoring her self-reliance after the shocking attack. Dogs and people would benefit from plenty of uplifting sunshine and fresh air, something she suspected they all needed.

"Stella would enjoy that," Hayley said, referring to

the young beagle. "And we can use the older goldens to show her and the puppy how it's done." The training center currently had two experienced golden retrievers in house for search and rescue recertification.

"Once Tyler arrives, he and I can set the course," Danica volunteered. If she was lucky, he would open up to her and she could then set Shane's mind at ease. Avoiding an official questioning was her top priority for Tyler's sake.

When Tyler finally showed up and knocked on her office door, she saw that his eye was a kaleidoscope of color under the flop of hair. "Looks worse than it feels," he told her.

"It looks like it needs an hour with a raw steak," she replied as they walked outside to set up the agility course.

"Ha," he said. "I don't want my face licked off by the puppy."

Smart kid, she thought, smiling to herself. Though he was quiet, he didn't seem any more restless than anyone else at the training center today. She was pleased he relaxed a bit as they hauled various brightly colored obstacles around to set the course. Despite ample opportunity, he stubbornly refused to volunteer anything about the bully who'd clocked him last night.

"Why don't you let them know we're ready?" she said. "And then bring the puppy out."

"Me?" He froze, staring at her. "Seriously?"

"Yes." Didn't he know how much she trusted him? "Is there a reason you don't want to?"

"No." He loped across the yard, as if afraid she'd change her mind.

Alone. Danica held her ground, studying the course

when she wanted to turn and check the fence and the trees crowding it. No one was back there. She could do this. She could stand here by herself and remember what it felt like to be safe. Her palms started to sweat and she wiped them on her pants, refusing to give in to the urge to go inside.

After minutes that only felt like hours, Hayley walked out with the golden retrievers and Stella, followed by Tyler and the puppy. Danica took Stella's lead and the beagle obediently sat at her foot, attentive as Hayley walked the retrievers through the agility course.

Naturally, Tyler didn't have as easy a time with the puppy, who was eager to get out there and play with the other dogs. At her silent encouragement, Tyler managed to get the little guy to lie down.

Danica considered it a promising sign that the puppy's ears were perked and he was alert to the action. When the goldens finished their second circuit, acting like the professionals they were, Danica started around with Stella. Other than balking at her first pass of the brush jump and skipping a few of the weaving flags, the beagle managed everything else with eager aplomb.

Hayley and Tyler let the dogs play for a few minutes while Danica set up a beginner's run for the puppy. It was a simple runner with treats and toys placed at regular intervals. "Bring him over," she called to Tyler. "Remember how we do this?"

He nodded, eyeing the simple course. The puppy was already inching toward the first treat.

"Just relax," she reminded him. "There's no real pressure." She forced her mind away from the twitch between her shoulder blades and looked him square in the eye that wasn't bruised. "Eventually, we want him to go from you to me without having him detour at the treats or toys."

"I know," Tyler said with a dubious look at the puppy. He gave the command to heel and walked down the runner, patiently encouraging the puppy to stay with him. At the end of the runner, he had the puppy sit and rewarded him well.

Tyler led the puppy down the runner twice more with only a modest improvement. Danica didn't care. Together, she and Tyler worked with the puppy on a few basic skills with a little more success. Her only real goal today was to have a little fun and give everyone a positive experience. The retrievers were lying down at the edge of the agility course, watching the action of the puppy and the beagle until Hayley gave them another turn on the course.

"All right," she said as Tyler returned to his end of the runner. "He knows what we want. Let's see how he does on his own." She secretly hoped the puppy failed spectacularly. The first failures always made for hours of laughter among the staff. Right now, they all needed the smiles more than the pride of immediate success.

Tyler gave the puppy the command to sit and stay. Then he slipped off the lead. With a nod to Danica at the other end of the runner, he gave the puppy the command to go. The little guy looked up at the lanky teenager as if he couldn't believe his luck. Tyler repeated the command.

"Come," Danica said, patting her thighs to get the puppy's attention. "Come."

Hayley had Stella on the lead and stood back with the retrievers to watch. The young Malinois didn't let her down. There were only three toys and two treats on his route, but he lost his focus and diverted to explore every single one. He gobbled up the treats, batted at the ball, and spun in happy circles when he found the squeaker. Danica was crying with laughter when the puppy finally waddled up to her end of the course, trailing a hank of rope.

For a few minutes, she and Tyler and the puppy just had fun, letting him romp about and playing tug for a bit. She pulled a lead out of her pocket and sent Tyler off to walk him, reinforcing the basics while she reset the run with more tempting challenges for the retrievers.

When Hayley was ready, Danica had the Malinois pup sit and watch the three other dogs triumph over temptation and get lavished with praise and rewards.

The puppy did better on his second solo attempt. He stole only one treat and romped with all the toys, and she let him move on to something different. Tyler, with Hayley's supervision, worked with the puppy on a short tunnel obstacle. He proved adept at that challenge, following Stella's example and then doing it all by himself over and over.

It was approaching noon and Danica realized she hadn't seen or heard from Shane. He was surely working the investigation and she hoped he had some good news to share soon.

Shane had spent the morning at his home office, going through the interviews from the training center staff and trying not to think about kissing Danica. Since she was at the heart of the investigation, it wasn't possible to put her out of his mind entirely.

He had a case to solve and he should be thinking of her only in the context of a witness and expert assistant. She was a Gage, for crying out loud, and from what he'd heard, she'd idolized her grandfather. None of that changed the way his pulse raced when he thought of kissing her again.

The case wasn't even close to stalled, but he needed a break and a fresh perspective. He called Stumps, and they walked over to the police station together. In the bull pen, he sought out Brayden and Echo. Of all things to bring his half siblings together, it seemed Demi's predicament and the ongoing Groom Killer case were the catalysts they needed. He and Brayden in particular were forging a new bond.

In recent weeks, he felt as if he was gaining family and it was a strange sensation after all this time. Growing up, family had meant only him and his mom. When she'd died while he was in prison, he was too angry to let anyone else close. Having a brother was turning into a positive thing, knowing someone cared about him as more than the kid who'd been screwed over by the system. Knowing that particular someone also understood the challenges of shaking free of a murky childhood and less-than-stellar past made the biggest difference.

"Got a minute?" he asked, reaching Brayden's desk. "I may have done something stupid last night," Shane admitted.

Brayden sat forward, lowering his voice. "If it's about the stolen puppy, tell it to the chief."

"Huh?"

Brayden scowled. "There was another attack at the

training center last night. The new guard's in the hospital and a Malinois puppy is gone."

"I know about that," Shane said. "Stumps and I should get over there." He was thinking of the Larson office, rather than the training center. In the back of his mind, when he wasn't thinking about Danica, he'd been debating how to handle another visit with the twins.

"So you saw something or followed someone?" Brayden asked in a whisper.

"Without calling it in? Are you kidding?" Shane said it lightly, and though his temper lit at the assumption that he would take that kind of chance, he didn't let it show. His first week in prison had cured him of revealing much emotion.

"You said you did something stupid and all you do is work." Brayden shrugged a shoulder. "What else is on your mind?"

Shane mentally regrouped. He could interview suspects with ease but he didn't know quite how to ask his brother the right questions about Danica. "What do you know about my witness on this case?"

"Danica Gage?" Brayden's eyebrows arched toward his hairline. "About as much as you, I guess. She's well-respected around town and among the police force. Dedicated. She's a remarkable trainer, but you know that." He reached down and gave Stumps a rub under the chin. "What is it you're really after?"

Shane wanted to know if he could trust her. More, he wondered if he could trust himself around her. His hatred for her grandfather, and her family as a whole, seemed etched on his bones after a decade of wearing that hate and fury like armor. He respected her and he didn't want to get close only to lash out from habit and hurt her. Better if he could forget that kiss, forget Danica and forget this conversation.

"Hey." Brayden gave his shoulder a shove. "You need a coffee or something? Either talk to me or get out of here so I can get to work."

"What work?" Shane teased. "Only dogs have gone missing around here lately." This experience of having a brother had perks. "And I know where they are."

"Yeah? Prove it, hotshot." Brayden shoved him again. "Talk."

"Right." Shane cleared his throat. "Danica just isn't what I expected. Outside of the training center, I mean."

Brayden whistled, earning the attention of both Stumps and Echo. "You like her."

"Shut up." He was a professional investigator looking for background on a witness. Of course he'd come to Brayden for personal advice, too. "Not on purpose," he confessed. He didn't get involved with clients or witnesses. Or anyone. "Besides, she's a Gage."

Brayden chuckled. "It's not like she had any more choice about being a Gage than you did being Rusty's kid," Brayden said. He sat forward. "Is she convinced that Demi's guilty?"

Naturally, that singular factor would be a priority for Brayden to develop an opinion about anyone in town. "I don't think so," Shane replied. That really should have been a primary concern for him, too. "She claims she believes Demi's innocent, though she is grieving her brother."

"Then what's on your mind?" Brayden pressed.

"Do you know if she was ever in any trouble?"

Brayden shook his head. "Not that I know of," he replied. "Always a sweet kid, dedicated, as I said. She and her grandpa were inseparable. Everyone around here was surprised she didn't join the RRPD. What sparked all these questions?"

"I'm not sure." If he could talk to anyone about this, it should've been Brayden. He knew his half brother wouldn't fly off the handle. Yet the idea of wrecking her reputation by sharing her claim that she'd killed someone turned his stomach. "I'll figure it out once Stumps and I find and catch the dog thief."

Brayden snorted. "We will all bow to your expertise."

"As you should," Shane said, puffing out his chest. They both laughed.

Shane supposed this conversation, his questions about Danica, boiled down to missing his mom. She'd been his rock, encouraging him at every turn to ignore his circumstances and dream big. He couldn't put all the blame for her death on Sergeant Gage, though he'd often wanted to. In his darkest hours, when Shane needed her most, Sergeant Gage denied him just as the law allowed. He'd never had another private conversation with his mother. Shane couldn't fault Gage for that piece of the fiasco. It had been one of the few parts of the process done right. It was, however, one more reason Shane considered his primary task making sure the police force did their job right the first time.

"Daydream somewhere else, man." Brayden turned to his computer. "You've got a thief to find."

"Right." Shane bent down and gave Echo some attention.

"Better not let it go three for three," Brayden mocked as only a brother would.

"I'll camp out in the kennel myself if necessary," Shane said, ignoring Brayden's eye roll.

At this point, solving the case seemed simple compared to figuring out what to do next with Danica. He supposed if there was going to be something personal between them, it would depend on her. Whatever last night's kiss did or didn't mean, they still needed to track down her attacker.

He went over the facts as he knew them so far as he and Stumps left. His next stop had to be the Larson office. The brothers had been bold enough to keep Nico in plain sight. He had no reason to think they'd bother hiding a puppy.

After the microchip debacle with Nico, there wasn't much point in taking a scanner over. If they had the puppy, they would have changed the chip by now. Really all he could do was go have another chat with the twins. If they had a new Malinois puppy, he could develop a plan to expose how they acquired it.

He and Stumps checked in at the RRPD secretary's desk on their way out. Lorelei Wong was one of his favorite people in the department. She loved all the dogs and she never treated Shane like a second-rate officer. "Did anything come in from the Larson realty office?" he asked her. "I'm expecting a receipt for a recent Malinois purchase. Probably would have been addressed to Chief Colton, but it could have been addressed to me."

She looked through email as well as the Received box on her desk. "Nothing here, Shane."

"All right. Thanks for checking. Hopefully they'll follow through soon."

The chief had tasked him with recovering Nico, and although he knew where the dog was, he couldn't see a clear, legal path to reestablishing the training center ownership and getting the animal back. He thought of Danica's face when they'd left Nico with the Larson brothers yesterday. He couldn't bear a repeat of that with the puppy. No matter that her feelings shouldn't be a factor in how he worked the case—he couldn't put her through that grief again.

Who was he kidding? He couldn't do it to himself. Mad, he could handle. Sorrow, as well. Bad stuff was part of life and people had to deal with it. But when Danica's eyes had filled with that overwhelming worry for a good dog left to the control of the Larson twins, he'd hated feeling helpless. Yes, he needed to meet with the Larson brothers, but he'd prefer going in armed with more than a reminder to send him a copy of a receipt.

He let Stumps snuffle and poke along during the walk back to the house. Walking didn't cost him much more time than driving and it gave him space to think. More important, walking was another affirmation that he was free to come and go whenever he wished.

The only fences and boundaries he wanted in his world were for the sole protection of his K9 partner.

Chapter 9

When lunchtime rolled around, Danica volunteered to pick up the food for everyone. The order placed, she insisted on taking Tyler with her. It wasn't because she was afraid, she told herself. It was to protect Tyler in case Shane came by the training center with an update as she expected. She didn't want Tyler to get caught unaware or feel pressured by even a casual conversation. She could give him some space, if nothing else.

She carefully avoided any and all reference to his black eye, the bullies and the second theft. She didn't want him to feel ganged up on, either, so she kept the conversation on the agility training, pleased when Tyler laughed with her as they relived the more humorous moments.

Hayley had chosen the restaurant today, which meant they were headed for a posh little place in the middle of Red Ridge, right across the street from the office building the Larson twins owned.

She wanted so badly to march into that office and just take Nico back. One more reason to be grateful she'd brought Tyler with her. The Larson twins always made her feel nervous with the entitlement and ownership that radiated from their expressions when they looked at certain people. It reminded her of the imminent threat of smoke creeping under a doorway.

Having been on the receiving end of those barely-veiled threatening expressions yesterday, she hoped she never had to feel such a creepy gaze directed her way again. Plenty of rumors had circulated through her school years about the crude stunts the twins often pulled on their girlfriends and others, as well. She didn't know how they managed to close real estate deals. Given a choice, she wouldn't sign a contract with anyone who made her wonder when the knife would strike.

She parked the car at the curb and she and Tyler climbed out. A sharp yip had them both turning toward the unmistakable sound of a puppy. Across the street, a Belgian Malinois puppy had spied Tyler. He reared up, his front legs scrambling as he fought the leash holding him back.

"That's him," Tyler said, stunned. "The stolen puppy."

Danica inventoried the black face, fawn body and a white spot on the chest and had to agree. "We don't know for sure," she said.

Reflexively, Tyler moved toward the puppy. Danica caught his arm just in time as the person on the other end of a retractable leash came into view.

Evan Larson.

Danica swore under her breath. She pulled out her phone and called Shane. The phone rang once, twice. "Come on. Pick up," she muttered.

"Shane Colton."

His voice, all business, gave her hope. "The Larsons have the puppy," she said without preamble.

"How do you know?" he asked.

"I'm staring at him right this second. We're near the Larsons' office to pick up lunch and the puppy is right there on the corner."

"The dog is loose?" Shane asked, incredulous.

"No." She swallowed, determined to maintain her composure. "No, Evan Larson has him."

"Don't confront him, Danica."

"He's recognized us," she said. "The puppy recognized us." Her voice cracked as Evan retracted the lead and tugged the puppy roughly, turning to walk him in the opposite direction. "Shane, we have to do something. He has no idea how to treat a dog."

"Nothing is the best thing you can do right now." He paused. "The *only* thing."

She hated that he was right. As much as she wanted to charge after Evan, she couldn't put Tyler in that situation. "Doesn't feel like it."

"I know." The palpable empathy in his voice went a long way to soothing her. "We will get both dogs back."

"Evan doesn't even like the dogs," she grumbled.

"I know that, too," Shane said. "Pick up the food and get back to the training center as soon as possible."

"Okay." She blinked away tears of frustration.

"One more thing," Shane said before she could end the call.

"Yes?"

"Who is 'we'?" he asked.

"Tyler is helping me pick up lunch."

"Good." Shane sounded too relieved by the news. "Both of you get back to work and stay there. I'll be over as soon as I can."

"All right." She ended the call and shoved the phone into her pocket.

Tyler was still ready to spring into action. "Well? What do we do?"

"We pick up the food and let the authorities handle it."

"We are the dog authorities," Tyler insisted. "There are two of us," he added.

She tipped her head toward the restaurant. "I thought the same thing," she admitted. "But if we go after the puppy, we could be charged with harassment or worse. I'm sure the dog is microchipped and registered to Evan or Noel already."

Tyler swore, echoing her own thoughts. She didn't have the heart to remind him to watch his language. His expression dour, he withdrew into himself as they collected the lunch order and returned to the training center.

They'd just finished distributing food to everyone when Shane walked into the break room with Stumps. Danica could see from his thunderous expression that his day wasn't going much better than hers. She had the outrageous urge to greet him with a kiss. Surely that would improve the day for both of them. Fortunately, she remembered where they were and what they were to each other. After greeting Stumps, she offered Shane half of the sub sandwich she'd ordered.

"I could eat. Thanks." He pulled out the chair next to Tyler, who offered to get him a drink from the refrigerator.

"Water is great," Shane said. His eyebrows arched as if Tyler's courtesy surprised him.

"Does Stumps need anything?" she asked.

"He's good," Shane replied. "I gave him a break and some water before we left the hospital."

"Did you learn anything about the thief?" she asked.

Shane gave an abbreviated shrug. "Not a lot to go on, but we'll keep working every detail."

Tyler returned with the water and sat down. Although she was curious about the guard's statement, she decided more questions could wait. She didn't have to remind Shane that recovering the dogs was paramount. To her surprise, he kept the conversation light and friendly and chuckled a bit when Tyler relayed the remaining puppy's initial failures on the agility course.

"He'll get it," Shane said with confidence. "Half the time when we try those courses with Stumps, I swear he goofs off just to test my patience."

Danica leaned over and grinned at the corgi lounging at Shane's feet. It was a fair assessment. "Stumps could have been good at a thousand things," she explained to Tyler. "I think he revealed his preference for evidence collection for the sake of variety."

Shane also glanced down at his partner, who was obviously soaking up every minute of being off duty. "I believe it." Shaking his head, he turned back to Tyler. "How'd you get the shiner, kid?"

Tyler shoved a french fry through a puddle of ketchup. "Typical bully crap," Tyler replied.

"Need a hand?"

Tyler's dark eyebrows knitted as he frowned. "What do you mean?"

"Help. I could give you an assist," Shane said. "When a bully knows the target has backup nearby, it usually makes a difference."

Tyler shrugged.

Danica sensed another prison story there, if not a blatant reference to her grandfather's bullying of Shane through the case. She added it to the column of things she didn't feel she had the right to ask him.

"You have an older brother?" Shane asked.

"No."

"Good friend who's bigger than you?"

"Uh, no." Tyler's gaze darted to Danica and then down to his empty paper plate. "I'm good. It's over." He gathered the remains of his lunch and shoved it all into the original sack. Pushing back from the table, he picked up the trash. "Thanks for the offer."

"Consider it open," Shane said as Tyler walked away.

Danica studied him. "Did something the guard said change your mind, or is this an attempt to slide past his defenses?"

"That would be a neat trick," Shane murmured. "The kid has substantial defenses." He stuffed his mouth full with the last of the sandwich.

Having brothers, she recognized the ploy to avoid answering and waited him out. "Which is it?" she pressed when he finished chewing. "Interrogation or olive branch?"

"A little of both, really. He's important to you."

His stark honesty startled her. "Oh." She didn't expect him to lie. She just hadn't expected him to be quite so forthright. And why did Shane care who was important to her? He wasn't known for soft-pedaling the facts with his clients.

"If the kid is involved, my guess is the situation has gone way beyond his comfort zone," he added.

She leaned forward. "He *isn't* involved," she whispered.

"Are you going to eat that pickle?" Shane asked as if she hadn't spoken at all.

Apparently, having half a sandwich had merely sparked his appetite rather than satisfying it. "Go ahead." She glanced down at her plate. "Take the rest of the sandwich, too, if you want."

His sandy eyebrows furrowed at the offer. "You didn't eat much."

Her appetite hadn't returned after seeing the way Evan handled the puppy. "When I called, I got the impression you already knew the Larsons had the puppy," she said.

Shane nodded, wolfing down the rest of her sandwich in big bites. "I'd gone by about an hour before you called. No sense bothering to take the microchip scanner after yesterday." He balled up a paper napkin in his fist, his mouth an angry slash across his handsome face. "I didn't think they'd have the audacity to walk the dog through town in the middle of the day or I would've warned you."

"They've always wanted people to know they have the power," she said. "With any luck their arrogance, will give us an opening."

"Agreed." The slash turned to a warm, charming smile.

She blinked, her thoughts scattered by the expression. "So, um, what's next?"

"Work, I guess," he replied. "You enjoy the rest of your day and Stumps and I will enjoy the rest of ours. We'll compare notes later," he suggested.

"You know that's not what I meant. Do you have a plan?"

"Oh." He sat back, his gaze so steady she wanted to fidget. "Since it's Friday, I was thinking something traditional like dinner and a movie."

Was he asking her out? She felt her mouth drop open as she floundered for the right response.

He reached over and tapped her chin. "Speechless I can work with. Thanks for lunch. I'll pick you up at seven." Clearing the trash from his place and hers, he and Stumps walked off.

For several stunned minutes, Danica sat there wondering if hell had just frozen over. In the past few minutes, Shane had been almost as charming and warm as he'd been before the murder trial. Admittedly, she'd really only seen that side of him from a distance.

Then she realized that last night's kiss, though it felt like spontaneous combustion on her side, likely had been delivered only to shock her. Dinner and a movie aside, Shane couldn't be putting as much romantic significance on that kiss as her fluttering heart wanted to put on it.

Logic alone dictated that not every toe-curling kiss signaled the beginning of a relationship. She might not have had too many kisses that left her obsessing, but this was *Shane*. The dinner-and-a-movie thing was probably a ruse to lull her into helping him get information out of Tyler. Or even out of her. She had told him she was a killer, after all.

Her momentary happiness doused by a more sensible theory, she perked up again as another possibility occurred to her. They were teamed up for a stolen dog case. Dinner and a movie could serve as good cover for rescuing Nico and the puppy. If that was it and they succeeded, it would be the best Friday night date she'd had in a long while.

That hopeful thought, combined with the realization that Shane hadn't hassled Tyler, put a boost in her step as she went to tackle the rest of her workday.

While she was covering the front desk in the early afternoon, Danica saw the florist delivery van arrive. It was hardly an uncommon sight. Every Friday, an enormous bouquet of flowers arrived for Hayley. The woman drew admiring men like flies to honey. She buzzed Hayley in her office to come out and pick it up. Hayley and the delivery driver reached the front desk at the same time, a cloud of fragrant lilies and aromatic greenery filling the air.

"From anyone in particular?" Danica queried out of habit as much as curiosity when the driver had gone. Her brother's body had scarcely been interred before his almost-widow started receiving overtures from other men, if they'd ever stopped at all.

It wasn't Hayley's fault. She had no more control over the genes that turned her into every man's daydream than Danica had control of the genetics that had shaped her into a short, slim tomboy.

"The card isn't signed," Hayley replied. "It's been anonymous for a while now." Her smile wobbled a little. "I almost wonder if this isn't something Bo arranged before…" Her voice trailed off as she breathed in the rich scents of the bouquet.

Danica was fairly certain weekly extravagance had not been synonymous with her brother, but what did she know? She'd thought he'd found his perfect match with Demi Colton.

On the desk, her cell phone buzzed and the display showed a call from Carson. She picked it up as Hayley returned to her office.

"I need a favor," he said as soon as she answered. "I've been called to another assault. The victim is alive, but everyone is edgy."

"Oh, no." She glanced up to see Shane and Stumps coming down the hallway. She hadn't realized they were still here.

"I've sent a text to Shane for an evidence team. Naturally, people are already muttering about the Groom Killer, though the victim should survive."

"That's a plus. What do you need?" she asked, already suspecting the answer.

"Can you please tell Vincent to knock it off with Valeria? They were seen making out behind the ice cream shop yesterday. It's no secret they're still set on getting married. I don't want to get called out to a scene like this one and find him."

Her stomach twisted at the thought of losing another brother. "I've tried," Danica reminded him. "We all have."

"I know, but try again. Please?" Carson said.

"I'm on it." What else could she say? Carson ended the call with a hurried thank-you and she set her phone aside. "That was Carson," she said, looking up at Shane. "He said he texted you."

"Yes." Shane and Stumps had stopped at the desk, waiting for her to finish the call. Shane looked rather edgy himself. "I hate to ask, but can we reschedule for eight?"

"Absolutely." There was no way she would miss a chance to recover Nico and the puppy.

He started for the door and stopped halfway through. "What's up with the flowers Hayley was mooning over?"

"She loves flowers." Danica waved it off. "Good thing, too."

He opened his mouth and his phone sounded, cutting him off. He scowled at the display, his mind clearly moving on to the new case in town. "Stumps and I need to go."

"Happy hunting, you two."

Shane didn't like having to delay the date with Danica, even by an hour. Having seen her face shift through a variety of expressions, giving her reason to doubt his motives seemed like a bad thing to do. On the way to the crime scene, he used his hands-free option and cancelled the reservation he'd made just after sharing lunch. He'd just have to save the fine dining option for the second date.

"What am I doing?" he wondered aloud. In the rear-view mirror, he saw his dog cock his head, ears high and alert. There were times when he wished his K9 partner could offer advice. Teaming with Stumps was the closest relationship Shane had taken a risk on since his release from prison.

His mom would have been disappointed by his near-recluse choices had she been alive to weigh in. Holding back, living fully only on the professional side of life, went against everything she'd tried to instill in him.

Shane parked at the curb, last in the line of RRPD cars at the newest scene, and twisted to speak to Stumps. "Ready, bud?" It was time to put his mind on the job. He could evaluate and overthink whatever was going on with Danica later.

The uptick in person-on-person crime was unreal lately. As if having a killer running amok wasn't bad enough, personal assaults like this one were on the rise. The first assumption with every report these last few months was how it might link up with the Groom Killer case, and rightly so.

This latest crime scene was no different. The victim, Tommy Sutton, claimed he was not engaged to anyone, nor had he recently broken off an engagement. He'd been found trying to crawl out of a delivery alley on Rattlesnake Avenue, just a block off Main Street. Shane and Tommy weren't particularly close, but he was considered a decent guy. They'd gone to high school together until Shane had been forced to finish his GED as a ward of the state.

Before Shane set Stumps to work, he discussed the assault with the officers on the scene. At first glance, no one could come up with any reason for someone to attack Tommy. His memory was foggy at best, typical of a head injury. He remembered seeing a black gun barrel, but he couldn't recall hearing a gunshot and the wound in his thigh was superficial, doing more damage to his pants than his leg. The crime scene unit had yet to find a bullet casing.

According to the officer who'd taken his statement, Tommy had no idea how he'd wound up in the alley. His last memory was deciding to take a smoke break outside his office at a restaurant supply company across town. That was as far as the questions went before the paramedics insisted on taking him to the hospital.

Shane and Stumps were to search the alley for the weapon used against Tommy. That was the first priority. Anything to identify the attacker or any sign of the gun Tommy had seen was considered bonus. Based on the results of their searches, Shane could decide how to proceed.

As Shane planned the search, his mind cycled through the similarities of his cases. Both Tommy and the new security guard at the K9 training center had been severely injured by blows to the head with currently unidentified objects. Whatever weapon had been used against the guard had not been around when Shane and Stumps had searched the training center. He was eager for a success here.

Unlike the guard, Tommy had been scored by a bullet. Too early to tell if that was by accident or design. Being single should have removed him from the Groom Killer's sights. Unless the killer believed otherwise. Secret relationships were becoming the norm in Red Ridge. Tommy also wasn't into stealing dogs and had never run in the same circles as the Larson twins.

Shane had to consider that either the Groom Killer or the dog thief might be trying to muddy the waters with random violence. If Tommy had been attacked near his office, the last place he remembered, someone should have seen something when he was dumped over here. *Not my problem.* Other officers were already canvassing the area for potential witnesses.

The only thing Shane knew without any doubt was that his sister could not have managed these recent attacks. She might have a hot temper but she lacked the motive, as well as the strength. As he walked up and down the alley, giving Stumps a chance to acclimate, he couldn't come up with anything that connected the stolen dogs to the Groom Killer case, other than the blunt-force trauma in these recent incidents.

Finding the answers, peeling back the layers to reach the truth, was what Shane lived for. The pungent odors of spoiling food and general refuse fought to dominate the alley. It was a rare day when he felt sorry for his dog's keen sense of smell, and this was one of them. His poor partner deserved a romp in the backyard at home and plenty of savory treats when the work was done today.

Giving Stumps the command to search, he watched his dog lean into the various smells permeating every inch of the alley. The corgi progressed up and down the scene, his waddling gait relaxed and easy until he caught an intriguing scent. Moving with clear purpose, Shane had to lengthen his stride to keep up.

Stumps went unerringly toward a row of garbage bins, and Shane feared his dog had been overwhelmed by the situation until Stumps sat, his long nose wedged as far between the bins and the brick wall as he could get. His back straight, he wouldn't do anything more than breathe until Shane gave him the command to release.

He used his flashlight to peer into the shadows and the light bounced off what appeared to be a plumber's wrench. "Winner, winner," Shane murmured, taking a picture with his phone. He called Stumps off, giving him praise and a treat.

"I think we have one weapon." Shane called over one of the crime scene techs. Why bash a victim over the head when a gun had clearly been in play?

He and Stumps watched from a safe distance as the tech worked to retrieve the wrench. Shane saw the bloody bits of hair and skin as the wrench was bagged. To the naked eye, the hair was the same color as Tommy's, though a lab report would be necessary for it to hold up in court. For now, it was enough to keep Shane searching.

"Now we just need a motive and an assailant," he muttered to Stumps. "Who could have dumped Tommy back here? And why not leave him where he was?"

According to the initial background information, Tommy was now a lead salesman with the restaurant supplier he'd started with as a delivery driver when he was a kid. Although he still made the occasional delivery, the majority of his time was spent managing the bigger accounts in the area from the office.

They already knew he hadn't come here to deliver anything. Neither the supply truck nor Tommy's car was anywhere near the alley. His thoughts swirling, Shane walked Stumps a block up and down Rattlesnake Avenue, then a block up and down Main Street. What businesses in the area would order from Tommy? The obvious connections were the restaurants, and the police were handling those interviews. Shane didn't expect those to amount to much. An assault in a public place around lunchtime should have resulted in an uproar.

"Who else, bud?" Shane murmured, repeating

the circuit. His gaze landed on a printing shop. They most likely ordered cocktail napkins for weddings and events from Tommy's company. Still, with the rash of wedding cancellations courtesy of the Groom Killer, Shane didn't think an emergency delivery of napkins was very likely and definitely not without a vehicle.

"No way this is the primary scene where Tommy was attacked," he decided. Shane returned to his SUV and opened the back door for Stumps. "None of this is making much sense." He slid into the driver's seat and realized his error immediately. The smells from the alley had followed them, permeating his clothing. Behind him, Stumps sneezed and then gave a hard shake from nose to hindquarters.

"Let's hope you finding the wrench will lead them to a solid suspect, buddy." Shane wanted to close at least one of these new open cases. In theory, a case like Tommy's should be simple to resolve. He would focus on that, since it was freshest.

"Let's see what we can find over at Tommy's office," he said to Stumps.

The dog bounded into the front seat and put his front paws on the dash, peering through the windshield. The little guy loved working. "You know you can't ride shotgun," he told Stumps. "Go on."

Shane started the engine as Stumps resumed his safer place in the back seat. Checking the clock on the dash, he hoped the next search didn't take them too long. He needed to shower and get the smell out of the car. "You'll need a bath, too," he said to Stumps, "or Danica won't want to hang out with us tonight."

It was a brief drive to the restaurant supply warehouse planted in the light industrial district on the other side of town. People liked to pretend Red Ridge was only the clean and polished Main Street and newer business and shopping districts where Tommy had been found. Plenty of hands-on labor was accomplished over here, though the buildings weren't as pretty.

Shane deliberately parked so he could keep his back on the shabbier side of town. There was nothing for him there anymore. Not even his dad wanted to see him. Of course, that had as much to do with Shane's grief as it did with his career choices. His mom had been his rock growing up on this side of town. She couldn't give him the address in the nicest neighborhood, but she'd provided well. She'd made sure that their house was neat and tidy and that Shane developed common sense, compassion and a solid work ethic. How often she'd reminded him that nothing was free and life wasn't supposed to be easy. He'd started mowing yards and picking up odd jobs by the age of ten and when trouble tempted him, it was the dread of disappointing her that kept him in line.

Though she was clear that she didn't want Shane to follow in his father's shoes, she never bad-mouthed Rusty or called Shane a mistake like some of the other single moms in the neighborhood had done in front of their kids. Officially, her death certificate listed the cause as a heart attack, but Shane knew it had been heartbreak. He knew she'd wanted to believe he was innocent, but the trumped-up evidence and inability to help Shane had been too much for her to overcome.

Muttering a curse, Shane dragged his thoughts back to the present. This type of melancholy was why he preferred to work his own cases or work with Stumps on county cases as far from Red Ridge and his grimy past as he could get. He'd thought of leaving, yet moving away would only have given the ultimate victory to the Gage clan for driving a Colton out of town.

With Stumps at his side, Shane walked into the restaurant supply front office. A woman with classic round pearls at her ears and throat, dark brown eyes and steely gray hair gaped at him. "Shane Colton. My goodness, you're a sight."

"Ma'am?" According to the nameplate on her desk, this was Irene Mixon. Her face was vaguely familiar, but he couldn't place the name.

"Oh, you don't need to remember me," she said with a careless flap of her hand. "I remarried and it's been ages since you've clapped eyes on me." Standing, she peered over the counter to see Stumps. "Isn't your partner handsome?"

Stumps, sitting in perfect obedience, tipped his head. Shane made the introductions, adding, "He's a flirt when he's off the clock."

"Then you two are well matched," Irene laughed. "You were incorrigible as a little boy, certain that big smile would get you out of any trouble."

Smiling hadn't been nearly enough once Sergeant Gage decided he was a killer. Being over here was bad for him. He focused on the receptionist. The case. Anything but the past.

Something about her eyes, twinkling over the rims of her half glasses, clicked for him. "You lived next door," he began.

She beamed indulgently. "And you nipped blackberries off the bush that grew through the fence."

Shane felt his mouth curve as the fonder memories rushed in. "You didn't mind that," he said. "It was whenever I ran my bike over the flowers out front that made you mad."

Her gaze narrowed. "It was indeed."

He felt about ten years old again, sheepish and wishing he hadn't taken the shortcut to catch up with the bigger boys. He barely kept his shoulders straight and his hands out of his pockets. "Sorry. Again."

She chuckled. "Why do you think I hired you to mow the grass?"

"I figured Mom begged you," he replied.

"She didn't beg," Irene clarified sternly. "We both thought it would instill a sense of pride that would prevent further mishaps."

They'd been right, though he never realized it until now. The statement reminded him of Danica's commitment to Tyler and the other kids at the youth center. Maybe he was letting the kid's background have too much influence over his assessment.

"What brings the two of you out this way?" she asked.

"Tommy Sutton was attacked a few hours ago. Stumps and I are following up."

The news startled her and her face paled as she pressed her hands together in front of her mouth. "He's alive," Shane said quickly. "He's been transported to the hospital after giving the police a brief, disjointed statement. I don't think his injuries are life-threatening."

"Well, thank goodness for small favors." Irene

glanced at her computer monitor tucked discreetly under the counter. "I thought he was in the office all day."

"No appointments on his calendar?"

She shook her head.

"He said he went out for a smoke and the next thing he knew, he was in a delivery alley just off Rattlesnake and Main."

Irene pointed toward the front window. "How did he get over there? That's his car. It's been here since he got in this morning."

"That's one of my questions, too," Shane said. "Stumps and I are here to see if we can find any clues." He wasn't about to admit he was looking for the original crime scene and upset her further.

"Oh, of course," Irene said. "Whatever we can do to help. We all adore Tommy."

Shane gave her his professional, reserved smile. "Could we take a look at his office, please? Maybe there's an appointment or note on his phone that didn't make it to the company calendar yet."

Irene rolled her eyes. "That happens more than I'd like." Irene dropped her cheaters to hang from the beaded chain around her neck as she stood up. "This way."

Shane and Stumps followed her through a set of double doors. The warehouse stretched out into a long open space, the concrete floor dark with age and racks loaded with boxes and crates stretched to the rafters on either side. A forklift hummed along, moving between the warehouse and the open bay door at the loading dock.

The offices at this end of the building were tidy and up-to-date. Tommy's office was about what Shane expected. There were files on the desk, samples scattered across the credenza and bookshelf, and framed certificates of education and accomplishments on the walls. The faint odor of cigarette smoke lingered in the air and Shane considered it a vast improvement over the smells from the garbage-filled alley. When Irene left, Shane let Stumps search, but there wasn't anything that caught his interest.

Shane applied his P.I. skills while Stumps took a break. Finding a short list of passwords printed on a sticky note under the desk calendar, Shane unlocked Tommy's computer and did a quick search. The man seemed to be all business with a few personal days scattered among his full schedule. His only true commitment seemed to be a weekly poker game with the guys. Not a bad life and clearly no sign of a fiancée in his present or recent past.

"Who would want to hurt you?" Shane muttered. There was always a motive. Maybe one of those occasional dates was married to a plumber, he thought, recalling the likely weapon. If so, why would a furious husband bother to move Tommy's unconscious body?

Shane poked through Tommy's client files and matched up one of his recent dates with a point of contact for a well-known French restaurant down in Rapid City. Huh. Shane had wanted to try that place for some time. It would be a haul, but maybe he and Danica could head down there one night soon. He could picture her in a dress with a short skirt and high heels that would bring her kissable mouth a little closer to his. The idea of going on dates beyond this evening startled him. He hadn't intended to kiss her, but now he could hardly think of anything other than the next opportunity.

"Get a grip, Colton," he muttered to himself. Case first, lust second.

A chime sounded, muffled, but unmistakably a cell phone alert of some sort. Shane followed the sound and nearly gave a whoop of victory when it led him to Tommy's cell phone. Even better, Tommy didn't keep his phone locked. Shane skimmed through his personal calendar and texts, hoping for any lead on a motive for the attack.

He stopped skimming at the sight of Hayley Patton's name and number. Tommy had regular dates with her before she'd accepted Bo's proposal and started wedding plans. He'd even marked their last date with a stop sign emoji. Interesting.

Shane compared the personal calendar with the business calendar and started to get a better picture of Tommy's dating habits. Returning the phone to where Tommy had left it, Shane took Stumps outside to investigate further.

It was a simple matter of following the odor of smoke through a side door to find where the smokers congregated. A trash can topped with an ashtray had been installed under the overhang of the metal roof. At the moment, no one else was here, giving Shane ample space and time to study the area.

He took pictures, noting how easily a vehicle could approach. Just as he gave the command for Stumps to investigate, a cream-colored sedan with the company logo on the door rolled by, followed by a delivery van. Clearly, the area had consistent traffic.

Shane made more mental notes while they worked, a potential theory for the attack developing in his mind. Stumps sat suddenly, giving an alert and waiting patiently for Shane to investigate. There in the gravel just outside the deeper rut of tire tracks, a bullet casing gleamed. It bore none of the grime of nearby debris, making it stand out as a new addition to the area.

Shane phoned in the find while he continued to search for more clues. Sure enough, a few paces back the gravel was scuffed up as if someone had been dragged away.

Once he'd handed the area off to the crime scene techs, Shane went to the office to let Irene know he and Stumps were done outside. "It was great to see you again," he added, turning for the door.

"Shane."

"Yes?"

She pursed her lips, clearly having made some decision while he and Stumps had been working. "You probably don't know I bought your old house at auction after your mother passed," Irene said. "While your father cleared out most things in his way, I was able to protect some mementos of your childhood and the things that meant more to her."

Taken aback, Shane felt rooted in place. "Why didn't you tell me before? It's been nearly a decade."

"I don't have a good answer for you," she said with a weak shrug. "Blame it on fear or doubt."

"Of *me*?" He should be used to people assuming he must have been guilty of something even after the real killer confessed. Instead, knowing his old neighbor sided with rumor gave him a disquieting prickle of unease behind his sternum.

"No," she said with a snort. "I wasn't sure you'd be interested in anything from before."

Curious, Shane couldn't help asking what had changed.

Irene's brown eyes welled with emotion. "You stuck in Red Ridge and made something of yourself. Your mom would be proud you didn't let the circumstances and rumors run you out."

He'd been sorely tempted, especially in those early days. He glanced at Stumps. The K9 opportunity had been the cornerstone of rebuilding right here.

Irene clasped her hands over her heart. "Then you were so busy with your new life and business, I didn't want to drag you down with the weight of a past we couldn't change."

"Thanks," he said, meaning it. When he thought of those dark years, his only real regret was that his mother hadn't lived to see him exonerated. "It would be nice to see the things you kept," he said. Maybe somewhere in whatever Irene had kept he would find the closure that had eluded him all this time. He fished out a business card and handed it over the counter. "Call me and I'll come by whenever it's convenient for you."

"Nonsense." She read the card. "I'll have Mr. Mixon drop it off for you."

"Oh." Shane had to work to get words past the emotion clogging his throat. "Thank you." He wasn't sure how he felt about having anything from his life on this side of town invading the new life and home he'd established on the respectable side of town.

It was a relief to drive away, to return to the police station and the responsibilities that kept his mind safely away from the bitter and twisted paths of his past.

News of their discovery of the original crime scene at the warehouse had preceded them, and Shane and Stumps were greeted with a rousing cheer. Stumps pranced along, soaking up the celebrity status. It wasn't as if they'd solved anything, but Stumps deserved all the credit for making good progress.

Shane asked for a moment with Finn. "I may have a new theory on the Groom Killer," he said when the door was closed. "We've been looking for a killer with ties to Bo and the other victims. I'd like permission to look into ties to Hayley Patton."

Finn's brow furrowed. "Keep going."

Shane understood he needed to lay out a convincing argument. "Today's victim, Tommy Sutton, doesn't fit with the Groom Killer case the way it's currently defined."

"It's only been a couple of hours, Shane. You know this takes time."

"And it should," Shane agreed. "But I've found a connection between Tommy and *Hayley*." He explained what he'd found on Tommy's cell phone and personal calendar.

"All right," Finn said. "You can pursue that angle. Just don't spook anyone. Start by interviewing Tommy."

Shane stood and Stumps rolled to his feet, as well. "We're on our way."

"Do me a favor first." Finn got up and opened his office window.

"What's that?" Shane was sure he was going to bring up the lack of progress on the stolen dogs.

"Get a shower," Finn said. "Bathe your dog, and burn your clothes. The pair of you stink."

With a small chuckle, Shane agreed to clean up right away, his mind already moving forward with the potential new angle of the Groom Killer case.

Chapter 10

Danica wasn't sure what to wear for a date that would potentially turn into a dog rescue mission. When the alarm she'd set for seven o'clock sounded, she knew she was running out of time to decide.

Her stomach a bundle of nerves, she opted for dark jeans, flats and a sky blue top that twisted in the front to give her the illusion of a real cleavage and flared out again. It wasn't easy being a short girl with a distinct lack of curves, but she'd long ago decided to make the best of it. She was strong and smart and capable and someday, she'd find the man who appreciated what she was, rather than what she wasn't. Or so her father always said.

She didn't want to think about her father's reaction if he heard she was going on a date with Shane Colton.

The questions and doubts in her own mind were more than enough to cope with.

She pulled the front of her hair up into a clip and swept mascara over her eyelashes. She tucked a tube of lip gloss into her purse. When she checked her reflection, her dumb heart wanted to spin in happy circles that Shane could be that man. She reined it in. Blazing kisses and sexy smiles aside, there was too much old baggage between them for her to contemplate anything beyond the present moment.

Oscar demanded a snack and more attention and she obliged. He was a good companion, as loyal to her as any dog she'd known. She flopped to the floor in the living room and they played with his favorite toy, a ball with a bell that lit up when he smacked it. It wasn't quite enough distraction to keep her mind off Shane, Nico or the puppy.

At ten minutes to eight, she checked her hair one last time and applied the lip gloss. She used the lint roller she kept by the front door to clear away the inevitable cat hair Oscar left behind. She felt as ready as possible for the evening ahead, but her stomach pitched when she heard the knock on her door.

Smiling, she opened the door without checking the peep hole. Then she was stuck, confused, trying to make sense of Tyler standing where she expected Shane to be.

"Hey," she said, recovering quickly. "What's up?" He shuffled his feet and her stomach pitched again. She didn't see any sign of new injuries and his parents weren't known to be abusive, but too many hard-luck scenes spun through her mind. "What happened?"

"Nothing." His smile wasn't so convincing. "I was just out walking and—"

He stopped as the elevator chime dinged an arrival down the hall. "Come on in," she said, following her intuition. Tyler needed to talk and date or rescue, she wasn't going to push him off.

"No." He shook his head. "Thanks though," he added a beat too late. "I was just walking and uh, thinking about the agility course."

Shane walked into view, flowers in hand, and Tyler clammed up. "I'll tell you tomorrow." He winced. "Are you working tomorrow?"

"Yes." Tomorrow was Saturday, but she typically spent part of her weekends at the training center. Animals needed care and attention every day. She stepped into the hallway as Tyler shifted back, out of Shane's way. "Hang on a second, Tyler."

Tyler waved and then shoved his hand back in his pocket, shoulders hunched. "'Night." He hurried along, giving Shane a half-hearted greeting as he left.

"Everything okay?" Shane asked her.

"Who knows?" She held up her hands. "Probably. Though he's never come here before," she added, stepping back to make room for Shane to come in.

He looked fantastic in pressed khakis and a short-sleeved linen shirt in a forest green. It didn't seem like a good outfit for dog rescue, but he was the professional. Brow furrowed, Shane eyed the now-empty hallway. "What did he want?"

She didn't have any idea. Better to change the subject than say anything Shane would interpret as Tyler's guilt. "Are those for me?" she asked with a nod to the flowers. A bundle of white daisies and rosy-red tulips peeked above the paper stamped with the logo from the florist that delivered to Hayley every week.

"Yes." Shane did a double take, then bent his head and kissed her cheek as he put the flowers into her hands. When he straightened, he gave her a smile laced with charm and confidence. Thankfully, he didn't bring that one out often or she'd never have a clear thought in his presence again. "You look great."

"Thanks."

She closed the door and inhaled the soft scent of the flowers. The bouquet was modest compared to the arrangements Hayley received, but Danica was thoroughly delighted by the gesture. It was the first time a guy—*man*—had brought her more than a corsage. She was a little embarrassed to have to pull out a water pitcher in lieu of a proper vase.

Some romantic notion wanted to flutter to life and she quashed it. This could simply be his way of enacting distinct attention to detail to make this look like a real date. She supposed that kind of cleverness was an asset in his work as a P.I.

"I brought something for Oscar, too." He pulled a small white bag from his back pocket.

At the sound of his name, or possibly the rich smell of salmon emanating from the bag, Oscar padded over from where he'd been curled on the top of the cat tower near the slider.

Shane knelt down and fed him a couple of the treats while Danica stared, having no idea how to interpret the thoughtful gesture. The flowers made sense, reinforcing their date as a cover story, but no one other than her would ever know or care that he'd been nice to her cat.

"Shane?"

He rubbed her cat's ears, and Oscar's rumble of approval grew louder. He turned and grinned up at her when she didn't say anything more. "Danica?"

"What exactly is going on?" She winced at how rude that must have sounded.

"I'm making friends with your cat," he said as if it should be perfectly obvious. He stood up and the full force of his smile struck her again.

"That's…kind." She should be polite and simply accept it. "I thought Stumps would be with you," she said, seeking a safe topic.

"He's at the house. It's been a long, productive day. For both of us." Shane raised his chin to the flowers in the pitcher. "I'll bring a vase next time."

There was going to be a next time?

"Have I said something wrong?" he asked, tapping his finger to his forehead just above his nose. "You've got that furrow going on."

"What?" She rubbed the spot he indicated. "No. Nothing's wrong." Unless she counted the way he was slowly crowding her, much as he'd done just before he kissed her last night. She licked her lips, her body warming with anticipation at the sexy promises in his gaze.

"Can I kiss you again?" His rough voice went right through her.

She nodded, terrified she'd beg if she tried to speak.

He stroked his thumb along her cheekbone, traced the line of her jaw as he tipped up her face. Cradling her head in that big palm, he slowly, slowly brought his lips to meet hers. No, the kiss last night hadn't been a fluke or intensified by the wine or the argument. This kiss, equally potent, if more controlled, left her reeling as much as the first one.

She gripped his sculpted arms for balance when he broke the kiss and touched his forehead to hers. If the goal was to make her fall in love—or lust—to sell the ruse, it was working. "Let me grab my purse and we can go."

He stepped back, an odd, speculative smile lurking at the corners of his lips. She had no intention of asking what he was thinking.

"Thank you for the flowers," she said as he waited for her to lock her door. "It was thoughtful."

There, that gave him an opening to clarify the gesture. He didn't. He took her hand instead. "You're welcome."

This was starting to seem like a real date and she was feeling well out of her element. "Is there a plan?" she asked as they waited hand in hand for the elevator.

"Well, I thought it would be nice to have dinner out, before I had to push things back." He paused as the elevator arrived. "We can still do that if you'd rather."

"Or?" she prompted as they stepped into the car.

He punched the button for the lobby. "Feel free to say it's too creepy or too soon, but I picked up everything for a pasta dinner at my house and you can choose the movie."

Out front, he continued to hold her hand until they reached his SUV. He opened the passenger door for and waited for her to slide in. "You're serious," she said.

"I knew it was creepy." He waited with one hand on the roof of the car while she stared up at him. "Especially on a first date."

"I know you're not a creep." She could stand here

in the shelter of his body for the better part of forever.
A weird blend of unconditional security and sensual
danger wound through her.

"And yet you're not getting into the car."

She caressed his smooth jaw and realized if she
didn't move the whole town would be talking about her
the way they murmured about Vincent and Valeria. She
hopped into the passenger seat, her hands laced in her
lap. He closed the door firmly and she willed herself to
breathe while he rounded the car to the driver's side.

"This really is a date," she blurted out as he drove
away from her condo.

He arched an eyebrow. "What were you expecting?"

"Honestly?" She couldn't stop the silly giggle that
bubbled out of her. "I thought, hoped, this was really
a rescue operation."

He shot her a startled look before scowling at the
street ahead. "Maybe we're not on the same page after
all," he sighed. "I'm an idiot."

"You're not. It's me." She was trying to catch up
with the real intention for the evening. They were on
a *date*. He'd been clear. She hadn't quite believed it.
This didn't feel like the right time to explain her dam-
aged confidence and it definitely wasn't the time to
confess her teenage crush on him.

"I'll take you home."

She wasn't about to let this rare opportunity slip
away. "Don't you dare," she said emphatically. "A date
sounds like way more fun than a dog rescue."

"Gee, how flattering." He pulled into his driveway
and parked, cutting the engine. "Don't move."

She waited, her pulse fluttering, as he stalked
around the car to open her door.

He leaned in and kissed her soundly. "Do you feel that?"

She nodded. She wanted to feel it again and again.

"How in the world did you come to the conclusion that this would be a rescue?"

It wasn't something she could she put into words without sounding like a total loser. "Family conflict aside," she said, starting with the obvious, "I'm not the girl guys like you ask out."

"Bull." He kissed her again.

She laughed, feeling positively effervescent as he helped her from the car. "It's true. You do realize every male handler who has trained at our facility has asked out Hayley? A few of the women, too," she added, remembering.

"Then they're all blind." He guided her to the door, his palm warm on the small of her back.

She looked down as Stumps barked once and trotted over to greet them. "Hello," she said, crouching low to return the fond welcome. "I heard you had a big day."

"He found a potential weapon and the origin scene of an abduction today," Shane said proudly, dropping his keys into a woven basket on the foyer table.

"Way to go, Stumps!" The corgi flopped to his side and she rubbed his belly.

"He was the epitome of humble professional until the celebration ended with a bath."

She laughed, pushing her hand through the dog's thick, soft coat. "I thought he liked water."

Shane extended a hand to help her up. "Oh, he loves water. Just don't add shampoo to the equation. Welcome."

The house, originally a tidy bungalow, had been

remodeled into an open area perfect for a bachelor to entertain. It suited him, she thought, taking in the soft earthy color palette and furnishings a man his size could lounge on with ease.

A distressed leather sectional with bolsters and toss pillows in various fabrics was at the center of the living room. A big-screen television was strategically placed for viewing from the kitchen, and a corner of the dining area had been converted to an office.

Fragrant aromas were coming from the kitchen and she followed the scents of tomato sauce and garlic as unerringly as one of their drug-sniffing dogs. The marble countertops, tile floors and cherry cabinetry with stainless steel appliances were an unexpected discovery.

Shane turned the heat on under a saucepan on a back burner and set water to boil for pasta. Pulling two packages of fresh ravioli from the refrigerator, he said, "I took a chance with portobello mushroom filling. If you'd rather have plain—"

"Sounds perfect," she said. "Did you make the sauce yourself?"

"Yes. My mom's recipe."

"Wow," she said, sincerely fascinated by his efforts.

"You might want to wait until you taste it. I have a tendency to go heavy on the spices."

"I'll take my chances." She studied the space, impressed with more than his cooking skills. He had a pared-back style that still came across as homey. Everywhere she looked there was texture or visual interest. Had he always been that way or was it a result of his time in prison? "Anything I can do to help?"

"Open the wine and relax," he suggested. He gave

a nod to a bottle of red and two glasses on the kitchen island.

Wine she could handle. Maybe it would dull her impulse to break into a happy dance. She was on a date with Shane! She poured two glasses of wine and handed him one. "Cheers," she offered.

He tapped his glass gently to hers and watched her over the rim as he sipped. "I do have one question about Hayley."

"Of course you do," Danica said, rolling her eyes.

"You brought her up," he said, a teasing glint in his gaze. "Has she dated much since Bo died?"

"Not that I'm aware of, although she still gets plenty of flowers."

"Pardon me?"

"You saw it today." Danica swirled the wine in her glass. "Every Friday, a big bouquet arrives."

"Every Friday?" The teasing was gone now, but she recognized his interest was professional rather than personal. "From who?"

"The cards are never signed. If she is dating someone in particular, he's staying far from the training center, which isn't uncommon now that I think about it." Bo had been the only one of her regular boyfriends to come around the facility. "Today she suggested it was something Bo set up before he died."

Shane reached to dump the pasta into the boiling water and stopped. "Are you saying she thinks Bo knew he was going to die?"

"No, not that." Danica smoothed her hair behind her ear. "I think she meant that he placed a standing order before they got married. A gesture to celebrate every week of wedded bliss." This wasn't exactly the conversation she imagined having with Shane and yet she didn't want to change the subject. The entire town needed some resolution to Bo's murder and the attacks and deaths that had followed. Unlike other members of her family, she would prefer it if the facts cleared Shane's half sister.

"Hayley has always received flowers. Before, during and after Bo. Personally, I don't think a standing order is something Bo would do."

"Why not?"

"Not his style, for one thing." She took another sip of her wine. "He was more down-to-earth than whoever is sending her these extravagant bouquets."

Shane made a humming sound as he lifted the lid on the sauce and stirred it. "People in love can change."

"Maybe." Danica's stomach rumbled loudly and they both grinned at the sound.

"Good thing we're not on a rescue mission or that might have gotten us busted," he said, teasing her again.

"Probably." She didn't want thoughts of Nico or the puppy to ruin the evening, but she couldn't ignore the situation, either. "I wish we could do something."

"I'm working on it," he said. "Through legal means," he emphasized.

She held up a hand as if taking an oath. "I promise not to do anything dumb." When he checked to be sure she wasn't crossing her fingers behind her back, she laughed. Who knew Shane had this lighthearted side? "But if Nico or that puppy makes a break for it, I will catch them, microchips or not."

"That's fair," he allowed.

He popped thick slices of garlic bread under the

broiler and then set a bowl of mixed greens on the table. When he drained the cooked pasta, she carried over the wine, adding to each glass as he finished serving.

Thoughts of the case fled from her mind at the first taste of his mother's spicy tomato sauce. The flavors burst and melded on her tongue. It was all she could do not to moan with delight. "Shane, this is heavenly. Thank you."

"My pleasure."

The sexy, slow smile on his lips would have buckled her knees if she'd been standing.

"It might have been the thing I missed most," he said. "Prison food tends toward bland."

She set down her fork and picked up her wine. Despite all he'd said, maybe this wasn't about a new relationship at all. Even if he'd been honest in those kisses, in asking her out and cooking for her, there were things he deserved to hear before this went any further.

Forcing herself to meet his gaze, she gave him the words she'd held back for too long. "I'm sorry—"

Shane felt his face heating with embarrassment. "Stop." He pinched the bridge of his nose, unable to look at her. He didn't know why he'd said that. Maybe it was the conversation with Irene today, or the food. He should have grilled burgers.

"I'm not bucking for sympathy here," he said.

This was a prime example of why he kept everyone at arm's length. Inviting people into his world only made them uncomfortable when he slipped up and let down his guard. She didn't need to hear the gruesome details of those eighteen months behind bars.

Yet, now that Danica had been close enough to kiss, he wanted her closer still. If she had any sense, she'd get up and leave.

"Shane, I'm not trying to give you sympathy."

"Pity?"

"No, not that either."

He glanced up, surprised by the flash of raw misery in her soft green eyes. He'd seen that expression too often in his mirror. "Then what?"

She sat up a little straighter. "An apology," she said. "You should have heard it from my grandfather."

"Stop, please." His voice cracked. He couldn't do this. "You were a kid when that happened."

"We both were," she said.

He left the table and stalked back to the kitchen for something stronger than wine, then thought better of it. He wasn't going to disappoint his mother by facing every uncomfortable moment in life with a stiff drink in hand.

"I can call someone to pick me up," she offered.

That was the last thing he wanted. He turned to face her, watching for any sign that she'd lie to him. "Is that what you want?"

"Not really." Her gaze shifted to the stove top. "I was hoping for seconds."

He stared at her. She kept surprising him.

"You ate my lunch, remember?"

The shy tilt of her lips blasted through the tension locking up his muscles. "You offered it."

"True. And I'd do it again."

He walked back to the table, pulled out the chair next to hers and sat down. "Because?"

"You were hungry." She shrugged. "I lost my appetite when we had to leave the puppy with Evan."

He felt terrible that he didn't have a better solution on that front. Yet. "My prison food comment didn't ruin your appetite?" She'd let him kiss her a few times now, but he'd discovered some women were only interested in the perceived bad-boy factor.

"You are more than what happened to you, Shane."

No one had said anything so kind to him since his release. More, he could see she believed it. It wasn't even her first reference to his being a whole and worthy person. He desperately wanted her words, her view of him, to be true. "You're remarkable."

"Same goes," she said.

Hell, she meant that, too. "Think there's any chance we can salvage this date?"

"It sure can't get worse." She raised her glass. "To us."

He snagged his wineglass and echoed her toast.

They talked of more mundane things while she finished her first and second helpings. Though his two cases percolated in the back of his mind, she continued to surprise him with every shift in topic. He enjoyed her insights and observations and found himself completely enamored with her.

He started to clear the table, planning to leave the cleanup until morning, but she insisted on helping him pack away leftovers and wash dishes.

"You're thinking," she said, giving him a light elbow to the ribs.

"About you," he said.

"Liar." Her hands swirled through the soapy water

as she washed the pasta pot. "You had the judge and jury face on. Your mind is otherwise occupied."

He couldn't argue. "Do I want to know what the judge and jury face is?"

"Probably not." She rinsed the pot and handed it to him to dry. "Want to talk about it?"

"I think the victim in the assault case we picked up today is tied to Hayley," he said.

She immersed the skillet into the soapy water. "How so?"

"He dated her before she settled down with Bo." He put the pot away in the cabinet. "I'm wondering if the Groom Killer is one of Hayley's exes. Someone she dumped rather than someone upset about being dumped by Bo and determined to wreck the wedding business in Red Ridge."

"That clears Demi, but it casts a wider net," Danica said. "More than half the male population of Red Ridge has gone out with Hayley Patton or wanted to." She scoured the skillet. "When she and Bo got engaged, you could hear hearts breaking all over the county."

"Still, I think it's worth doing interviews," he said.

"You might not realize the enormity of the task." She rinsed the skillet and handed it over. "It's a much shorter list looking at the men who haven't gone out with her."

"I guess I'll start by speaking with her again." He was ready to table this and get their date back on track. "Tomorrow."

Danica snorted as she cleaned the sink and dried her hands. "Hayley doesn't think of her exes the way most women do."

"Meaning what?" he asked.

"She dates, serial-style. Until Bo, I didn't think she had any intention of settling down."

"You're saying men get attached to her, but not the other way around." He brought her hands to his lips, then reluctantly released her. "Thanks for helping with the dishes."

"Sure." Her teeth sank into her lower lip. "I could give you half a dozen names to start you off. Men she probably considers acquaintances only. Before she was engaged to Bo, men had things delivered all the time and they were sure to sign the cards so she'd know without a doubt that they were interested. Since his death, it's worse."

He played with her fingers. There was such strength in her compact hands. "How so?"

"It's as if every single man with a pulse wants to be who she leans on for comfort. Personally, I find the anonymous, clockwork deliveries unnerving. She generally finds it adorable."

He wanted to kiss that crease between her auburn eyebrows. "You don't think she's the killer, do you?"

"Be serious," Danica laughed. "Not only am I her alibi for at least one or two of the murders, she isn't capable of launching an attack that would chip her manicure."

"You don't like her much, do you?"

She blushed instantly and he felt the need to shelter that heart she wore so obviously on her sleeve. "I do, actually," she said. "She's great at her job." Danica sighed. "I'd come around to the idea that we were going to be related. She can be pleasant and thoughtful when she's in the right mood."

"Come on," Shane urged. "Spell it out for me."

"Fine." She folded her arms over her chest. "I've never put much stock in her pleasant or thoughtful moods. I've known her all my life. So have you." She nudged him aside and walked out of the kitchen. "Down deep, she's self-absorbed and considers that a personal strength. It's just who she is."

He did, but hearing it from Danica gave him the full picture. Even the season he'd been in prison, he'd heard about how Hayley had nearly destroyed the Red Ridge high school football team's bid for the state championship. She'd dated three different boys on the team, all top players, and they spent the week leading up to the game far more concerned about winning the girl rather than the title.

"Did she make Bo happy?" he asked, joining her at the sectional where she was doting on Stumps.

"Bo made her happy," she replied. Stumps wriggled around, giving her better access to his belly again. "Hayley was…" She spread out her hands as if smoothing a blanket while she searched for the right word. "*Calmer* is the best word. She was excited about the wedding, but there was a steadiness when she had Bo around."

Lots to consider, Shane thought. Later. Right now he had different priorities.

"You ready?" she asked, her gaze on his silly dog stealing all her attention.

"For what?"

She looked up, smiling at him as if he wasn't the sharpest knife in the drawer. "The names of the men I know she turned down around the time Bo proposed."

Shane went to his desk and grabbed the notebook. "Go."

It was a quarter to ten when she stopped rattling off names. With almost two pages of names of potential new suspects in Bo Gage's murder, Shane was almost sorry he'd asked. Almost. He could just imagine Brayden's face when Shane showed him all these possible routes to clearing Demi.

Chapter 11

Danica was exhausted by the time she finished. It felt like throwing a crowd of strangers under the bus. If any of the men on that list was the Groom Killer, Shane would track him down. The right way. And her family would finally have justice for Bo.

"I know it's late," Shane said, tossing the notebook aside. "If you'd rather do the movie another time, I understand."

She'd leaned back against the couch, her legs stretched out. Stumps had his head in her lap and she was stroking his ear. Going back to her condo didn't really appeal. Even with Oscar's company it was hard to face the night alone. "That depends on the movie you have in mind," she heard herself say.

"Horror, obviously," he said.

"Obviously?"

"So you'll let me protect you." He flopped to the floor next to her.

"Ah. You do know I can protect myself?" Maybe if she said it often enough, she'd start believing it again.

"Not from zombies or monsters that rise from murky lagoons," he said, his blue eyes lit with mischief. "Seriously, what sounds good?" He turned on the television and started scrolling through the options.

She chose a recent spy film, one of her favorite genres, and they moved to sit together on the couch, her thigh brushing his and Stumps at their feet. It was so comfortable and yet she was still a bit shell-shocked that she was here. She gave a start when he laced his fingers with hers, but she leaned in close when he shifted to curl his arm over her shoulders.

They were just past the halfway point of the movie when Stumps trotted to the back door. Shane had installed a dog door to the backyard for the times he was home alone, but Stumps didn't use it this time.

"He didn't get his walk after dinner," Shane whispered at Danica's ear. "He'll get over it."

A few minutes later, Stumps barked, racing back and forth between the door and Shane's feet.

"All right, bud. Settle down." Shane paused the movie and got up, crossing to the back door. He flipped the switch for the floodlights and swore. Stumps started barking again, but stayed inside at Shane's command.

"What's wrong?"

"Someone is out there," he said, keeping his voice low.

The icy shiver down her back pushed her to her feet. She was by his side before he could tell her to stay put. "Do you want me to call the station?" Where was her phone?

"No. It could be anything," Shane said. "There's a walking trail back there."

Right. She had to calm down. "And a fence to keep them on their side of your yard," she said. "Was the person in your yard?" She knew the answer without his confirmation. Stumps wouldn't have been that upset if the person hadn't been inside his territory.

Shane went to get the dog's lead and returned with his gun, as well. "Stumps and I will go out and search," he said. "Then I'm taking you home."

It wasn't how she'd hoped the evening would end, but she could hardly argue. "Should I call anyone while you're out there?" she offered again.

"No sense calling unless and until Stumps and I find something." All the ease had drained from his face and the familiar, cold detachment in his gaze was back.

Danica wrapped her arms around her middle to ward off the chill that came over.

Shane took a moment to clear the immediate area from one corner of the yard near the house to the other. He didn't want anyone sneaking up behind them. He wanted to catch whoever was out here on sheer principle for ruining his date.

Not that he hadn't come close to wrecking the evening all by himself. This was different.

Moving off the patio, he gave Stumps the command to search, wary of what might be waiting for them beyond the reach of the floodlights. He had the lead in one hand with the flashlight and the other hand on his gun. He knew every inch of his yard, had repaired the fence himself, making it safe for Stumps.

The corgi knew his boundaries, but Shane didn't trust neighboring cats or dogs, and local wildlife could be a problem, too, on occasion. If someone had jumped the fence and been close enough to the house for Stumps to notice, Shane wasn't going to take any chances.

When he'd hit the floodlights, he'd seen a shadow scramble back toward the walking trail. Hopefully whoever had been trespassing was smart enough to get away and not look back. That assumed trespassing or petty theft was the only goal.

Reaching the middle of the yard, Shane called a halt and Stumps stopped. Glancing over his shoulder, he confirmed what he'd suspected. Anyone back here would have a clear view of him and Danica on the couch, distracted by the movie. Right now, even with the floodlights in his face, he could see Danica framed by the window, her hands clutching her cell phone.

He put Stumps back on the search and followed the trail of footprints in the spring grass illuminated by the beam of the flashlight. Shane kept Stumps on that path and the dog dropped into a quiet alert right at the fence.

"Stay," Shane said. With the aid of the flashlight, he spotted the scrap of fabric Stumps had found caught in the fence. Shane took a picture with his phone and kept searching. It was probably time to call in an RRPD team, but he was hoping for more. Carefully, he peered over the fence, sweeping his flashlight across the dirt and tall grasses between his fence and the walking trail.

There, as if planted just for him, he found a clear

footprint. He took a picture and hopped over the fence. With gun in hand, he found two more clear prints. At least there'd been only one person here.

He climbed back into his yard knowing his evening had just taken a turn that might drive an insurmountable wedge between him and Danica. Considering the bad blood between their families, that was saying something.

Releasing Stumps, he praised his partner and let him romp around the yard for a minute before heading back to the house for the good treats. Danica was waiting, her lower lip rosy from where she'd chewed on it. He wanted to kiss her first, before she started arguing with him over what he'd found.

Knowing the drill, she let him give Stumps his reward and more praise. "What did he find?" she asked.

Reluctantly, Shane pulled up the pictures and handed her the phone. "Piece of T-shirt caught in the fence and a clear print from a shoe."

"Looks like a Converse shoe."

"I thought the same thing," Shane said. The sole pattern on those shoes remained distinct. "Give me a minute to change clothes."

"Why change?" she asked as she trailed him down the hallway.

If she followed him into his bedroom, he might just wait until morning to haul in his prime suspect. With more self-control than he thought he possessed, he closed the door in her face. She was waiting, clearly perturbed, when he opened the door dressed in his jeans and a work shirt, his badge clipped to his belt.

He rolled back his sleeves as he slipped past her to get his backup boots from the front closet. After prison, he'd known he would never be comfortable in a real uniform. As a P.I. attached to the RRPD K9 unit, he had a little leeway when it came to official attire. The plain gray work shirt and badge were as far as he could go without hyperventilating. The boots were practical since crime scenes and searches could take him anywhere in the county in any conditions. Right now, the boots were going to take him back to the old neighborhood—after he dropped Danica at home.

Danica pursed her lips, hands on her hips as her gaze swept over him. He wasn't too proud to admit he hoped she liked the view.

"You're going to make an arrest?"

Apparently, he failed to appeal. "Only cops can do that." She didn't need the reminder. "I'm not a cop. I'm just going to have a conversation."

"With?"

He shot her a look. She already knew. "Tyler Miller," he said anyway.

"Shane, you can't."

"Can and will. Grab your purse." He needed to get her out of the house and away from the happier, sexier thoughts his mind would rather entertain. "He was wearing those shoes when he was at your place earlier."

She blanched. "Nearly every kid in town wears those. You probably have a pair. Or you did once. Can't this wait until morning, at least? He'll be at the training center."

"No." If he looked at her again, he'd be tempted to give in. He clipped his holster into place, snapped his fingers for Stumps. "This is what I do. He trespassed on my property. He's been following you and he's involved in the thefts."

"You're blowing this out of proportion," she snapped. "Where's your proof?"

"I'm about to get it."

"Shane." She'd lowered her voice to a quiet plea.

"Stop defending him, Danica. The kid is hiding something."

"I'm coming with you," she stated.

He muttered an oath and then counted to ten, searching for the patience he'd developed in prison. "Whatever you think, I'm not planning to water board him."

"I'm coming with you."

"Fine." Not exactly a ringing endorsement of him as a person, but that would have to wait. Her riding along wasn't a horrible idea. Tyler trusted Danica and with any luck, the kid would open up if she was nearby.

She gave him the address and then didn't speak again on the drive across town. The silence wasn't a problem for him. He wasn't feeling chatty. In prison, where it was never quiet, he'd learned true silence was invaluable.

The closer they got to the house, the worse Shane felt. They passed his father's bar and wound along the dark streets, deep into the shabby neighborhoods he knew too well.

Maybe, when this was done, he should leave Red Ridge and make a real fresh start. He'd proven all he could prove here, anyway. If people still gossiped about his time as an inmate after nearly a decade, sticking around wasn't going to change anything.

Danica reached over and laid a hand on his arm when he parked in front of the house. "He's a good kid, Shane."

"He's hiding something." In the dark, under the wavering gloom of the weak streetlight on the corner, the house didn't look too bad. Shane figured it probably looked worse in the daytime when sunlight highlighted all the flaws and neglect.

She gave a nearly imperceptible nod of agreement. "Probably. Regardless, you can't mention that he was at my place. Please."

He started to snap at her and stopped. If someone had given him the benefit of the doubt, or double-checked the sergeant's work, he might have graduated with his class and enjoyed a completely different life. "Why not?"

"He often sneaks out and walks around town."

"To spy on you?" Shane asked.

"No," she replied indignantly. "He's biding his time until he's in control of his future. You remember how it was."

Yes, Shane remembered the feeling. And he remembered having his plans derailed by her grandfather's blind determination to close a murder case. "You said the parents aren't abusive?"

The curtain rippled at the front window. Someone had noticed their arrival.

"That doesn't mean they care," she said. "Tread lightly. You know how feeling cornered brings out the worst in people and dogs."

Was she kidding? He'd been the cornered kid, not much older than Tyler. During his time as an inmate, he'd seen it happen time and again. If a man couldn't fight, he was considered fair game or wasted space.

"Let's go." Better to get this over with before it grew any later. With Stumps trotting between them, he and Danica approached the house.

The front door opened before he could press the doorbell. Tyler stood there, his eyes full of worry. "What are you doing here?"

Shane noted the red T-shirt and flip-flops the kid wore now, rather than the darker shirt and Converse shoes he'd had on when he was at Danica's condo and in his backyard. "I need a word with you," he said.

Tyler looked to Danica. "I'll talk to you at the center tomorrow," he said in a hoarse whisper. "Please, not here."

"No, not here and not tomorrow. Right now and at the station," Shane clarified. "This has gone on long enough. You'll need a parent to join us."

"What the hell is the problem?" a deep voice boomed from somewhere in the house.

Tyler swore. "Tomorrow," he said, trying to close the door.

Shane, noticing Stumps had dropped into a quiet alert stance, shoved his boot into the dwindling space. "Now."

A light flared overhead and exposed the cracked and peeling linoleum of the entry floor, along with what might have been white-painted walls hazed yellow from perpetual smokers. The assessment was confirmed when the owner of the voice stalked up behind the kid, exhaling a plume of smoke. "What do you want with my kid?"

Tyler's dad was taller than Shane with the bulk of a man who preferred beer and burgers to fresh air and exercise. "Sir," Shane began. "I'm working a case for the Red Ridge Police Department and I need to speak with Tyler for a few minutes."

The man's beefy hand covered Tyler's narrow shoulder with a hard grip. "What the hell did you do now?"

"Nothing, Dad."

"You hurt this girl?"

"What?" Tyler said as Danica gave a resounding "No."

"Tyler works with me at the training center," she began, but Mr. Miller wasn't in the mood to listen.

"You're the Miss Good Samaritan, huh? Thinking you can give my boy something I can't?"

Shane bristled at the long look Mr. Miller aimed at Danica. On instinct, Shane moved to shield her. "I have a few questions for Tyler, pertaining to an official case."

A woman in torn-up jeans and a dingy sweater pulled tight across her body shuffled into view, a cigarette hanging out of her mouth. Her hair was pulled back into a severe ponytail and the circles under her eyes were likely beyond any help.

"He's a minor." Her voice, rough as sandpaper, flowed out of her along with a trail of smoke. "You can't take him anywhere without us."

"I'm not arresting him," Shane said.

"Damn straight," she interrupted.

"I believe Tyler may have information essential to a case," Shane finished as if she hadn't spoken.

"Talk to him here." She smacked her husband. "Out of the way so they can come in."

Shane had no intention of allowing his dog or Danica into this house. He had an irrational urge to grab Tyler and run. Suppressing the ridiculous reaction, he infused his voice with all the authority he possessed and insisted the three of them come to the station. "If I need to, I can have an officer escort you," he finished.

For a moment, he thought Mr. Miller would protest again, but Mrs. Miller intervened, her eyes angry slits through the haze of smoke. "We'll be right behind you."

Tyler was forcibly jerked back and the door slammed in their faces.

Shane waited until he saw a side door open and the light under the carport come on as Tyler and his parents piled into a pickup that had seen better days.

"You weren't kidding," he said when they were on their way, the Miller family behind them.

"They either don't know or don't care what a good kid they have," she said sadly.

"They have a kid who was trespassing and, according to you, sneaks out regularly."

"Every kid in town sneaks out or tries to at his age."

She wasn't wrong. He would've done that and worse if his mother hadn't been so vigilant and dedicated to his growing up right.

"Can you think of any reason Tyler would have been in my yard?"

Her jaw set, she gazed out the window.

"Danica, that kid needs your help here. If there's a reason, tell me so I can adjust."

"A little late to consult me." She gave a gusty sigh. "I honestly don't know what is going on with him. He wouldn't have come to my place—or yours—if there wasn't something on his mind."

"Will he talk in front of his parents?"

She shook her head. "I doubt it. They're likely to

believe the worst, however you handle it. We should have talked to him at home."

"Not a chance," Shane said emphatically. "This is already the worst first date on record. I wasn't going to compound it by letting you walk into potential danger."

The sound she made couldn't be classified as laughter. "Why did you ask me out?"

He checked his rearview mirror and then shot her a wicked grin as he waited for the traffic light to change. "I figured my mom's red sauce was the best chance you'd give me another kiss."

"You stole the first one," she said. "And a few after."

"Did I?" He saw the smile tugging at her lips. "Maybe you should press charges." He pulled forward as the light turned green, his mind getting back to the issue at hand. "Later."

"We'll see."

He hoped that didn't mean any future kisses were dependent on how this conversation with Tyler went. Tempted to ask, he thought better of it. Just having her here was enough of a distraction. If he started watching her reactions more than the kid's, the interview was doomed from the start.

Steeling himself for the task ahead, he shoved the personal stuff aside and escorted the unhappy kid and unhappier parents through the front doors and into a conference room.

Danica didn't have much to go on other than the stories shared by the police officers in her family, but she could tell this wasn't going to be a successful interrogation. She appreciated Shane's calm approach, though Tyler remained sullen and uncooperative. She was also aware Shane had no obligation to honor her request about keeping seeing Tyler at her condo to himself.

No matter how informal Shane kept it, no matter how he focused questions on the dogs, Tyler refused to provide helpful answers.

Shane asked for his whereabouts on the nights Nico and the puppy were stolen and Mrs. Miller answered for him. Tyler just deferred to her with a shrug. Mr. Miller grew agitated with his son, claiming Tyler should answer so they could all go back home.

Danica left the room at one point to get everyone water from the vending machine, including Stumps. It was the only time Tyler became the least bit animated, as she let him care for the dog. The compassionate gesture only served to confirm her assessment that whatever was going on with him, it couldn't possibly have resulted in harm to the dogs or training center.

Shane tried another tack, barely skirting Tyler's tendency to walk around town at night, and still the boy wouldn't crack.

She desperately wanted to give Shane a signal to drop it, but she didn't dare. He was the official and she was only here because…well, she wasn't quite sure why he'd let her come along. Sure, the chief had told him to work with her, but she wasn't helping with the case, other than to identify Nico and the puppy.

Tonight would have been a far better first date if they'd attempted a rescue, she thought.

She was having zero success as a soothing presence on anyone in the room, except Stumps, who sat beside her and let her rub his ears. Hard to be soothing when she was still overwhelmed by Shane's admission that he wanted to kiss her again. Her mind drifted, seeing the hard-knock similarities between Shane and Tyler and wishing things could be simpler. What she wouldn't give to be two normal people attracted to each other and free to pursue it rather than a Gage and a Colton on opposite sides of yet another legal matter.

Her brother dead, his sister accused. Two dogs missing, one kid choosing the wrong time to get moody. It was all such a tangled mess. Even if Shane had somehow managed to see beyond her last name, would it last or would the Groom Killer case or another dog theft drive them apart?

Could she really trust him to do the right thing?

Yes. The answer whispered across her senses, releasing the knots of tension in her neck, carrying her out of this awkward interview to the moment they'd stood together in the Larson offices. He might have a different approach or even a different agenda, but every step was thoughtful, planned and right, she realized.

As the clock on the wall ticked past midnight, Shane hadn't made any progress. Tyler slumped in his chair, his feet stretched out under the table and his arms folded defensively over his skinny chest.

Mrs. Miller leaned across the table toward Danica. "Do you think my boy attacked you?" she demanded, clearly hitting her limit. "Is that what this is about?"

"Absolutely not," Danica replied before Shane could intervene. "I trust Tyler completely."

Shane stifled a curse. She wasn't *helping*.

"You can't hold him here." Mrs. Miller glared at Shane. "I watch *Law and Order*. I know he has rights."

This wasn't a damn television show, Shane thought.

This was life and death and hard crime in the real world. Shane was tempted to make something up just to get the kid away from his useless parents. If Tyler had had any interaction with the Larson twins or their operation, no matter how remotely, he was in significant danger.

"He's not being charged with any crime, Mrs. Miller," Danica interjected with far more patience than the woman deserved. "Tyler might not even realize what he knows."

"He's not saying another word without legal counsel," Mr. Miller stated.

Shane had expected them to use that line earlier. He understood the disadvantages kids like Tyler dealt with. Shane's mother had been solid, but his dad was pretty much king of the rough side of town, drinking away any profit he managed to turn at the Pour House.

Shane looked at Mr. Miller. The man reeked of alcohol. Given a few minutes alone, he was sure he could find a way to connect with this kid, but that wasn't going to happen. Too bad he hadn't listened to Danica earlier.

"Last chance, Tyler. Tell us what happened the night Nico was stolen."

The kid's sullen gaze remained on some point on the wall between Shane and Danica.

"Tyler, whatever happened, you can trust us to help." It wasn't the first time she'd made such a claim.

"I've had enough of this circus," Mr. Miller said. He hauled Tyler up by his arm.

Mrs. Miller slapped the table as she stood, as well. "We're leaving."

Shane figured they'd had enough time without nicotine. There was nothing he could do. "We appreciate your time," he lied with a smile.

He left Stumps with Danica as he walked them out of the station. When he turned back, she was right behind him with his dog.

She looked as exhausted as he felt. "That went well," she said.

"You were right," he admitted as they loaded into his SUV for the short drive to her condo.

"We both were," she said.

Uncertain what she could possibly mean by that, he let the comment go. His thoughts were reeling with what if's and what now's. Still convinced Tyler was into something, he'd only managed to alienate Danica and the kid. He couldn't remember the last time he'd let his temper ride roughshod over common sense on a case.

He parked in front of her condo and cut the engine. "We'll walk you up. There's something I need to say."

"Whatever." She pushed open her door. "I'm too tired to argue."

"Good. You can listen."

He ignored the hard look in her eyes as they rode the elevator to her floor. She unlocked the door and he counted himself lucky she didn't slam it in his face.

The menacing growl from somewhere overhead had him doing a double take. He followed the sound to the top of the kitchen cabinet, where her cat perched, looking as if he'd leap down and claw out Shane's eyes at any moment. Shane picked up Stumps to protect him.

"Oscar, that's enough," she said.

"Can you crate him or something?"

She gave him a look as lethal as the cat's glare. "He's startled and he hasn't met Stumps."

She made the introductions as if the cat were a child. "This is Shane's partner, Stumps. He won't hurt you. You'd probably like him if you came down and said hello."

The cat rumbled.

"That's enough," Danica warned in a perfect mom-voice.

Stumps whined, but not in fear. It was the sound he made when he was eager to try something new. His rump wriggled as he shifted in Shane's hold, wanting a better view as the cat moved across the cabinet tops.

Danica walked the length of the galley kitchen and opened the door on the far end. Shane caught a glimpse of shelving before she bent over, distracting him with the view of her trim hips.

Yanking his thoughts away from that dangerous canyon edge, he eyed the cat.

"We'll go," he decided. "I'm sure we'll both be more rational in the morning."

She turned around, holding a water bowl and a dog biscuit for Stumps. "You only want a reprieve so you have time to come up with a better explanation."

"Danica, I swear—" He stopped yet another attempt to convince her Tyler was in over his head when the huge cat dropped to the counter with a predatory silence and padded closer.

Stumps wriggled, ears forward, nose twitching. Shane stared into a golden feline gaze that unnerved him. Stumps seemed oblivious to the cat's do-not-disturb warnings, eager to make a friend.

"He won't eat Stumps?"

Her green eyes blazed. Great, he'd offended her again. Not the way to win her to his side of the Tyler issue. He walked into the living room and set Stumps down gently. "Sit."

The dog obeyed, and though he patiently awaited the next command, Shane knew Stumps wanted to slobber all over the cat until they were best buddies. The cat watched from the countertop. He released Stumps to relax, explore and enjoy the treat Danica had for him.

Stumps lapped up water and munched the dog treat while Danica crooned to her cat that Stumps was no threat. As she spoke and Stumps behaved himself, Oscar grew more receptive to the intrusion.

"You bring dogs here often?"

She glanced at him and then chuckled. He realized it sounded like a cheesy pickup line paraphrased. It felt good to laugh along with her after the night they'd had.

"Beer?" she offered. "It's the middle of the night, after all."

"Sure."

She brought out two longneck amber bottles from a local microbrewery. It was his favorite variety simply because the Pour House only stocked the cheapest beer possible.

She curled herself into one end of the couch again, leaving the animals to work things out. He supposed if she trusted her cat, he would, too. He sank into one of the facing chairs, wondering if she'd ever give him another chance. "Stumps alerted when he saw Tyler."

"I saw it. Hard to know what it means." She pushed at her hair. "You do realize you won't get anything out of Tyler now." She turned the beer bottle in little circles over her knee.

"Why won't he talk?" His fingers wanted to trace that same pattern, right there, and erase the chill left behind. With a mental shake, he pulled his focus back to the reason she'd let him in here. Tipping back his beer, he waited for her to connect the dots.

"Tyler has been working with me long enough to know the men and women with K9 partners are steady and calm. He won't fall for your blustering, impatient routine."

His impatience wasn't a routine. His gut instinct was insisting this wasn't over. Not just because a trained attack dog was currently under the dubious control of the Larson twins. Someone had drugged Danica, left her outside and later used more violence against a professional security guard. The break in the Groom Killer case might be right in front of them along with the potential to link some serious crime to Noel and Evan Larson. If the culprit believed Danica remembered something, she would be in the crosshairs.

"You can't sit there and tell me you believe this was coincidence. Two thefts in two nights screams inside job. I've cleared everyone else at the training center."

"Tyler didn't steal those dogs."

"I'm certain he helped the man who did."

She held up a hand. "We've been down this rabbit hole enough already. You have a theory. I think it's bogus."

He took a deep breath and exhaled slowly, striving for that calm she was so convinced he had in spades. When it came to keeping her safe, he was starting to realize he didn't have nearly enough. "Then give me another theory to work with," he said.

Her lips pressed together, turning them from that soft peach color to almost white. "Maybe Tyler saw something when he was out walking. Maybe he heard something around town."

When he snorted, Danica rolled her eyes and stood. Crossing the room, she ignored him in favor of the view through the sliding glass doors.

"Why are you so willing to defend him? You've said it yourself that something is going on with him."

"You saw his parents," she said without turning. "It could be anything."

Her voice was so low, he wouldn't have heard her if he hadn't come to stand behind her. He caught a whiff of the exotic ginger and sweet honey scents in her golden-red hair. Outside, the nearby mountains loomed, deeper shadows in the darkness, like the case that was leading them in circles. Instead, Shane focused on the faint reflection in the glass, which underscored his height advantage. That was the only advantage he had on Danica. She had the benefit of solid family and professional support. People generally liked her and steered clear of him.

Maybe it was the beer, or the late hour, but he gave in to the urge to open up. "I don't want to talk about Tyler anymore." If he leaned in, he could kiss her hair. Or move it off her neck and discover what her skin tasted like under the heavy veil.

She spun around. "You took a big risk tonight, doing everything but calling him a thief." She thumped his chest lightly with a fist. "You of all people in this town should know that what is 'obvious'—" she actually used air quotes on the word "—might not be true."

He caught her smaller hands in his and pinned them to her hips. Her eyes widened. Then he claimed her mouth, plundering and reveling in the textures of lips, tongue and teeth. He brought her hands up to circle his waist, moaning as her palms swept up his back, clutching at his shirt.

That felt too good. He pulled her close as she kissed him back. Nothing gentle or careful or curious here. Need crackled through his system and he set out to learn what made her sigh with delight and pleasure. The low sound she made in her throat had him ready to rip the clothes from her body and take her right here against the cold glass door.

So much for the myth that K9 officers were steady and calm.

He broke the kiss, quaking with his reaction to her. Unhappy with the sense of wonder and longing coursing through his veins. He brushed his lips over her brow, her cheeks, her nose, fearing he was already addicted. No. If he left now, walked away, they might both come to their senses.

Any second now, he would release her hands, take his dog and leave. Then she looked up at him through her lashes and everything changed. The awkward pressure deep inside his chest shifted and clicked into place, as if he hadn't been looking at life from the right angle before.

She must have sensed it, too, because she moved in, pressing that slender body flush to his. He boosted her up and she wrapped her legs around his hips. Her head fell back on a wild laugh that he swallowed with another searing kiss. His mind blanked of everything but her.

Her teeth nipped his ear and goose bumps raced down that side of his body. "I have condoms in the bedroom," she said between fluttering kisses along the sensitive skin of his jaw.

"Good." The single syllable was all he could manage with his arms full and his body aching. He found her bedroom and moved straight to the bed. He laid her back and stretched out over her. Together they were a tangle of limbs, hot touches and blazing kisses as clothing scattered. Her skin, warm and smooth over the supple, subtle curves, lit a fire in his blood.

"You're glorious," he whispered along the sweet column of her throat, down across her breasts.

She murmured something that might have been doubt and he set out to prove his sincerity. He drew one pebbled nipple into his mouth and she arched into him. For such a small woman, there was so much to explore. When she was gasping his name on a shattering climax, he applied the condom and sank deep into her welcoming heat. She overwhelmed him and sensation built with every thrust and sigh until she crested again and at last he gave in to his release.

After disposing of the condom, he returned to the bed and pulled her into his arms. She didn't say a word as she snuggled in. He didn't want to think or analyze his actions, not now. He just wanted to feel, to enjoy her as the passionate rush faded into an easy comfort.

Chapter 12

Danica heard Stumps's nails on the hardwood floor as he trotted with Shane to the front door. Though he surely thought he was moving almost silently, she heard the door open and close. Heart heavy, she waited a few minutes before getting up and locking the door behind them.

What had she done? Well, the sex was amazing, but she'd really crossed a line.

She was a fool. Worse, she was behaving like an idiot on par with her little brother. Shane would always be out of her reach. That he'd walked out without a word only proved the point. She could practically hear Grandpa Gage rolling over in his grave. Shane couldn't be her Mr. Right.

She climbed back into bed and curled into the pillow, inhaling the masculine scent he left behind. Her heart, apparently cut from the same cloth as Vincent's, had gotten caught up in some wistful fantasy that love could heal all wounds.

Love wouldn't give Shane back the time stolen by a legal system that failed him. Love wouldn't bring back the mother who'd died believing he was a killer. Love couldn't change that whenever he looked at her, he surely saw the root of all that pain and injustice.

They were consenting adults who'd been swept up by stunning passion. They'd shared an amazing, memorable moment she would treasure for the rest of her life. No need to make it anything more significant than that.

She pressed her lips together, recalling his mouth on her skin. Tears for what would never be soaked into the pillow beneath her cheek.

Tomorrow would be a new day. A fresh start with her eyes wide open where Shane was concerned. They had a case to solve whether he wanted her help or not. She might not be able to identify her attacker, but if Tyler did know anything, she was the only one he would talk to.

Shane hated sneaking out of Danica's bed without a word, but his mind wouldn't settle. Tossing and turning would only lead to both of them being grumpy and ineffective come morning. He was a block away from her condo when he realized he could have left her a note.

Idiot.

Not that a note would have done much. How could he explain the overwhelming sense of being trapped while he'd held her in his arms? No, he didn't have a key to her condo, but he hadn't been a prisoner there, either.

Shane swore, frustrated with himself. His self-control had turned to dust at the taste of her lips and the feel of her sweet, strong hands on his skin. Coltons and Gages were worse than oil and water. The times when they didn't repel each other, they corroded and corrupted everything from the inside out.

Demi and Bo had been engaged, had broken up, and now Bo was dead and Demi the prime suspect. Valeria and Vincent were the latest in a line of doomed relationships. Everyone in town knew it, even if they refused to accept the facts yet.

The idea of finding any lasting satisfaction or peace with Danica was absurd. Not only was he a Colton from the wrong side of the tracks, he'd been wrongfully imprisoned by her beloved grandfather.

"Doomed," he muttered to Stumps as made his way out to the cemetery.

It wasn't fair of him to waste Danica's time. Together, they didn't stand a chance. Too much bad blood, too many people ready to judge them and toss that bad blood back in their faces. People told him to move on, as if they couldn't see him doing just that. In the past nine years, he'd finished his education, trained as a P.I. and K9 officer, and did all in his power to keep the police around here honest.

He'd been advised that creating a new life could be easier if he left Red Ridge. Maybe it was time to give that more serious thought.

He turned the corner and leaned into the upward slope. At his side, Stumps adjusted his pace to match

Shane's. "You and me," Shane said to the dog. "We work."

At one point, Shane hadn't been sure he could manage the commitment even of a dog. Reclaiming his freedom had meant no ties, no boundaries. After being locked up for eighteen months, he'd wanted to be able to roam without sparing a thought for anyone or anything but himself.

Then the loneliness had set in and Brayden had shown him that working with a K9 had multiple benefits—companionship being first and foremost. Stumps was always game for a walk, no matter the hour. Having the dog's company whenever he was overwhelmed by the invisible walls closing him in gave him solace no person could provide.

In prison, Shane had learned to protect himself—body and mind. He'd learned emotions of every variety got men killed in the zoo that was life behind bars. Get too happy and a guard or inmate would find a way to steal the joy. Wallowing in depression made a man vulnerable to the smallest attack. Anger and pride clouded sound judgment and made a man stupid, but honesty... well, there was no place for honesty in a prison.

It was one thing to know the truth and another to talk about it.

Which led him right back to Danica. He wanted her—that was true. Also true was how much he didn't want to feel anything for her. Their professional situation was a requirement. The rest of his feelings for her should be irrelevant.

"I've messed up, Stumps." He stopped at his mother's grave. "I let her get under my skin and I can't lie to myself about it anymore."

He sank down beside his mother's headstone. Rusty had done that much at least for his third ex-wife. The shred of decency in his father had surprised Shane. Upon his release from prison, Shane had expected Rusty to ask for reimbursement for the service and burial. Instead, he'd poured Shane a beer and raised his own glass in a silent toast to his mother. That was the last time he'd crossed the Pour House threshold.

Although this corner of South Dakota was full of nocturnal wildlife, the Red Ridge cemetery remained in a perpetual hush. The night stretched out, wide open and full of possibilities. Stumps stretched out against his hip, making his head available for Shane's hand.

Shane indulged the dog and let his mind wander over the past and the present. Not the future. It had taken only a year and a half behind bars to cure Shane of that kind of dreaming.

Maybe Danica had a point and he was assuming the worst about Tyler. "She definitely had a point," he said to the dog. "Otherwise I would have kept my cool."

It irritated him to admit it even to Stumps.

"He's hiding something and if it is related to the cases I'm working, he should understand there will be consequences."

When Danica's grandfather had hauled Shane in for questioning, he was eighteen, a legal adult, and his mother couldn't intervene as Tyler's parents had done. He didn't think it would have made a difference on the outcome, but it would have been nice to see someone going to bat for him. The list of things Shane couldn't find a way to forgive was long, but the one that burned hottest was that Danica's grandfather had convinced Shane's mother he was a killer.

That she could think him capable of such a crime had shattered the last of Shane's faith in the world at large and Red Ridge in particular.

"I hope you know how things turned out, Mom. I miss you."

The sun was warming the eastern horizon when Shane and Stumps went home for a few hours of sleep.

Danica had no intention of skirting her responsibilities at the training center, but losing Nico and then the puppy dumped more guilt on her than she could manage gracefully. When the morning slipped away with no sign of Tyler, her guilt multiplied. She'd been on the verge of losing her temper time and again this morning. Despite the cloudy weather, she'd taken herself on a walk into town to clear her head and regain her composure.

If she happened to walk by the shiny glass office building the Larson brothers owned, that could be simple coincidence.

Danica told herself the ache in her heart was all about the dogs and had nothing to do with a certain P.I. who was conspicuously quiet and absent today. Both dogs had so much potential and she didn't want to see it wasted. She couldn't stop thinking about how to get them back.

Stealing dogs—or anything else—from the Larson twins was tantamount to a suicide mission. Everyone in town suspected them of illegal activities, yet RRPD couldn't get any charges to stick. In Danica's mind, that meant it was time to fight fire with fire. If someone, namely Shane Colton, would give her a better option, she'd happily take it.

It the meantime, she'd clear her head and do a little recon simultaneously. The Larson brothers had four dogs now. That didn't mean they knew how to deal with them. And Evan was far less confident, especially around Nico, than his brother Noel. It was a recipe for a disaster.

All morning she'd considered reaching out to Evan, by phone or email, warning him of what Nico was capable of. She'd mentally drafted letters and quickly tossed them out the proverbial window. Anything anonymous would be ignored and anything she signed left her wide open to any number of retaliations. Noel and Evan were too bullheaded to heed a warning anyway.

So she walked the area where the puppy had recognized Tyler yesterday. It wasn't quite lunchtime and she had started to feel a bit like a shark as she circled the block repeatedly. Any minute, she was sure someone was going to call her out for loitering. Hopefully she'd spy something worthwhile before that happened.

At last, she heard the yips of a young puppy and the grumbling voice of whoever held the other end of the lead. Danica started walking toward the sounds, keeping a tight lid on the well of deep emotions throbbing in her veins. She saw Evan with both dogs today. Nico was alert and heeling well, though Evan kept leaning away from him. His reluctance toward Nico wasn't grossly obvious today because he was so distracted by the puppy's refusal to obey his commands.

Whatever they were trying to do with the little Malinois wasn't working. She considered it a small improvement that he wasn't on a retractable leash today. For a rambunctious puppy a retractable leash posed more problems than it solved. Then Evan stopped and yanked the leash hard, tightening a choke collar on the puppy.

Danica winced at the resulting pained yip and whine.

"Get back here, runt," Evan said in a menacing voice that left the puppy cowering.

"Hey, Evan," she called out. Striding across the street, she prayed her bravado held up. "Cute puppy."

He glared at her. "What do you want?"

Danica was tempted to answer honestly. "Nothing." She stuffed her hands into her pockets where she had always had a treat stashed. The puppy remembered. He sat and peered up at her expectantly.

"About damn time," Evan said.

"Out on an obedience run?" she asked.

"Apparently, I'm chief dog walker now," he muttered. "Noel calls it bonding." The angry gaze he directed at the puppy held far less confidence as he glanced at Nico. "Only one of them knows how to behave."

She wondered if Evan had any idea how much easier she could make his life. "Puppies have so much energy."

"And tiny bladders," Evan groused. "Go do business," he snapped at the puppy.

"True." Although it wasn't the command the puppy had been taught, he'd caught on fast. Survival instincts were strong. For a moment, she imagined the thrill of victory if she just scooped up the little guy and ran off. The reality that she'd probably be shot by Evan or, worse, or attacked by Nico before she made it to the end of the block burst the happy-thought bubble.

"You know we teach obedience classes, right?"

"Get over it, Gage. These aren't your dogs. We've proven it."

She rocked back on her heels. "Yeah, sorry about that. It's tough when so many dogs look alike," she said with more calm than she thought possible. "Even an expert can make a mistake under duress."

The puppy had finished "doing business" and was snuffling around every blade of grass. "Does Nico— I mean, the dog that reminds me of Nico—know the purpose of this outing?"

Again, at the sound of his name, his gaze slid to Danica.

"He's fine. Leave us alone."

"Attack dogs smell fear," she said conversationally. "Is there a reason this guy makes you nervous?"

"Maybe I'm just a cat person at heart," Evan snapped. "Get out of here."

"Sure. I was just passing by."

"Right." Evan stepped forward. "Probably best if you don't pass this way again anytime soon." Nico came to his feet, his ears perked and his gaze intent on her, the object of Evan's ire.

This was the real threat and one she anticipated. "You need to calm down," she said. "That dog is well-trained even if you aren't."

"You don't know anything about *this* dog, because it is not yours!"

Nico growled and the puppy, now on alert, was watching from the strip of grass with clearly confused loyalties. Damn it. She couldn't risk a dog fight or an attack.

She held her ground and raised her hands, a sign

Nico should recognize as surrender. "Hold," she said under her breath in Dutch. It wasn't a command or motion that would guarantee her safety. If Evan gave him the command, nothing would stop Nico from attacking her. If she let that happen, Nico would likely be put down as dangerous and uncontrollable. No matter what Evan said, no one would believe it if he claimed he'd let Nico loose as self-defense against Danica.

Look at that—there were advantages to being short, after all. Of course, Shane's conviction proved people didn't always trust fact as much as presentation and circumstance.

"I'm going," Danica said. "If you want to take that obedience class, call the center and ask for Hayley."

"You know what?" Evan grabbed her wrist with the hand holding the puppy's leash. "I think we should go upstairs and wait for the cops. This is the third day in a row you've hassled me and my dogs."

Her mind blanked. She'd trained for years to be able to defend herself. If Nico wasn't here, she would hand Evan his ass on a platter. She couldn't let him take her off this street.

"No one hassled you yesterday," she protested. She wanted to shout for help but that would only compound the risk with Nico. "We didn't come near you. Let me go."

"Not a chance." Evan's grip tightened and he started dragging her back toward the office.

"This is the wrong move, Evan."

"Threats now, Danica? I'd like to see you—"

He broke off, his face blanching at something behind her. He released her so fast, she tripped backward.

A familiar hand at her back steadied her. Shane. At

his heel, Stumps was in working mode, ears perked and stance forward. By the hard line of Shane's jaw and the furrowed eyebrows over his sunglasses, she could see he'd already decided she wasn't here by accident. Caught, she could only hold her ground and hope for the best.

"Hi."

Shane ignored Danica's greeting. Inside he was fuming that she'd taken such a risk confronting Evan while he was out with both dogs. She didn't know it, but she'd managed to interrupt his own search for the exchange between the thief and the Larson brothers.

"Evan, were you harassing Miss Gage?"

"The opposite, in case you're out here in the interest of justice," Evan snapped. "She's been harassing me."

He spared her a glance as he moved a half step in front of her. "She's hardly a threat to you. Especially when you're protected by your dogs."

Evan sneered. "Of anyone, I'd think you'd be willing to take my word on this. You know how the Gages like to spin fact from fiction."

Shane felt the old anger at Sergeant Gage flame through him. This time less of it spilled over to Danica and it sputtered out almost as quickly. He'd figure out what that meant later.

"You need to put your dog at ease, Evan." He kept his voice friendly, but businesslike. "We don't want any mishaps."

He turned to Danica. "I'm glad I bumped into you. I could use your help if you're free for a bit."

"Of course," she replied, seizing the lifeline he'd thrown.

He put himself and Stumps between Evan and Danica as they walked down the block.

"Stay away from us," Evan shouted after them.

Shane didn't say a word and thankfully Danica kept quiet, as well.

He'd slept for all of three hours before taking the list of men Danica had given him into the police station. After he had a brief conversation with Finn, the names had been split into manageable groups and assigned to various officers to clear for the recent attacks and murders.

Shane had worked on his part of the list for a time before he turned his attention back to the dog thefts. He wanted to clear Demi's name and bring her home, but he found himself equally motivated to protect Danica and get those dogs back under her care. All of the vets on the list she'd given him were checking out as legit. He'd been working on a possible connection point when he stumbled on her and Evan. Her stunt might have jeopardized any small forward progress he was making.

The disappointment flattened him. He simultaneously wanted to take her in his arms and kiss her until he believed she was okay and shake her until her teeth rattled. "What were you thinking?"

"I was going to give him a couple of tips. For the dogs."

Shane choked. "Of course you were. I didn't want you on this case," he said through clenched teeth. They turned a corner and the police station came into view. On the rise beyond the station, he could see the roofline of the training center.

"I know," she replied, squeezing his hand.

He didn't recall lacing his fingers with hers. Rather than pull away, he gave her a squeeze back. "What were you thinking?" He paused to collect himself. The fact was he'd been terrified when he came on that scene. "I trusted you."

"Oh, you did not," she shot back. "You don't trust anyone in my family."

He sucked in a breath. For the first time, he actually wanted to deny it. "I trusted you not to jeopardize the case," he said instead.

"Oh."

With her gorgeous hair pulled up, the sun fighting through the clouds lit the gold mixed in with all that red in her sleek ponytail. It gave him an excellent view of her profile and the little tick in her jaw.

He was feeling a similar muscle twitching in his jaw, too. "Were you trying to steal the dogs back?"

"Rescue," she corrected him firmly, making him laugh despite himself. "And not really. I knew that would backfire."

"At last logic prevails," he deadpanned.

"What were you doing out there?"

"Stumps and I went over to see if we could find any sign of the place where the thief handed the dogs over."

She brightened, her smile hopeful as she turned her face up to him. "That's a smart idea."

"It might have been, but now I'll need to stay away."

Her smile evaporated and her gaze fell to the sidewalk. "I'm sorry. What now?"

"I'm not sure," he admitted. "The dogs didn't levitate over to the Larson office."

"And the new microchip indicates they had some vet intervention. Any luck on that?"

He shook his head and her shoulders slumped. The pose made her look like a sorrowful elf. Damn it. He would not let her down. "I don't suppose you thought to ask Evan about the acquisition or vet care."

"No." Her ponytail rippled as she shook her head. "Turned out I was more interested in helping him manage the dogs so he doesn't command Nico to kill anyone by accident."

"He doesn't like the dogs, does he?"

A grin toyed with those tempting lips. "Looked mutual to me."

"You're the expert," he said, smothering a laugh. "No wonder I never liked him."

"What now?" she asked as they stopped in front of the police station. She crouched down to give Stumps some love.

"I guess we both go back to work. And stay there," he added, in case she misunderstood him. "Despite the microchips, we know the Larson twins have the stolen dogs. That means there is a connection between them and the thief. Finding the thief is still our best option."

"Is there anything I can do to help?"

"Only if you can find the thief's contact at the training center." He halted her immediate protest with a shake of his head. "Stop fighting the truth. We both know someone helped the thief get in."

She pursed her lips. "I'll go back to work and I won't let anyone know you suspect them *all*."

He was grateful his sunglasses hid his reaction to that comment. "The goal of investigating is to make sure we pinpoint the right suspect. Do I need to walk you to the door?"

She stared at him a long moment, hands planted

on those slender hips. "Did you know I wanted to be a cop?"

"No." He wondered why she thought it was relevant. "Was it a height issue?" he asked, baiting her. Baiting himself, really. He kept wanting to pluck her up and kiss her.

"It was a Colton issue." She drilled a finger into his chest. "Specifically you. I didn't want lives riding on my decisions, good or bad."

He waited, sensing she wasn't done, and noticed that she pulled back. There was more to it.

"People make mistakes," she said, her voice rough. "I know you know that." She stopped again and gathered herself. "I decided to train dogs so I can help people make fewer mistakes."

Since working with Stumps, he'd wondered if an evidence dog might have helped prove him innocent long before the district attorney filed the charges against him. "I'm out here every day to make sure the cops get it right."

"I know," she said. "And I commend you for it." She turned on her heel and walked away.

He stared after her, stunned. Why did she continue treating him like a human being? She hadn't even railed at him for slipping out without a word last night.

The petite spitfire was making him rethink everything he'd taken for granted since his return to Red Ridge. In the back of his overtired brain, he thought he heard his mother laughing softly.

Chapter 13

Shane hated doing it—it felt like tattling—but he let Carson and Finn know where he'd bumped into Danica and what had happened. All three men wanted to dump Noel and Evan behind bars and they would, just as soon as they could get a charge to stick. When Carson offered to speak with Danica, Shane waved him off. "I don't think she'll pull that kind of stunt again."

Carson snorted. "You don't know her like I do."

No. Shane knew her very differently. He wasn't about to tell her brother what he felt for her when he wasn't sure of the right words himself. Shane focused instead on the fear he'd seen in her face once she realized she was stuck, again, with no way to successfully defend herself. "She won't do anything that would potentially harm Nico," Shane said.

"Well, that's true," Carson agreed. "Did you and Stumps find anything near the Larson office?"

Shane shook his head. Having hit this latest wall on the stolen dog case, he turned the conversation back to Hayley and his new theory. After a brief discussion, in light of Danica's insight, they decided not to interview Hayley again.

"I have a short list of men I'd like to speak with in person," Carson said. "I could use some help on those interviews."

Shane agreed and took the information on three men in town. It would keep him and Stumps busy for the rest of the day. Probably best to take a step back. They both needed some breathing space after their protracted worst first date in history.

Well, worst first date right up to the moment when they'd spontaneously combusted in her bedroom. And if he didn't put that memory out of his mind quickly, another Gage was likely to try to put another Colton in an early grave in the interest of brotherly protection for a sister. He left the station and, with Stumps in the back seat, drove out to Harrington Energy to speak with Devlin Harrington.

Shane's curiosity had been piqued when Danica mentioned that Hayley had turned down the wealthy lawyer who stood to inherit even more when his father retired or died. He certainly had the money to send flowers week after week, but wouldn't he want Hayley to know? The whole thing felt like a stretch to Shane, especially since the local rumor mill had Devlin happily dating Shane's cousin Gemma.

Shane had called Devlin's office from the police station to verify he'd be in on a Saturday afternoon.

When they arrived, they were shown back to Devlin's office suite almost immediately.

"You're a miracle worker," he whispered to Stumps. The dog had charmed the receptionist, turning her from aloof to a puddle of corgi adoration in ten seconds flat. Shane counted it as another of his dog's many talents.

If he'd thought the Larson brothers had decorated with an eye to luxury, Harrington Energy could have given them lessons. Shane supposed it was the typical old money versus new money thing. Everything about Harrington oozed quiet opulence without being ostentatious.

Devlin came out to greet them with a smile and a firm handshake. "What brings you and this little guy out this way?"

"Detective Gage wanted some help crossing the t's and dotting the i's on the Bo Gage murder case," Shane said, refusing to use the sensationalized Groom Killer label in this interview. It would only perpetuate the local fears and he'd decided to keep this as casual and friendly as possible with a light layer of professional on top. But Shane had no doubt Devlin's father, the even wealthier Hamlin Harrington, was keeping tabs on the case. Hamlin was supposedly dating Shane's cousin Layla Colton, and Layla's father—Shane's rich, entitled Uncle Fenwick, the mayor of Red Ridge— was constantly badgering the chief to get the Groom Killer case solved so Layla and Hamlin could marry. Word was the union was more about business than love. Hamlin had to be twice Layla's age.

"Anything to help," Devlin replied. "The sooner we

put a stop to the Groom Killer, the sooner the rest of us can get on with our lives."

Shane managed to smile when he wanted to wince. "Does that mean you're thinking of proposing to Gemma Colton?"

Devlin's expression brightened. "It's early days for that," he said. "I admit proposals and weddings are on my mind because of the, ah, case, but I certainly wouldn't propose now and risk making her a widow before we exchanged vows."

"Fair point," Shane allowed. "How close were you to Bo Gage?"

"Not very close at all. We ran in different circles, had different interests."

Shane referred to his notes. "Hayley Patton mentioned that you reached out to her recently." Of course Danica was his source, but Devlin didn't need to know that. "She said you were interested in the K9 training center."

"I was thinking of getting a dog to hike with me," Devlin said. "That would mean training classes. Hayley was very helpful."

"Did you plan to purchase one of Bo Gage's dogs? Well, it's Darby's business now, I suppose," Shane corrected himself. "She has the best German shepherds around."

"No." Devlin leaned back, a wistful smile on his face. "Hayley thought a retriever or heeler would be a better hiking companion for me. I think Gemma would be more comfortable with a breed with a less aggressive reputation."

"Good choice," Shane agreed. It must be serious if Gemma's opinion was affecting Devlin's long-term choices about dogs. "If you haven't decided yet, you might consider a corgi," he suggested. "Stumps is great on a hike."

Devlin smiled at the dog seated beside Shane's chair. "On those short legs?"

"Amazing but true," Shane said. "Do you know Tommy Sutton?"

Devlin frowned. "The name sounds vaguely familiar."

"Sutton Heating and Cooling," Shane supplied. "That's his dad's business, but that's where most of us know the name. Tommy was attacked yesterday around noon." Shane tapped his notebook.

"Are you asking me for an alibi?" Devlin asked, clearly amused. "My assistant can—"

"Oh, that's not it," Shane said cutting him off quickly. He'd already checked with the receptionist anyway. "Tommy wasn't engaged so we don't have an immediate or obvious motive for the attack. Since I remembered he dated Hayley a long while back, the chief sent me out to notify all of her exes that they might be in danger, engaged or not. It's unlikely, but forewarned is forearmed and all that."

"Well, you don't need to worry about me," Devlin said. "Hayley and I never dated, only conversed a time or two about my future hiking buddy."

"Perfect." Shane flipped the notebook closed. "Thanks for your time, man." Shane stood and Stumps followed suit.

"Thanks for the warning," Devlin said.

"Be careful and hold off on that proposal as long as you can." Ever alert, Stumps moved with Shane toward the door. "It seems like a bad time to be in any kind of relationship in Red Ridge."

When he was back in the car, Shane used the voice command to call Carson at the police station.

"Any luck?"

"Not so far. Devlin Harrington didn't seem bothered in the least that I'd mistaken him for one of Hayley's exes. And he's got an alibi for the Sutton attack. From the sound of things, he's a workaholic looking to reform, and plenty of people are around who can confirm that."

"Well, at least we've knocked out one wild goose chase."

Shane bristled, but held his tongue. The police didn't have anything that pointed them *away* from Demi. He knew some of the officers were starting to look at the overwhelming physical evidence as a little too convenient, but the only way to clear his sister was to find the real killer. All he could do in the meantime was make sure the police didn't take the easy way on any aspect of this case.

On to the next name on the list.

Danica didn't hear from Shane Saturday afternoon or evening. They were both supposed to be working, but unless she started driving out to interview vets in the county on her own, she couldn't think of anything to help him with the case. What good would she be in an interview? Her family and Shane would flip out if they heard she'd driven around rural South Dakota alone, looking for someone cooperating with the Larson brothers.

Unwilling to deal with that kind of fallout, she'd

taken Hayley's overnight shift to make up for the crisis on Wednesday night. She considered it the first real test.

Sunday morning dawned clear and warm and she supposed she'd passed, if only because all of the dogs were still present and she hadn't allowed herself to have a breakdown when she'd been out in the yard alone in the dark.

She'd cleaned up and changed into a fresh uniform, prepared for a light day, when she found Tyler mopping the training room floor, looking as if his own personal thundercloud was about to drench him until he dissolved.

Danica understood the sentiment, though she had far different reasons for her moodiness. She'd had a one-night stand with the hottest guy in town and had to figure out how handle herself around him in the aftermath. Still, she remained resolute about hiding all signs of her insecurity over Shane. She'd just tuck those feelings down deep, buried alongside the persistent fear that she couldn't protect herself as well as she thought.

"Good morning," she said from the doorway.

Tyler didn't look up. "'Morning."

Though he'd never shown up with any signs of physical abuse until the black eye, Danica knew not all wounds were visible. She wondered if his parents had badgered him yesterday, or handed out some punishment he didn't deserve. "Was it bad when you got home?"

He shrugged and kept mopping.

"I'm starving. Why don't we go get breakfast?"

"I already ate." He continued to move the mop back

and forth with little enthusiasm for the task. "Not hungry."

That was a lie. Tyler was always hungry. "Great. More for me. Come on, Tyler." This wasn't the first time she'd taken him to breakfast. He was growing like a weed and needed all the good food he could get. No matter what he did or didn't eat at home, the staff kept snacks ready here.

He slammed the mop into the bucket in a rare display of temper. Water sloshed, spilling to the floor. "Look, I don't know anything, okay?" He immediately started cleaning up the mess he'd made.

How could anyone doubt he was a good kid? "Did I ask?"

He looked to the ceiling, lip curled, reminding her of Vincent at that age. It had the same effect of making her determined to succeed. "Let's go. We'll beat the brunch rush. Consider it part of the volunteer program."

"I'm not done," he said stubbornly.

"At the rate you were going, you would've been stuck in here all day. Convenient for you, I'm sure."

Tyler sighed with all the expertise of a put-upon teenager.

"Impressive," she observed. "Just leave the mop and bucket and mess. No one will be in here today. You can finish when we get back."

"Fine." He carefully put the mop in the bucket and brought the wet floor sign with him to leave at the door.

Whatever was going on with him, he hadn't lost his attention to detail or his normal concern for the people he worked with. She wanted to interpret it as evidence against Shane's persistent suspicion, but she knew she needed something stronger and more tangible to turn Shane's investigative nature in a new direction.

They went out to Danica's car and she drove them into town. Given a choice, Tyler preferred Peeps Diner for their hearty portions, platters of tender hash browns and wide variety of fresh pastries.

"You never told me how your finals went," she said, pulling out of the parking lot and turning toward the center of town. He was on the cusp of high school, and she had been encouraging him all year to strive for better grades so he'd have more choices when he graduated.

"Fine."

"What about—"

The glass in the rear window shattered, cutting her off. She checked her rearview mirror and saw only the forest at the edge of town. Swearing, she prepared to pull over when another loud bang reverberated through the air.

"Drive!" Tyler screamed.

"Get down."

He wedged himself into the space between the front seat and the dash.

They'd just passed the police station. Should she turn around or keep going? Uncertain, she hesitated a beat too long. She heard another gunshot and felt a tire go flat. She swerved and laid on the horn in warning and a plea for help. A bullet whizzed through the car, straight down the middle, leaving a hole in windshield.

She stomped on the accelerator, willing the three other tires to give her enough power as she yanked the steering wheel right at the next corner, getting out of the line of fire. The back end of the car screeched and fishtailed wide but they made it. She could only pray it was enough to move them out of harm's way.

Voices surrounded her. A faint thrum of exclamations and concern filtered through the ringing in her ears.

"Tyler! Are you hurt?"

"No." He started to squirm upright. "You're bleeding."

"Stay down."

She peeked at her mirrors. Three RRPD officers were racing toward the car. At just past eight on a Sunday morning, everyone on duty would have been at the station. She was sure other officers were headed out in search of the shooter's position.

Her priority was Tyler's safety. "You need to get into the drugstore," she said, pointing to one of Red Ridge's original retailers. The thick brick and friendly faces should be enough protection.

"Not without you."

Good kid. "You first. It's a straight shot." She cut the engine and left the keys in the ignition. "I'll be right behind you."

"Promise?"

"Where else would I go?"

He frowned as if it was a trick question.

With every second that passed without another gunshot, she breathed easier. Tyler opened the car door and uniformed RRPD officers escorted him off the street and into the store. She grabbed her purse and crawled across the seat. Just as she drummed up the courage to run for it, a familiar corgi nose met hers. "Hey, Stumps."

He licked her face. Clearly, he wasn't here in an official capacity. Shane's big hand came into her view and she accepted the assistance. She didn't miss the way he put himself between her and the origin of the gunfire.

"Do they have the shooter?" she asked.

"They will," he replied with unwavering confidence.

In the drugstore, it took all her willpower not to throw herself into his arms and take comfort from him. Why did casual sex have to be such a delightful pastime with bizarre emotional fallout?

Because nothing about Shane is casual, a little voice in her head replied. She ignored it.

"What happened?" His blue eyes were hot, but with fury rather than the passion of last night. At least he wasn't giving her that cold, emotionless judge and jury expression.

"We were headed to breakfast and—" she flung an arm toward the car "—that."

He smoothed her hair back behind her ear and turned her face to the light. "A scratch," he muttered as his thumb traced a stinging line across her cheekbone and ear. Abruptly, he drew her into his chest, wrapping her tightly within the safety of his arms. Startled by the public display, she almost forgot to hug him back. Almost.

"I heard the rifle," he murmured into her hair. "You…you…"

She waited, but he didn't elaborate. Under her cheek, she felt his breath move through his chest, heard his heart racing. The tension in his shoulders practically sizzled beneath her palms. "I'm okay," she murmured, though she couldn't be sure he'd heard her.

He released her reluctantly as the pharmacy technician on duty brought out first aid supplies. Danica looked around into the collective arched eyebrows and speculative gazes. Surely Shane noticed, but he ignored them. She followed his example.

She and Tyler gave official statements to Shane and a RRPD officer. As her car was towed away as evidence, she was lost. "This is crazy." Her knees weak, she leaned into him.

"I'll get you home," Shane said.

Tyler shuffled over. "I'm sorry. This is all my fault."

"Nonsense," Danica began. Shane silenced her with a gentle squeeze.

"You finally ready to talk?" he asked.

She couldn't scold Shane for being too stubborn about Tyler when the boy nodded. "Can we do it somewhere other than the station?"

"For now, yes," Shane allowed. "But if you've done something criminal, there could be formal charges."

"Shane," Danica said.

"It's okay." Tyler's gaze hit the floor. "He's right. My mom will have a fit no matter what happens."

Dumbfounded by Tyler's admission, Danica let Shane usher them into the back office of the drugstore. He locked the door behind them.

"I don't want anyone overhearing or seeing this conversation." His cell phone chirped and he stopped, Stumps sitting at his foot, waiting.

She, too, waited expectantly for Shane's next words. Unlike the dog, she didn't have the same confidence that she would like whatever he had to say.

He slid the phone into his pocket and met her gaze. "They found the shooter's position, but they don't have him in custody." He rounded on Tyler. "What do you have to tell me?"

Tyler looked at her, his eyes full of regret and sorrow. "I'm sorry. No one was supposed to get hurt."

Her stomach knotted. Shane was right all along. "Keep going," she said, though being tough with him cost her dearly.

Tyler hiccupped. "Some guy offered me a hundred bucks to leave the back gate unlocked at the training center the night Nico was stolen. He offered me another hundred to do it again and make sure he could get into the kennels the next night, too."

"Oh, Tyler. That's who hit you?"

He nodded. "I tried to back out of the deal after he drugged you. I know it was stupid." He shrugged her off when she tried to comfort him with a touch to his shoulder. He appealed to Shane. "I was trying to get some money so I could get out of here. I wanted to tell you the night I was in your yard, but…"

Shane nodded. "I understand."

Danica noticed Shane's gaze wasn't cold this time. His mouth was set in a grim, no-nonsense line, but empathy flickered in his eyes. Shane questioned Tyler, seeking details about the man who'd paid him.

Danica knew she should be listening, and she tried, but her mind was whirling. They'd been shot at. Really, there was no logical conclusion to the timing other than someone had been watching Tyler. He'd been hauled into the police station Friday night and today, he'd been targeted. Whatever he knew, someone wanted to keep him from talking.

He might have been killed for a desperate attempt to break free of a frustrating, neglected life? It was wrong. Tyler shouldn't bear the brunt of the punishment because someone older and meaner used his obvious weakness to steal for the Larson twins. If a judge threw the book at Tyler, what chance would he have? And the kid was good with the dogs. That unwelcome sense of helplessness dragged at her.

Unlike Tyler, Shane hadn't been guilty, but still he understood how important it was to have a second chance. "You have to do something," she whispered.

Shane's piercing gaze landed on her. "Pardon me?"

"Do something," she said with more urgency. "He made a mistake, but he's a good kid." Something ugly, something that resembled panic churned low in her belly. She couldn't let one lapse in judgment wreck Tyler's life. "He's only fourteen."

"I know." Shane tipped her face to his. "Hey. Look at me." He waited until she focused on that clear blue gaze. "I *know*."

A calm washed over her, radiating from his touch and slowly melting the icy sensation that prickled under her skin. "Okay." She leaned back, just enough to break the contact, and regretted it immediately. "Thanks."

"Let me make a call. Stumps, stay." Shane left the dog with them as he walked out of the office.

"I'm so, so sorry," Tyler murmured. "When I heard you were drugged, I should have said something."

"I'm fine," she said, determined to make it true. "We'll get to the bottom of this," she added, borrowing Shane's confidence. "We all make mistakes, Tyler."

"They'll never let me come back. I'm a security risk now."

She was afraid he might be right. "Trust Shane," she said instead. "I do."

It was true, she realized as the words came out. She trusted Shane to do the right thing for the case, for Tyler and for her, as well. She wondered how he'd react if she told him.

Chapter 14

Shane experienced profound relief as the RRPD launched into action to protect Tyler and his parents. Two officers picked up the kid at the drugstore and Shane had the report from the chief that the family would be in a safe house within hours. He didn't imagine it would be fun for them, but he wasn't about to lose his star witness who'd given a full description of what amounted to the first solid, criminal link to the Larson twins.

Danica posed a different problem. Since he'd helped her out of the car, the color in her cheeks fluctuated between too pale and too bright. Her green eyes would be focused one minute and distant the next.

Adrenaline from being shot at was clearly taking a toll. Although she was smart enough to realize it, he wasn't sure she was thinking clearly enough to take the right action. He couldn't get a read on her. When she spoke the tension in her voice bordered on panic. She claimed she needed to work, but even Stumps was giving her a side-eye full of concern.

How could he convince her to take the rest of the day off, preferably a week? "Did you have breakfast?"

Her mind had drifted again. She blinked rapidly. "We were headed to Peeps."

"Good idea. Why don't we go grab a sandwich?"

She pressed a hand to her middle. "I couldn't. I should get going. Unless you need me?"

Hell yes, he needed her, some primal instinct inside him shouted. He needed her to be safe, to be well, and to return to her sassy, smart self. He'd never forced or begged a woman to do anything in his life, but with her, he was about to break on one side or the other.

Once he'd explained the situation to the chief, the news had whipped through the department like a wild-fire. Danica's brothers had called nonstop offering help, but she'd insisted she was fine on her own.

It was obvious to him she wasn't fine at all. Worse, he and her brothers were concerned that she was in more danger. The shooter, keeping an eye on Tyler, had seen the kid with Danica. Firing on them this morning was likely an attempt to silence both of them, in case the kid had talked.

Except the kid was alive and the shooter had to assume Danica knew everything.

"I need food," he lied. "And I hate eating alone." Another lie. "Come on."

"You eat alone all the time," she muttered even as she fell into step beside him and Stumps.

The observation stopped him short. "What?"

"Every time I see you out, it's just you and Stumps."

She walked up the block while he processed what it meant that she knew that. Staring after her, he noticed a man cross the street. A burly man was striding toward her, head down, face shadowed by a red ball cap. The man was on a collision course with Danica, and at twice her size, would flatten her or nudge her into traffic with little more than a bump.

The man fit Tyler's description, but only by size. Red Ridge was full of men built tough from either hours in the gym or working on local ranches and industry. On either paranoia or instinct, Shane gave Stumps the command for a vocal alert. It was a new response they'd been working on and the stocky dog proved he was up for it.

He barked, turned a circle and barked again.

As Shane hoped, the sound drew Danica's attention as well as the attention of others on the street. She turned and hurried back toward Shane and Stumps.

"What is it?" she asked.

Behind her, the man checked his stride and veered off. "A little impromptu training opportunity," Shane said.

Her auburn eyebrows flexed as she frowned. "That's not the most effective method…"

He stopped listening, his thoughts locked on the stranger who had disappeared. It wasn't exactly proof of bad intentions, but it was enough to make up his mind. He put his hand to the small of her back as the three of them moved down the sidewalk once more.

"Please have lunch with me," he said. "At my place."

She wouldn't look at him. "Why?"

So many reasons. Fresh desire surged through him

with so much force he nearly kissed her right here on Main Street. "I'd like to talk." He'd like them both to be able to rest easy, knowing she was out of harm's way.

"About the other night?"

No. He managed to keep that answer to himself. "And today," he hedged. He opened his car door for her, keeping an eye on the area around them as he walked to the driver's side. When Stumps was settled in the back seat, Shane drove to his place.

It was a short drive, but Danica was nearly asleep. "You need some rest."

He pushed the button to raise the garage door and pulled inside. When they were parked in the dim space, out of sight, he started to breathe easier.

He let Stumps lead them into the house. Head high, the corgi trotted straight to the kitchen for a treat. He obliged his dog and then poured Danica a glass of water. He didn't bother asking about food. He simply made two thick ham sandwiches and pulled a bag of chips from the pantry. He carried everything to the table, sliding a plate in front of her and taking the chair opposite.

She ate, sparingly, while he devoured his food. Who knew worrying over someone could stir up such an appetite? "How adaptable is your cat?" he asked. He nudged the bag of chips closer to her. With luck the conversation would distract her and she'd eat a bit more.

"He doesn't have to adapt much," she replied.

The answer wasn't much help. "When you leave town, do you board him?"

"I don't travel too often." She nibbled at a chip.

"When I do, I usually have Vincent check on him daily. Why?"

Better to just get it out there, he thought. "I'd like you to move in here until the shooter is caught." The little progress he'd been making on feeding her ended right there.

She gripped her napkin in a tight fist. "You can't be serious."

"It's a good idea," he insisted.

She shook her head, fresh alarm stamped on her face. "No."

"You were attacked at work. Someone shot at you this morning after following you from work."

She waved that off. "How does moving in here solve any of that? I still have to go to work. The shooter was after Tyler."

He struggled for patience. "Think about it. You were in the station with me when I questioned Tyler. You work with the kid. If the thief is snipping loose ends, you must be on the list."

She paled and he cursed himself for being so blunt. "Then so are you," she managed.

"I'm an investigator. What Stumps and I find as evidence can and will be used in court, but I haven't had any direct interaction with the thief like you and the kid."

"You're crazy," she protested.

His temper simmered. "You were adamant I do something to protect Tyler and I did. Why won't you let me protect you, too?"

"I can take—" Her lips parted again but no sound came out. She closed her mouth and dropped her head into her hands. "You're right. I can't take care of my-self. But staying here isn't the answer."

He came around the table, kneeling beside her chair. Her hair curtained her face and he smoothed it back, careful of the deep scratch on her cheek. "Why not?"

She peeked at him, a wealth of undefinable emotion in her solemn gaze before she closed her eyes again.

"Why?" he persisted. "Staying alone is foolish under these circumstances."

She sat up, pushing her hands through her hair. "So is staying here."

"Oh. I thought better of you." He stalked away as his worst fears rattled through his head. He'd convinced himself she was different, that she actually accepted him as-is.

"Pardon me?"

He leaned against the counter, searching for a distance, a calm he could not find. "You're more afraid of gossip than a thief and would-be killer."

Her creamy skin flamed and her eyes sparked with anger. "That is *not* true."

He waited for her to elaborate. She didn't. "Tell me what is true," he demanded. "And do it fast."

"Or what?"

Or he'd haul her into his arms and kiss her until he found the strength to admit one night in her bed had changed something fundamental inside him. He gripped the counter to keep his hands to himself.

"I want you safe," he said, clinging to the last of his self-control. "Seeing you crawl out of that car…" He couldn't finish the sentence, couldn't go another min-ute without holding her.

One second his hands were locked onto the cool

granite countertop and the next he felt the warmth of her skin as he cradled her face in his palms. She was precious to him and he didn't even know when it had happened. Life turned on a dime and this time it was for the better.

He kissed her with all the tenderness he possessed, all the love she deserved.

"Danica." He whispered her name between kisses. Couldn't stop himself, even when he tasted salty tears on her cheeks.

"It's adrenaline," she said as he wiped them away.

"Of course it is." He kissed her again. "I heard those gunshots," he began. He had to start over as the images of the damage to her car filled his mind. "You scared the hell out of me."

She dropped her forehead to his chest. "I hesitated." She sniffled. "The shooter took out the tire. Tyler could have died because I hesitated."

He smoothed a hand up and down her spine as she cried. "He survived because of you. Never forget that."

When she sniffled again, he simply picked her up and carried her to the couch. She felt so small, though not the least bit fragile in his arms. It was a fascinating paradox. He held her until the waves of emotion were spent and her breathing evened out.

He held her while she slept, his mind working overtime. Getting nowhere, he turned his thoughts to Danica and whatever she was opening inside him. He never expected to find love. Hadn't felt worthy of it after his stint in prison. No matter that he'd been innocent, his time behind bars had left a stain on his soul. Nearly a decade since his release and it was still there.

Until she'd kissed him.

No, before that. Maybe it was when she'd stood up to the Larson twins and walked toward Nico with such confidence. Maybe it had been the way she'd stuck up for Tyler. He'd wanted to dismiss her commitment to the kid, toss aside her assurance in his skill as a person and a P.I. She'd made it impossible.

Good grief, he was in love with a Gage. Maybe what he was feeling was simply adjusting to the earth tilting on its axis. The image made him chuckle and she stirred.

He kissed her hair and soothed her back to sleep. She needed the rest and he needed the time to think. When she woke, he wanted to give her a coherent plan they could agree on, personally and professionally.

Knowing what he wanted gave him clarity. Now he just needed her to let him know what she wanted.

Danica came awake slowly, a familiar weight stretched across her feet. Oscar always enjoyed the days when she napped. She nestled into the pillow, thinking more rest sounded like a good idea when she realized the light was all wrong and the scents were too masculine.

She wasn't at her condo. Shane had brought her to his house. Rubbing the sleep from her eyes, she glanced down, expecting that weight on her legs to be Stumps.

Instead she met Oscar's golden gaze. He flicked an ear and ducked his head under a paw, making it clear he had no plan to let her up. "How did you get here?"

She heard a chair slide across a hard floor, by footsteps. "You're awake."

Danica turned toward Shane, momentarily blinded

by the easy smile on his face. Not an expression she'd seen often. "Tell me it's only been a few hours and not a few days."

His mouth kicked into a grin. "Only a few hours," he confirmed. "Feeling better?"

She wasn't sure how to answer. Physically, she felt much better and she gave him a quick nod. She didn't have any idea how she felt about her cat being here. "Where is Stumps?"

At the sound of his name, the dog sat up from where he'd been curled behind her bent knees.

Oscar gave him a wary look, but didn't move.

"That's unexpected," she said. "What kind of alternate dimension is this?"

"Same town, same dimension," Shane said. "I had Vincent bring Oscar over, along with an overnight bag with a few essentials."

Danica groaned, imagining what her little brother deemed essential. Not ready to face that certain trouble, she turned her attention to the cat and dog. "Tell me how you worked this miracle in just a few hours."

"I think having met at your place helped."

She eyed him dubiously. Is this how they were going to open the discussion of their one-night stand? She carefully withdrew her legs from under the cat.

"Could be Stumps is just that good," Shane said, tucking his hands into his pockets. "You trained him, so you would know."

The man knew how to give a compliment, she thought. Stumps gave her a pleading look and flipped to his back, inviting a belly rub. Danica indulged him and endured Oscar's glare. Better to focus on something she could control, rather than the unanswerable questions darting through her mind.

"I guess this means we're living together?"

Shane pulled the ottoman closer and sat down in front of her, their knees nearly touching. "Would that be so bad?" he asked, his eyes cool and serious.

No. "That depends on what my brother packed for me."

He laughed. When his eyes lit with amusement, the tension in his shoulders eased. "I'll take you back over whenever you like," he said. "I just don't want you going anywhere alone right now."

Whether it was the man or his miraculous way with her content cat, she couldn't drum up any outrage over his protective measures. "You're that sure something will happen?"

He nodded, the amusement replaced with professional intensity. "The one person who can identify the thief is out of reach. You might have been in the wrong place at the wrong time the night Nico was stolen, but you are now a wild card. The bad guys can't be sure what you know."

"I suppose whoever is behind this might also think I know where Tyler is hiding," she mused.

Shane closed his eyes a moment. "Also a possibility," he allowed.

An immediate urge to comfort him came over her, and she stood before she gave in. His kisses were wonderfully distracting, but they both needed to focus. "Did you make any progress on the list of Hayley's exes?" she asked, hoping to distract herself from everything else.

Shane shook his head. "Tommy hasn't recalled anything helpful about his assailant and likely won't. The chief has all of us working through the list by phone and face-to-face interviews. It will take time, but he didn't dismiss the alternate theory outright."

"Good." She trailed after him as he moved to his computer. The sooner they found a lead on the real killer, the sooner his sister could come home to Red Ridge where she belonged. "What now?" she asked, strangely uncomfortable that she was now effectively his roommate.

"Now we wait and see if they can track down the man who bribed Tyler to leave the gate unlocked," he said.

"I feel awful for him," she murmured, turning her gaze to the window. Shane had every right to say *I told you so* and berate her for her misplaced faith in Tyler.

"You were right," he said. "He's a good kid."

Startled, she whipped around, confused by the sincerity in his gaze. "You mean it."

"I do." He shifted forward, catching the tips of her fingers with his. He toyed with her fingers, that small, sweet contact stirring desire low in her belly. "We all make mistakes."

And like her, Tyler had made a big one. At least he would have help rectifying it. She would never be able to undo the damage she'd inflicted on her grandfather. Or Shane.

With Shane's gaze on their hands, she couldn't see his eyes, but the warmth was clear in his touch. How odd that she stood here with a man who'd been wrongfully convicted of murder, yet he was really the only innocent person she knew. No, he wasn't perfect, but of all the mistakes made through the years, Shane's being in the wrong place at the wrong time was the most benign.

"I'm sorry." The words tumbled from her lips, unbidden. She didn't even know what to do with them now that they were out there.

"For what?"

For being a Gage, she thought. If there were two people with more bad baggage between them, she didn't know who they were. "My grandfather owed you an apology. It should have been offered sooner."

"That's the third time you've apologized for him." He looked up, his eyes earnest. "You can stop now."

"I only count two," she said. Over his mother's amazing red sauce and just now. And both times she'd avoided confessing her part in making closure impossible.

He stood up and stroked a thumb over her unscathed cheek. "At the end of my first day training with Stumps."

Oh, that. She felt her face flame. "I…well. You, ah, didn't seem to hear me and I lost my nerve." Lack of nerve around Shane seemed to be her default.

"It took a whole lot of nerve just to say it at all. I was bitter and resentful that you were our instructor."

"Is that past tense?" she asked.

"I seem to be getting over myself." His lopsided smile sent butterflies pinwheeling through her belly. "Slowly."

"Some things shouldn't be forgotten," she agreed. If they could be, she would have found it easy to forgive herself for hurting Grandpa Gage and by default, Shane.

"Why do you look guilty when you think of him?"

"Him?" she asked, buying time.

"Your grandfather." He drew her along with him as he returned to the couch. Patting her knee, he sat back. "I'm an investigator, remember? You had nothing to do with the bungled murder case and yet you're the only Gage who's addressed the situation with me directly in nearly a decade. And you look guilty every time."

She desperately wanted to turn away from the subject and Shane, but he was right about the guilt. It had been eating her alive for years. "You heard my grandfather died of a heart attack, right?" At his nod, she continued, determined to get it all out this time. "That's my fault. I killed him." She pulled back before he could and clutched the quilt he'd draped over her while she napped.

"I'd like the whole story," Shane said with excruciating calm. "Please."

Investigator at work, she supposed. "When it got out what he'd done, how he'd manipulated everything about that case, I went over and just unloaded on him. He was my idol, my rock, and what he did to you crushed me." She swiped the tear from her cheek. Whatever she'd suffered was nothing compared to Shane's ordeal through the trial, in the court of public opinion and as a prison inmate.

"Oh, I let him have it," she said. "I said the most dreadful things, the way only a devastated and disillusioned teenager can say them. When he tried to apologize to *me*, I told him you were the one who deserved those words. He asked me to wait. He was struggling to breathe and rubbing at his arm. I didn't."

She braced herself for the worst part. "It was the only time in my life that I left him without giving him a hug and telling him I loved him." She forced herself to meet Shane's gaze. "He was dead hours later. My fault." Tears clogged her throat, but she would get it all out. "You can never have the closure you deserve because of me. I'm so sorry."

Her entire body itched to get up and run as far from Shane and this shameful moment as she could get. Her cat shoved his head against her fist until she opened her fingers and stroked his ears. At least Oscar didn't care that she'd been cruel and careless.

"You never told anyone else?"

"No," she said, voice trembling. She was such a coward.

"I'm the only one who knows?"

He'd clearly found his calling as an investigator. "Yes." A vise of emotions, old and new, squeezed her chest. She wanted to apologize over and over again for denying him that essential piece of healing when he'd returned to Red Ridge. She could never make it right.

"I tried to talk to Carson once and chickened out." Well, she was certainly full of confessions today.

"You do realize having an argument is different from actively ending a life, right?"

"If I'd stayed, if I'd been a decent human being and given him an ounce of the respect he'd earned despite his horrible error with your case, he might still be alive today."

"Danica." He nudged the cat out of the way and pulled her into his arms. "You don't know that."

"Neither do you." She hiccupped and despite her attempt to maintain control, the dam burst. She cried in earnest, her tears soaking his shirt.

He kissed the top of her head, smoothed her hair

back with long, soothing strokes and murmured comforting nonsense until the worst subsided. Stumps laid his chin on her knee in support.

"Is this why you didn't go into law enforcement?" he asked.

"Yes." How was she going to get out of this gracefully? "I couldn't bear the idea of wearing that uniform. It would have been like a slap in your face every day."

Something that sounded suspiciously like laughter rumbled in his chest beneath her cheek. "You have the sweetest heart."

She sat up, her palms braced on his rock-hard shoulders as she gaped at him. "What?"

"Of everyone involved in that disaster, you have the least cause to carry around any guilt." He helped her sit up and handed her a box of tissues.

She surely looked frightful, yet there was something in his gaze that made her warm all over. "Are you saying you've forgiven him?"

He sighed. "That may be a lifelong journey, but I'm getting closer. I was furious from the moment he pinned that girl's death on me. When I was finally released, I was determined to ruin him, to expose him as a fraud and a bad cop." He pushed a hand through his hair, his expression sheepish. "As you pointed out, none of his other cases were flawed or overturned."

"I don't know why he went off the rails with you." She glanced at Stumps, who had rolled to his back once her tear-fest ended. Bending, she gave the little dog a belly rub, smiling as his rear legs kicked at the air in happiness.

"You didn't see the crime scene." Shane's shuttered

gaze grew distant. "At the end of the day, why doesn't really matter," he said. "It happened. It was rectified. Now we all have to move on." He poked her shoulder lightly. "Even you."

"Ha ha." It was disconcerting to hear him speak so plainly, with none of the bitterness or smoldering temper that often colored in his voice. Maybe her guilty conscience had added those elements to their previous exchanges.

"I admit it has taken me longer than it should have to get to this point," he said quietly. "What I thought I lost in prison was nothing compared to what I gained."

She waited, petting Stumps with her toes while Shane searched for the words to explain.

"I lost time, definitely. And I was angry about it."

Rightfully so, she thought.

"Prison takes more than your freedom," he said. "It takes all the milestones, your self-respect, and if you're not careful, it steals your humanity. I went in there a hotheaded kid, knowing I was innocent and knowing my claim sounded like one more guilty man spitting in the wind.

"Losing Mom was the worst because she died thinking I was guilty. I considered it my job to be there for her and I couldn't be. So yeah, it piled on and I wallowed in that bitterness and self-pity for a long time until the K9 unit turned me around." He tipped her face to his. "Until *you* turned me around."

She shook her head, unwilling to take any of the credit. "You did that on your own. Well, you and Stumps."

"I couldn't bring myself to be a cop and wear a uniform either, but checking up on cops worked for me.

Investigating scenes the right way and dealing with the result no matter what? That I could manage. Then you whispered that apology to me and it all started to feel manageable, like I had one ally in this town, someone who wasn't waiting for me to start a crime spree. You gave me that."

He caught her hands in his and brought them to his lips, kissing her knuckles. "You apologized at the first opportunity and it took me nearly a decade to say thank you. Truly, Danica, your generosity is astounding. It made all the difference."

She could hardly process what he was saying as his touch sent sparks through her system. He wasn't judging her or smothering anger under layers of polite decency. His blue eyes, so frequently cold and distant, blazed with passionate heat that mirrored what she felt for him. More, she recognized a deep affection that made her want to dance with joy.

They moved together into a swift kiss full of newfound acceptance and healing. Needy hands sought tantalizing places, wringing out sighs and moans from both of them. She laughed when he swore in an attempt to discard his clothing and hers as fast as possible.

They left a trail all the way to his bedroom, where at last she could get her hands on him and show him the last few things she was afraid to put into words. Every hard plane and ridge of his sculpted body was a wonder. He left her in awe, helping her see the wonder in her body, too. She cried out as his mouth and hands exposed every sweet pleasure point. As a climax left her feeling splintered and sparkling, he caught her quivering body to his and sank deep.

Joined with him, her body, heart and soul were in full agreement. This man was exactly where she was always meant to be.

Chapter 15

Shane's heart pounded against his ribs as he fought for control, determined to be gentle. He needed to make her understand how different this was for him. She was too beautiful, her hair gleaming in the afternoon light pouring through the bedroom window. Her eyes, glazed with passion, held his as tightly as her body embraced him. For once, he was thrilled to be a captive. This woman was his all. Work might take him away, but his heart would be safe, with her, forever.

"Let go," she urged, a small smile on her lips as her body arched to meet his. "I've got you."

Let go? He was already in free fall, heart, mind and body. He rocked his hips, relishing her soft moan as her eyes closed. "Do you know when I fell in love with you?"

Her eyes flew open and the shock and wonder in

those green depths made him want to laugh. "Guess that's a no." He rocked again, slowly in and out, torturing them both.

Her inner muscles squeezed tight and her fingers dug into his back, her knees hugging his hips. "Shane."

The way she said his name, half plea, half demand, shattered his self-control. She felt so good under him, the scent of her skin and their mingled arousal drifting through him with every thrust and sigh. The release ripped through his body and pitched him into a whole new world.

A world that began and ended with Danica.

When he could move again, he rolled so that she was sprawled across him like a blanket. He flipped the bedspread over them so she wouldn't get chilled. She stacked her palms on his chest to pillow her cheek. He could stay right here for days and not miss anything of the world outside this room.

"When did you fall in love with me?" he asked, curious if she was dazed enough to answer.

"The day you met Stumps," she murmured, snuggling into him.

He managed to hide his shock over her response. Her back rose and fell on a heavy, contented sigh, as he put the reply into context. With her body so close, he felt the moment she realized what she'd said.

"Hey. That wasn't fair." Her smile belied any real aggravation. "You're sneaky."

"Sometimes P.I.s do sneaky things," he said without any remorse. "Why that day?"

"No. Nope. *Nuh-uh.* That's all you get." Though she tried, she couldn't hold on to a stern expression as he stroked her spine and caressed her hip with his palm.

"Is it?"

Her auburn eyebrows drew together as she frowned. "Are you really in love with me?"

"Color us equally surprised." He pulled her along his body until her lips were within reach and kissed her soundly. "Yes, Danica. I love you, though it sounds like you have one hell of a head start on me."

He lost himself to the taste of her kisses for several long minutes. "How much of a head start?" she asked, a little breathless. "Think you'll ever catch up?"

"I'm on my way." He rolled so they were lying side by side, facing each other. Her high cheekbones, the sultry mouth and those changing-sea eyes gilded by the soft light fascinated him.

"I've tried to ignore you for years," he admitted. "Training and retraining with you has been a challenge."

"Understandable. I'm tough." She tapped his lips, then hers. "Plus redheads are hard to miss. And then the Colton-Gage thing is a real hurdle."

He kissed her nose. "Good thing I'm an expert at knocking right past hurdles and obstacles."

Her cheeks went pink and he couldn't help himself—he kissed her again.

"Just tell me," she said, laughter dancing in her eyes. "Or are you scared?"

"I'm scared," he admitted. But it was the good kind of scared. The scared that was full of promises of great things just over the horizon if he only had the guts to climb up and discover them. "Pretty sure I fell hard when we found Nico and you stood up to Noel. At the very least, that was the moment I knew ignoring what I didn't want to feel for you wasn't going to work anymore."

"Hmm."

"What?"

"As love stories go, that's less than romantic. A girl has to have standards." Her hand slid down his torso, teasing and tempting.

"Guess I'll work on it," he growled against her throat. He let her push him to his back and make love to him, and he took inspiration from every touch.

At the sound of a soft whine, Danica was almost afraid to open her eyes and find herself alone again. Then she felt the mattress sag a little. Shane kissed her shoulder before he rolled out of bed to take care of Stumps.

She sat up, startled to discover they'd slept through the afternoon. Twilight had fallen as the sun sank past the ridge, and the stars would be out soon. Her body felt glorious and satisfied.

"Didn't mean to wake you." Shane tugged his jeans over his lean hips. "I closed the dog door so Oscar wouldn't try to go home."

It was one more thoughtful gesture. He might look hard on the outside, but the guy was pudding down deep. "Thanks." She checked the clock. "We should feed them. Us, too."

"I'll get started."

"Mind if I shower? I'll be quick."

He stared at her so hard, she thought she'd managed to say the wrong thing. If she was living with him while they searched for the shooter, he had to expect her to bathe occasionally.

"You can be quick this time," he said, crossing the room to pull her to her feet.

The soft denim of his jeans, the coarse hair on his chest, tickled her bare skin. He nuzzled the sensitive spot just below her ear. "Next time, we'll test the limits of my hot water heater."

The words gave her a thrill. Reluctantly, she slipped out of his arms and dashed for the shower, his low, sexy chuckle chasing her.

A few minutes later, she was clean and dressed in jeans and an old T-shirt with the training center logo on the front, her damp hair coiled and secured up off her neck. It was clear she'd need to make a run to her place for more clothing, but Vincent had managed the essentials pretty well.

Stumps munched his dinner, occasionally pausing to trot over and check on Oscar's progress. Her cat was making snorting and snuffling sounds as he gobbled his dinner. "He's happy," she said, stroking his back lightly. "You didn't have to feed him on the counter."

Shane shrugged. "He was already there and it seemed easier than starting a new training session with Stumps tonight. I figure it's love you, love your cat, right?"

Her heart did a happy spin in her chest and she felt the glow rise in her cheeks. Hayley was right—she really shouldn't ever play poker. "Right. I can fix dinner."

"I've got leftovers started," Shane said. "Just take it out of the oven if I'm not back in time."

He brushed his lips across hers in a fast kiss as he bolted for his turn in the shower. She set the table and poured wine for each of them while she waited. It felt so natural and so strange at the same time. She tried to focus on the natural part of the equation.

It was easier when Shane breezed back in with less than a minute to spare on the oven timer.

"Perfect timing," she said.

"I've discovered life sort of takes care of the timing if we let it."

She would agree, unless they were talking about Nico and the puppy currently subject to the Larson twins' treatment. Depending on the training techniques employed, both dogs might never have valid working careers.

"You're thinking of Nico," he said as he set both plates on the table.

She couldn't deny it. "Every day means less chance of a full recovery. I won't stop thinking about him or the puppy until they're both safe at the training center again."

"The way Noel was going, the training center might need to invest in more steak," Shane said.

She knew he was trying to make her laugh, and it worked a little. "If that's the worst of it, I'll cover the expense out of pocket."

He reached over and touched her hand. "We'll get the dogs back. You'll see. And then you can work your magic."

His confidence was contagious and it washed over her, easing the persistent frustration with the unresolved situation. "Any new messages from Demi?"

He shook his head.

She noticed the tension bracketing his mouth. "As worrisome as it is to have so many people injured or killed, it must be convincing more of the RRPD that she's innocent."

"That is one positive." They finished dinner, and after taking Stumps for a walk, they returned to Shane's house to watch the movie that had been interrupted when Tyler had been skulking around outside.

By the time the credits rolled, Danica decided Hayley had been right. It was much better to take a chance and claim love without worrying about how long it might last. They'd purged the past and cleared a path for something new, something that gave her hope.

She'd never experienced a relationship that filled her with such a sense of peace to balance the excitement. She'd never given herself permission to seek that kind of relationship, really, burdened as she was by the guilt of her grandfather. Of course, love or not, she wouldn't look far into a future with Shane. It was way too soon for that.

For now she was happy to be happy.

"I'll let Stumps out," she said as Shane turned off the television.

Stumps went racing out into the yard and did a big circuit that made her laugh. When the corgi decided it was playtime, he did it with the same exuberance and gusto he applied to every working and training activity.

She walked inside and right into Shane's embrace. The unknowns on resolving the case would be waiting for them in the morning.

From his pocket, Shane's phone hummed and his face turned thunderous as he read the message.

"Is that news on the shooter?" she asked hopefully.

He shoved the phone back in his pocket. "The initial trail away from the shooter's position went cold. I'm not sure how he managed that. And the trail in town went cold, too."

"You could have told me earlier." She wasn't fragile.

"We had more important things to discuss when you woke up."

"Right."

He stepped close. "You realize you're even more beautiful when you blush?"

She looked away.

"Yes, just like that."

"Stop teasing me." She knew what she looked like.

"Maybe in an hour. Or three." He scooped her up and carried her back to the bedroom.

Shane came awake from a deep sleep in the span of a single heartbeat. Alert, aware of a threat, he listened for the source without moving a muscle.

Stumps growled low. The dog was close. Beside the bed or under it?

Shane surreptitiously reached out for Danica to warn her to keep her still and found the sheets where she'd been were already cool. It was the only fact that mattered. Someone had taken Danica. If she'd left willingly, Stumps wouldn't be growling.

He slid out of the bed to the floor.

"Hold it, hotshot," a low voice threatened. "One more move and I kill her."

"Danica?" The only answer was a shift in the darkness near the bedroom door. "Let her go," Shane demanded.

The lights came on and Shane held up a hand against the glare. When he could see Danica, his heart stuttered in his chest. A man in black, bigger than Shane, wore a mask over his face and held Danica tight against his chest. A hunting knife gleamed at her throat.

Shane shut down his emotions and his mind switched to the cold tactics of survival.

"Let her go," he repeated.

A tremor rippled through Danica. Her eyes rounded as she met his gaze. He knew what she'd heard. Yes, the cold, calculating Colton was back, but it was the only way he knew to save her.

The masked man gave her a shake, the knife pressing into the tender skin under her chin.

Behind him, Stumps let loose another low growl, and this time a strange sound caught between a yowl and cry joined in. Her cat, Shane realized, hiding under the bed from the sound of it. Perfect. He could use all the help he could get here.

The man jerked back another step and Danica's toes came off the floor. She was completely at the man's mercy. One slip and the knife would end her, whether or not that was the goal.

"What do you want with her?" Shane asked. Questions often interrupted a violent thought pattern as the brain automatically tried to provide answers.

"Loose ends," the man replied. "Where's the kid?"

"She doesn't know."

The man gave Danica a shake and Shane's heart kicked, certain injury was imminent. "You do."

"I don't," Shane said. "I swear that information is above my pay grade."

"We'll play it your way," the man said. "Thought she meant something to you." The man started backward once more. The dog and cat growled in a threatening chorus. Danica reached out and grabbed the doorjamb, fingers digging in.

"Wait!" Shane lurched forward, only getting as far as the end of the bed, before Danica's pained cry stopped him short. "She means everything," he declared. "What do you want?" he asked, watching the small trickle of Danica's blood well up over the knife edge.

"Where is the kid?"

"Let her go and I'll tell you," Shane promised.

From here, he could close the distance and use the doorway as choke point as soon as he had a distraction. Prison had taught him how to use anything in a fight, refining skills he'd first practiced in his old neighborhood.

"Tell me and I'll let her go," the man countered.

"Don't—" Danica's attempt to speak was cut short by her captor. Her fingers twitched and flexed into the hem of the T-shirt she wore.

It was all the distraction Shane needed. He gave Stumps the bark signal and lunged forward as the dog turned into a whirling dervish.

The raucous noise from Stumps set off Oscar. Scared and mad, the massive cat bolted from the bed like an arrow from a bow.

Shane ducked low, hoping the man's instincts would draw the knife down and away, leaving Danica room to escape.

Shane heard a shrill scream as his shoulder connected with the big man's knees, knocking him into the door frame. Then they were through to the hallway, just Shane, the man and the knife.

With Danica out of danger, Shane used the small

space and his long reach to full advantage. He wrapped up the man's legs as he tried to scramble away, rolling him toward the wall.

Light from the bedroom skated over the knife, giving Shane the split-second warning he needed to evade. With the knife buried to the hilt in the wall, he overpowered the intruder and pinned him to the floor.

"Danica?"

"I'm fine."

Thank God. "There are cuffs—" He had to stop as the man tried to squirm free. "Cuffs—"

"Foyer table. I know." She tiptoed around the men on the hallway floor and returned quickly.

Once he had the man's hands secure, he hauled him up against the wall. He walked to the bedroom and got his gun, handing the weapon to Danica. "Shoot him if he moves."

"Tiny here doesn't have the guts to pull a trigger," the man said.

Shane glared at him, almost smiling when Danica flicked off the safety and pointed the barrel at the man's crotch. "You're wrong." He called Stumps over to stand guard with Danica.

"Where are you going?" she asked.

"Cord for his feet," Shane said without looking at her. If he did, he'd break and he didn't trust this guy not to pull a Houdini move to escape. "He's evaded everyone and their K9 trackers. I'm not taking any chances."

He returned with the electrical cord he'd pulled from his bedside alarm clock. He kneeled, bound the man's feet, hauled him out to the living room and left him trussed up on the floor.

Danica followed, along with Stumps and Oscar.

He turned to her and his control snapped when he saw the blood on her throat and the neckline of the T-shirt.

Carefully, he turned her chin so he could see the damage. The wound was barely more than a scratch, and a waterfall of gratitude and relief cascaded over him. "You're okay?" He couldn't put more than a whisper into the words.

"Alive and unharmed." She smiled. "Thanks to you." She wrapped her arms around his waist.

They were barely dressed and he needed to get some answers out of this guy, not the least of which was how he'd bypassed his security system.

"Go get dressed while I call this in."

Her hand slid across his bare waist. "Better wait until you're dressed, too."

"Right." He didn't care if anyone caught him in only his briefs. "You first." He wanted Danica to be comfortable as much as he wanted a few minutes alone with this jerk on his floor.

He crouched in front of the man who'd invaded his home and held Danica hostage. The woman he valued above his own life. Nothing like a violent intruder to put priorities into perspective. "How did you bypass my security system?"

"The hacks are as easy as a Google search."

Shane knew better, but it was a narrow suspect pool for who was directing this guy. "Why?"

The man had the grace not to pretend he didn't understand the question. "Loose ends are bad for business. The kid talked or he wouldn't be hiding now. I'll find the safe house and I'll—"

"You'll be twiddling your thumbs in lockup," Shane corrected him. "Tell me how the Larsons hired you."

"Don't know anyone by that name."

Danica returned looking fresher than she should in cropped yoga pants and a matching tank top, her feet bare and a pair of his jeans in her hands. "Figured you wouldn't want to leave me alone with him again."

He could tell by the sharp glint in her gaze she would happily have found a reason to pull the trigger if she needed to. He understood the sentiment.

"Remind me to give Oscar fresh tuna," she said, staring at the intruder.

"Huh?"

She pointed to the man's face and he laughed. Oscar, in his panic over the barking stunt, had somehow managed to rake the side of the man's head. His ear and the scalp above it were bleeding. He might even need stitches.

"Cat scratches are nasty," Danica said as breezily as if she was discussing a summer day at the beach. "You probably want to take care of that."

The man swore. "You'll never see your mutts again, you bitch."

With a kick to the man's knee, Shane put an end to destructive conversation. He asked a few more questions while they waited for the police to haul the man away. Unfortunately, they didn't get anything useful out of him.

"Now what?" Danica asked when they were alone again.

Shane gave Stumps a big reward, Oscar too, wishing he had a good answer. She'd been victimized in his home, a place where she should have felt safe. "Would you feel safer at your condo?"

She shook her head. "Not really. I imagine he went there first, unless he knew I was already here."

Neither he nor Vincent had made any attempt to keep it secret that she was at his place after the morning's shooting. "What a day," he said, rubbing a hand over his hair.

"I recall a few high points." Her body chose that moment to start quaking from the adrenaline surge.

He opened his arms and she walked into him, resting her cheek against his chest. "You were amazing."

Did she know what she was saying? How would she ever forgive him for letting her down? "I was terrified," he admitted.

"It didn't show," she assured him. "I could tell you were working out the solution."

"Thanks for trusting me."

"With my life." She burrowed deeper into his embrace. "Let's check the locks and go back to bed," she said.

He wasn't about to argue with that suggestion. They found the intruder had come through the back door, which made sense, but however he'd bypassed the alarm, the lock pick he used had barely left a scratch. "New locks tomorrow," he said, verifying that the door closed properly.

Though convinced the house was secure, with a patrol unit from the RRPD parked out front, neither one of them seemed eager to go back to the bedroom. "You sure about staying here?"

She squeezed his hand between both of hers. "My

self-confidence took a beating the night Nico was stolen," she admitted.

"That's natural."

"Leave it to you to understand." She smiled. "As independent and capable as I feel most days, I realize it's okay to have limits, too. To ask for help."

He kissed her head. "You'll be able to sleep after all this?"

"As long as you're beside me," she replied.

Shane couldn't believe her strength or her unceasing faith in him. "Count on it."

Danica was so grateful for Shane's easy compassion and though she didn't understand it, she was delighted to feel more like her capable self rather than diminished by Shane's solid presence.

"I don't understand how he got by Stumps to begin with," Shane said. "I'm a light sleeper these days."

Assuming sleeping light was one more lingering effect of life behind bars, she smoothed a hand up and down his arm. "I was on the way to the kitchen for water. I heard the break-in and when your alarm didn't sound, I sent Stumps to you."

Shane stared at her. "You know he could have given a verbal alert."

She appreciated the blend of heat and worry in his blue eyes. "Stealth worked out," she replied. She'd been so afraid the intruder would shoot Stumps if he'd barked. She couldn't bear to deal Shane one more loss.

"Aw, man." He hugged her close. "You thought he'd kill Stumps."

She nodded against his bare chest. She wanted to tell him she admired his ruthless fighting skills, but she didn't want to offend him or bring up more bad memories.

They headed down the hallway, passing the hole where the knife had landed. In the bedroom, the rumpled covers mocked her and terror tried to creep in. The intruder could have killed her outright. So much could have gone wrong and yet together she and Shane had been victorious.

She'd hang on to that. Breathing deeply, she inhaled the pure comfort and security of his masculine scent as she stretched out beside Shane's tough body in the bed. Being close to him gave her a sense of confidence she hadn't entrusted to others in years. Putting confidence in others had come naturally until her grandfather had let her down in stunning fashion by mishandling Shane's case.

Life had a way of coming full circle, she thought, drowsing within Shane's embrace. After nearly a decade of burdensome guilt, she could finally look at Shane and feel only affection and love. It was a beautiful new awareness.

How much could change in a day? *Everything.*

She'd known it when her grandfather's sterling reputation was suddenly tarnished. She'd faced the shock on the day her brother had been killed.

"You asleep?" Shane's voice rumbled softly through the darkness.

"Not really," she murmured.

"Change your mind?"

"Not about you," she replied. Her palm rested over his chest and she felt the sigh flow through him, relaxing all those wonderful muscles. It made her smile. "What are you thinking?"

He sighed again, his arm banding around her and then easing. "You make me feel like the luckiest man in the world."

A profound statement from him. Before she could sort out how to reply, he was snoring softly. What a bizarre, exhausting day. She couldn't think of a more apropos start to a relationship with a man like Shane Colton.

Chapter 16

The morning after the home invasion, Shane and Stumps drove Danica to work at the training center. She'd kissed him goodbye, wished him a good day, and promised to meet him for lunch. It was so normal he almost didn't know what to do with himself.

He and Stumps went straight to the police station to catch up with the intruder's interrogation. The man claimed he'd been working alone and then invoked his right to an attorney. It would be interesting who showed up to defend him. At least the police had the statements from Shane and Danica about his talk of the dog thefts and his violent interest in Tyler. The kid had been brought in long enough to identify the intruder in a lineup, but the man refused to flip on whoever had hired him.

Still, having the thug in custody meant fingerprints

and evidence they could work with and build on. It wasn't open and shut on the dog thefts, but it sure would be on the home invasion. Though slow, it was forward progress.

Shane was heading out of the police station when he caught sight of one of his wealthier cousins walking up. Anders Colton didn't necessarily have to work, but he continued on as foreman of the Double C Ranch. Shane knew he even kept to the modest foreman's quarters rather than stay in his rightful place in the main house.

Shane couldn't throw stones about family and choices. Not with his less than stellar background and certainly not when he had hopes to convince Danica Gage to marry him as soon as the Groom Killer was caught.

"Shane, just the man I was looking for," Anders said, extending a hand.

Shane swallowed the reflexive doubt and met the handshake. Related or not, his cousins rarely made an effort to look up any of Rusty Colton's kids. "What's up?" At his heel, Stumps sat, relaxed and curious.

Anders glanced around. "I think I've got a needy thief out at the Double C."

"Meaning?" Shane's curiosity piqued now.

"Someone has been stealing leftovers from the fridge. A gallon of milk went missing, along with a blanket and pillow." He stepped closer and lowered his voice to little more than a whisper. "We had an old baby cradle in the barn and it's disappeared."

Shane felt a flare of hope for his sister. Demi was rumored to have been a few months pregnant when she'd fled town. Her baby would be a newborn. In need of a cradle. He kept waiting to hear any news. "You're thinking it might be Demi?"

"It crossed my mind," Anders replied. "Can you and your dog check it out? Unofficially."

"Unofficially?" Shane echoed, surprised.

"I'd rather not file any formal reports unless I have to."

Shane appreciated that more than he could express. It still worried him that the police would shoot first and ask the right questions later when they found Demi. Although more people in the RRPD seemed to be entertaining the idea that she was framed, Shane wasn't ready to count on that opinion holding up during an active manhunt.

"Stumps and I will head that way now and let you know."

"Thanks." Anders gave Shane his cell phone number and with a resigned expression, he returned to his truck.

Shane suffered a moment's guilt over not discussing this with Brayden at the very least. He justified his decision, knowing that he'd report any signs of Demi immediately. To Anders, Brayden, the chief and Detective Gage and in that order. If anyone fussed, he'd remind them that his P.I. license gave him every right to take private cases.

Checking his watch, Shane decided he could get a preliminary search in before he was due to meet Danica for lunch. He headed out of town, taking the back roads around to the Double C Ranch so he could investigate without being spotted on the property. It meant more of a hike, but Stumps was up to the task.

He and Stumps searched the property, especially the

area around the barn and outbuildings that Anders said had been pilfered. Though Stumps worked attentively when given the command to search, he didn't alert on anything in particular.

That could mean the person in need had been here long enough to be part of the norm in Stumps's professional K9 opinion, or it could mean they weren't searching in the right places. Shane widened the search area, moving with deliberate caution toward the trees that bordered this side of the ranch. He saw signs of people moving through the area, but it could be hikers or workers.

Shane wasn't sure if he felt more relief or disappointment as he sent the text with his inconclusive results to Anders. He drove back into town, eager to take Danica to lunch. With her attacker in custody, there were things they needed to discuss, regardless of the status of any other troubles in Red Ridge.

Having made up his mind about the future, he didn't see the point in stalling. Rebuilding from the lowest point in his life without any family support hadn't been easy. It wasn't as if his branch of the family was blooming with exemplary relationships. He wanted to change that moving forward and he wanted Danica to change that with him.

His palms went damp on the steering wheel as he parked in front of the training center.

With a killer taking out would-be grooms still on the loose, this might be the worst time to propose, but he'd made himself a promise when he was released that he wouldn't waste a minute of the life he had left. He'd known the first time he kissed Danica that she was the one, though he'd been slow to admit it even to himself.

Stumps gave a soft *woof* at the driver's side window. Shane turned, watching Danica walk to the car. What if he was rushing things? What if she said no? He didn't have a ring for her and couldn't safely give her one until the Groom Killer was found and captured.

Her smile seemed to brighten an already clear and sunny day and he felt his entire body relax. Whatever she said to his proposal, she would know without any doubt where he stood on the issue.

He opened the door to greet her and his phone chirped with an incoming text message.

The baby is fine. Working on finding the real killer. Hope home soon. D

Demi. He had to take this to the chief right now.

Danica greeted him and reached behind his seat to greet Stumps. When she looked up at him, worry clouded her gaze. "More trouble?"

With her face tilted up at him that way, she was irresistible. He brushed his lips to hers. "Hi."

"Hi back."

The kiss shifted the worry in her green eyes to such a warm affection he kissed her again, pulling away before he drew a crowd. "I could do that all day," he confessed.

"I wouldn't argue."

A lifetime wouldn't be long enough to enjoy that smile. "Lunch," he reminded himself why he was there. "I need to stop by the police station first."

"Sure." She went around to the passenger side door and Stumps jumped to the back seat to make room for her. "Did you hear something?" she asked.

So much had happened since Demi had become a murder suspect, he thought. And yet Demi's desperate situation was running secondary to the sudden events in his life. He reached across the seat and took her hand, enjoying that he could do that, feel that physical connection and the deeper undercurrent.

She shot him a curious look, but she didn't press him. He handed her the phone. "I just got a text from Demi."

Danica read the brief message. "Oh, thank goodness they're both all right." She scrolled up and down. "That's it? I mean, I'm glad they're fine, but I want details. The baby can't be more than a few weeks old, if that."

Shane chuckled. "I know. She doesn't even say if we have a niece or nephew," he added.

"And she's out there searching for a killer?"

"Seems to be." He parked in front of the police station and they walked inside to share the text message with his siblings and colleagues.

Although there was still no hope of tracing the phone Demi had used, a general sense of relief filled the room. Not everyone was as convinced as Shane and Danica that Demi was innocent, but the Gages and Coltons all agreed that it was good news that both baby and mother were healthy and feeling fine.

"We can't let up," Finn said. "Guilty or not, we need to find her and put this case to rest."

As everyone returned to work, Shane, Danica and Stumps walked out. As various ways to state his hopes flitted through Shane's mind, he tried to sort out the right words that would convince her to say yes.

She slipped her hand into his, reminding him she

accepted him, loved him, already. He didn't have to get every word perfect. He just had to get them out there.

Danica realized something other than Demi's predicament was weighing on Shane. She gave his hand a squeeze, hoping to reassure him. Life had been so hard on him and the Gage family hadn't made it any easier. It was miraculous they'd found this amazing love in each other and now she couldn't imagine her days or nights without him.

They walked on toward town, hand in hand, Stumps trotting along on his other side, right past his car. It struck her as more than symbolic that she and the dog were flanking Shane, making a statement to the community that he was theirs and he belonged. Though Shane was constantly stepping up to protect her, she never wanted him to doubt that she had his back, too.

"You're quiet," he said as they passed the drugstore and veered closer to Peeps.

"I'm basking in happiness," she said.

His lips quirked. "I like that about you."

"My basking?" She tilted her head as he stopped at a bench edged by beds bursting with cheery spring flowers. He sat, tugging her to sit with him, and Stumps sat at his feet, at ease but ever alert. She supposed it would be a long time before any of them could fully let down their guard.

"Your happiness," Shane said. "This isn't how I thought it would go," he said quietly.

"Life?" she queried, amused by his odd mood.

"That, too." He leaned forward to rub Stumps's big ears.

"Life is full of surprises," she replied. "Fortunately,

you and I have found not all of them have to be unpleasant."

His low, rusty laugh had her vowing to make him laugh more day by day. "I didn't expect to fall in love with you," he said.

Her pulse stuttered and skipped at the words. "You didn't want to love me."

He turned his head, his lips fighting a losing battle with his sexy smile. "I'm supposed to believe you can make a different claim?"

She leaned over and kissed his cheek. "You know I can't." He was acting so strangely, it was starting to make her nervous. She focused on the dog's sweet face and intelligent eyes.

If he was dumping her, pushing her away now that they'd caught the man who'd attacked her, he was going to find himself hip-deep in another battle. She wasn't going to give up on him. *Them.* Couldn't he see that they had something special? She took a deep breath and looked up at the sky, searching for calm and the part of her that trusted him implicitly.

If he couldn't see what they had...well then, there was no point chasing after him. She used her toe to poke at a crack in the sidewalk.

"Danica?"

"Hmm," she replied without looking at him.

"In prison, I decided if I ever got out, I'd never take anything good in my life for granted again."

She bit her tongue, waiting him out.

He rubbed his hands on his jeans. "This might feel rushed, but I don't think I believe in perfect timing anymore."

"No such thing," she agreed, wishing he'd get to the point.

He leaned close, their shoulders touching, and whispered in her ear. "Will you marry me, Danica?"

For a moment she was lost in that heady sensation of his scent, the brush of his words against her skin. He'd proposed? She was braced to handle the breakup talk with grace and dignity, to give him the space and freedom he valued above all else.

He'd proposed?

"You want to get married?" she whispered, lips barely moving. "To me?" Fiancés and grooms were an endangered species right now.

He draped an arm over her shoulders. "I know it sucks that we can't tell anyone yet."

"Obviously." She didn't want a target on his back any more than he'd wanted her in the crosshairs.

"That's why I didn't bring a ring. But I have one in mind."

She met his gaze and could have happily drowned in the love shining in his blue eyes. "You do?"

"Obviously," he echoed her. His lips curved into that wide-open smile full of temptation that made her want to leap into his arms. "You can have it, eventually, if you give me an answer."

Oh, yes, she wanted to give him an answer. She linked her fingers with his and tried to pretend nothing earth-shattering was happening here on this little bench surrounded by flowers. "Yes," she whispered. "It will be our secret." The idea held far more appeal than she might have thought.

"They'll catch Bo's killer," he promised. "We won't

be living under the shadow of the Groom Killer forever."

She believed him. "Your sister and cousin will be thrilled to be back in business." Wedding ideas spun through her mind.

"Both our families will be relieved when Bo's killer is brought to justice," he said, his gaze drifting down the street.

"Then we can spoil that relief with our news," she teased.

"Shouldn't we leave the *Romeo and Juliet* spotlight to Valeria and Vincent?" he teased back.

This was the side of him she loved most, the confident man who would shelter her from every danger and was willing to let her protect the vulnerable spots he hid from the world.

She was the luckiest woman on earth, to have a steady future ahead despite the unanswered questions about the Groom Killer and the dogs she wanted safely back in the custody of the K9 training center.

"I love you, Shane Colton."

He pressed a kiss to the top of her head. "I love you, too, Danica Gage...Colton," he added in a whisper.

She kissed him again as they sat there in the warm afternoon sunshine, both of them awash in happiness. There was so much life ahead today, tomorrow and in all the days ahead.

* * * * *

LET'S TALK

Romance

For exclusive extracts, competitions
and special offers, find us online:

 facebook.com/millsandboon

 @millsandboonuk

 @millsandboon

Or get in touch on 0844 844 1351*

For all the latest titles coming soon, visit
millsandboon.co.uk/nextmonth